BRUSHED
UP ON
MURDER

BRUSHED
UP ON
MURDER

A Mobile Cat Groomer Mystery

Ruth J Hartman

LEVEL
BEST BOOKS

To Garry, my husband and best friend who always reads my manuscripts. Whether he wants to or not! And to all the cats. The ones who are pampered and the ones looking for their forever homes. I love them all!

Chapter One

I waved to Veronica Waters, my assistant, on my way to the door. "Be back soon. Going to the auction."

"Okay, Molly. See ya later."

A gray Persian meowed as I walked by. I gave her a wave, earning me a whisker twitch. Not a smile, but it would do. The cat wasn't known for her good moods, but then, her owner was a little high-strung herself. Maybe the cat wanted to be like her mom?

The door to my pet grooming shop, Fabulous Feline Salon, squeaked as it closed behind me. I really needed to get that fixed. What was a girl to do when she ran a grooming business along with a pet-sitting service? There was only so much time in a day. The squeaky door could wait.

I saw clients in the shop, but also did work out of my mobile grooming van. Some of my clients' pet parents preferred me to come to them for their convenience. I didn't mind. It gave me more options to take care of the cats, plus to get out of the building for a change of scenery.

I decided to hike to the auction instead of drive. It was being held in the courtyard of Whitewater Valley's library. Their board of directors hoped to get lots of people bidding on donated goods and services to help them fund the library's new wing. I was donating a free cat grooming session for the cause. Since our town was so small, I reached the building in no time. My short journey was spent waving at other townspeople, the majority of whom were friendly.

As I rounded the corner to the library's courtyard, I nearly plowed into an exception to the friendly rule.

Durbin Haines.

The man wore a perpetual scowl beneath his perfectly groomed mustache, like a bad-tempered walrus. "Oh. Molly. It's you."

I took a step back after almost having been stepped on by his spotless black dress shoes. "Nice to see you too, Durbin."

He waved his hand toward the growing crowd assembled on the lawn. "What brings you to the library? Are you one of those readers?" He made readers sound like something he might step in that would soil his shiny footwear.

"Um, actually, I love books. I want to support the library."

As I stepped closer, which forced me to tilt my head way back in order to see him, he peered at me through squinted dark eyes.

"And I believe I saw something in the program about you donating a grooming session from your shop," he said."

Shoot. Although I wanted to give the session to someone for their cat, Durbin was, unfortunately, my least favorite client. His cat, Jasper, was extremely sweet, but Durbin had the habit of standing right next to me as I did the grooming, giving me unsolicited advice as well as plenty of criticism of my work.

Even though the man was exasperating, I tried to be kind when I was with him. My dad had told me that when I was a toddler, I'd wandered into the street and was nearly hit by a car. Durbin happened to be nearby and scooped me up, taking me out of danger's way.

For that reason, I owed him my best attempt at patience when we were together. "Yes, that's right. I'm donating a session." Feigning interest in the crowd behind Durbin, I tilted my head toward the auctioneer's podium. "Although, I'm sure there are lots of *other* really great things to bid on too. I happen to know there's a gift card for Carrie's Coffees. Also, Evan Lakes is giving away a family portrait session."

He scowled. "Don't care about those other items, but I do want the session for Jasper." Durbin shook his head. "It's so odd. Every morning I brush him and tie on a clean bandana, with a different color for each day of the week, of course. Then every evening when I return from work, his fur is messy, and the bandana wrinkled. What do you think about that?"

I opened my mouth to speak, but he went on.

"Part of me wonders if my wife is the culprit."

I frowned. "Culprit?"

"You know, trying to drive me crazy by making sure Jasper doesn't stay presentable. It's particularly important to me, as you well know."

It took everything in me not to laugh. Yes, Durbin always made a show of being without wrinkle, stain, or flaw. It was no surprise he'd want his pet to appear the same. However, I did agree with one thing. Cats were fastidious animals. It would be highly unlikely Jasper wouldn't keep his fur smoothed down with the numerous daily tongue baths cats gave themselves.

Durbin stood taller, his chest puffing out. "And though I do want to win your donation, the main reason I'm here is even more monumental than that." He crossed his arms and waited.

Oh, did he want me to say something now after interrupting me before? He stared at me.

"What might your monumental reason be?" I asked.

"I'm determined to win the bid to oversee construction of the library's new wing. It's what I've decided should happen. So, it will."

Wow. What could I do with so much self-confidence? Probably all sorts of important, stupendous feats. Wait, though... Durbin's schemes often got him into trouble. I'd better not be envious of anything the man did.

My uncle, Russ, wanted to win the contract for the library construction too. Of course, I'd root for him over Durbin. Those two had a bad history between them. From what Russ had told me, just last week, they'd had a loud argument at a construction site. Now they were both up for the same library contract. With the way Durbin felt about my uncle, it surprised me he still wanted me to groom his cat.

I checked around the grounds, hoping to see Russ. No luck. Maybe I'd spot him later.

Relieved when the auctioneer took his place at the podium, I pointed in that direction. "Looks like they're ready to start." Maybe now Durbin would latch on to someone else to spout his opinions, conclusions, and evidence of his importance and wonderfulness.

Durbin nodded. "Yes, I feel it in my bones. Today, I shall win your prize. And soon, when they announce who gets the library contract, I'll be awarded that as well." He lowered his eyebrows. "Well, Molly, aren't you going to wish me luck?"

For one thing, if he felt it in his bones, why did he need luck? Also, I couldn't very well wish him luck when I didn't particularly want him to win my auction prize, or the library contract either. Instead of speaking, I gave him a thumbs up. Maybe that would pacify him for the time being, and he'd go away.

Durbin nodded. "All right, Molly. I'm sure I'll be talking to you soon."

I let out a relieved breath as he turned to leave.

When Durbin headed right, toward the crowd, I veered left and spotted Jillian Wells, my best friend.

She looked over and grinned. "Hey there. Thought I'd see you here."

"Yep. Want to be here when they announce who gets my session." After glancing over my shoulder to make sure no one else was close, I whispered, "Durbin Haines wants to have it."

Jillian rolled her eyes. "Of course he does. So he can tell you how to do your job again. I'm afraid I wouldn't be as patient with him as you are. I have a hard enough time with library patrons who constantly complain."

"I'm not always patient. I try, honest, I do. Maybe it seems I'm patient on the outside. But inside?"

She tilted her head. "Yeah?"

"I'd like to smear some dust on his too-tidy shirt."

My friend snorted, which produced curious looks from two older women who had me do mobile groomings for their cats. I waved, earning me a smile from Florence Makes and an exaggerated wink from Lottie Campbell.

The two ladies lived next door to each other, each alone. Yet, they were always together. Made me wonder why they didn't save on house payments and live together. Maybe they liked their own spaces. I understood.

I'd lived alone since college. Well, Percival, my long-haired black cat, and me. Sometimes he liked to ride along with me on mobile cat visits because he was so nosy. He didn't seem to have a problem with other felines, which was good. If I was ever gone from home for too long and he was stuck there alone, I got an earful when I returned. It was less stressful for him and, in effect me, to take him.

Jillian and I approached the rest of the bidders, opting to stand near the back. I'd never been comfortable in large groups of people. Put me in a room full of cats, however, no problem. Jillian didn't like big groups of people either. We'd each been loners and a little shy in school. A teacher had put us together as desk mates, and we'd been bonded as friends ever since. Kids used to poke fun at us for being opposites in appearance. I was short with long dark hair and brown eyes. Jillian was tall with long blonde hair and blue eyes. We didn't care, though. Since we had each other, we were happy.

A movement caught my attention from the other side of the crowd. Uncle Russ waved and made a goofy grin. I laughed. He and I had always been close. He was my uncle but was only fifteen when I was born, so when I stayed with my grandparents, he was often there. He was more like an older brother, really.

The auctioneer's voice drew my attention. She described a gift basket from Pastries by Paula to the crowd. Several hands went up, giving their bids. I didn't blame them. Her cinnamon scones were heavenly.

I glanced at the program Jillian had handed me. I wanted to search for the order of items to be auctioned. There was mine. Good. Near the top. Maybe I wouldn't have to wait too long to see who got my offer. I had a grooming appointment for a white Persian named Lulu in a half hour and didn't want to make her or her mom, Agnes, wait.

Plus, I wanted to be ready in case whoever won the free session happened to want it done later today or, hopefully, this evening. I normally scheduled appointments ahead of time, but this was a goodwill gesture on my part. If it was claimed by one of my regular clients, it would only serve to make them happy, and they'd spread the word about Fabulous Felines. Also, if someone else was the winner, I could always use new clients.

Items were announced and held up, and each one was given to the highest bidder. Jillian elbowed me when the auctioneer held up the poster I'd made for the free session. "You're up."

I nodded, then stood on my tiptoes to see over a tall woman standing in front of me. As the auctioneer called off higher and higher amounts, people's hands went up. Enthusiasm lessened as the number kept going. Finally, there was only one hand in the air. Durbin's. Of course.

Muffling a groan, I gave Jillian a pat on the shoulder and tilted my head toward the courtyard entrance. "Talk to ya later."

She grinned. "Have fun with you know who."

I rolled my eyes. "Gee, thanks." I waved to Russ as I left.

He and I had plans soon for our weekly lunch. I treasured those and always found time in my work schedule to see him.

Halfway back to my shop, my cell phone purred in my purse. I dug it out of the outside pocket and looked at the screen. It was Durbin. That was fast. Well, I was prepared for possibly having the winner redeem their grooming later today.

"Molly. I got it."

"Yes. I know."

"Jasper's in dire need of the full works. I assume the free session includes everything?"

"Of course."

"I can swing by my house, pick him up, and be there in ten minutes."

Good grief. I wasn't even back to the shop yet. "But—"

"See you then."

With a sigh, I sent a quick text to Veronica to set out the supplies I'd need for Jasper, stuffed my phone back in my purse, and increased my speed. Because, if Durbin showed up and I wasn't ready, much less not even there yet, there'd be fireworks, and not of the happy, cheerful, colorful kind.

I ran the last few yards to my shop and flung the door open, startling a short-haired Russian Blue sitting in a carrier.

Veronica's eyebrows were raised over dark eyes. "Are you okay?"

I opened my mouth to speak. Nothing came out but a gasp. Surely my heart rate would slow down any second. Veronica grabbed a bottle of water from a basket on a side table, rushed toward me, and thrust the bottle beneath my nose.

After a few guzzled slurps, I nodded. "Thank you. Did I make it before—"

A door squeak came from my left. In strolled Durbin, as he held Jasper's carrier. Veronica headed back to the counter.

After he placed the cat carrier on the floor at my feet, Durbin studied me. "You don't look particularly good. Are you in the midst of some sort of attack?"

I forced a smile, then shook my head. "Nope. Fine. Everything is wonderful."

He eyed me for a few more seconds. "If you say so." He rubbed his hands together. "Can we get this show on the road? I have things to do."

It was then I remembered Agnes and Lulu were due any minute. While Veronica could take the cat and would do an excellent job, some of my clients only wanted me. This was one of those times. Durbin tapped his shoe on the wooden floor, obviously impatient with the possible wait. Agnes liked things to run like clockwork too.

Now what?

Veronica waved at me from behind the counter, her other hand on top of a Calico's back. Did she want me over there?

I raised my eyebrows. She nodded.

Then I turned to Durbin. "If you'd like to get Jasper from his carrier, I'll be right with you." Hopefully, the smile I gave him brimmed with confidence instead of the panic rising in my throat at the thought of upsetting one, if not two, clients if someone had to wait.

When I reached Veronica, she ducked her head lower, so I did the same. She looked over my shoulder for a second, then back at me. "Don't worry. Right before you got here, Agnes called to reschedule. She said a family emergency came up and apologized for any inconvenience it might cause you."

I slumped against the counter. "Inconvenience? I may just give her a free session next time for making my life easier with Durbin today."

Veronica giggled. "I thought as much. Now, I have everything you need for Jasper set out in back. I know you usually work out here, but with you gone earlier, I didn't want to work in back and leave the front room unattended."

"You did exactly right. Thank you. You're a gem. Have I ever told you that?"

"Only at least weekly. However, if it would make you happy, I can always hear it more." She gave a cheesy grin.

I laughed and patted her arm. "Anytime. Well, wish me luck with...." I gave a slight head tilt behind me.

"You got it."

I turned around, ready to get the grooming session over with. Durbin could never seem to help himself from giving me play-by-play critiques while I worked. "Okay, Jasper, ready to get more beautiful?" I asked.

The gray-striped tabby cradled in Durbin's' arms winked.

"See?" Durbin slightly jiggled the cat. "He's a genius. Must run in the family, huh?"

My eyes widened, but I refrained from comment. "Let's head into the back room. Everything is ready to go."

We were halfway to the back when Durbin's phone pinged. Did he receive a text? I pivoted and held out my arms, taking Jasper so Durbin could check his phone.

I waited while he read the message. "Is everything all right?" I asked.

His eyebrows lowered. "I think so. Right now, I need to go check something out. Jasper, will you be all right with Molly while I'm gone?"

He was leaving?

I so wanted to grin but somehow refrained. "We'll be fine, won't we, Jasper?" I took the cat's paw and waved it at Durbin, which earned us an uncharacteristic grin.

"Thank you," he said. "If you don't mind... when you're finished, can you drop him at my house? What I need to do shouldn't take long, and I'll wait there for you."

"Sure. No problem."

He huffed out a breath like he was relieved. What was in the text that had him racing out of here?

I placed the cat on a soft towel in the center of my worktable and removed his bandana. He squeaked out a sneeze.

"Bless you." I ruffled the gray-striped fur between his ears.

Jasper sneezed two more times. Either he was having a reaction to some new scent in the shop, or he was coming down with a virus. Good thing Veronica and I were diligent in our scrubbing surfaces and rooms after every cat to keep them from spreading something to other clients. I'd have to remind Durbin to get him checked out.

Once the cat had been washed and brushed, had his ears cleaned and claws trimmed, and a fetching green bow tied around his neck, I nudged him back into his carrier. "Time to go back home, little man."

Jasper peered at me, large green eyes wide and unblinking. He really was a sweetie. Even though I didn't enjoy spending time with his human, I did like hanging out with the cat.

The drive across town didn't take long, even though Durbin's house was at the opposite end from Fabulous Felines. I parked my van in front of his house, noting the car—spotless, of course—which sat in the lane. Hoping Durbin was happy with the grooming job I'd done, I pressed the doorbell and waited a few seconds.

Nothing.

I tried again, this time allowing my finger to stay on the button a little bit longer.

No answer.

Weird. Durbin had specifically told me he'd be here when I arrived, ready to have Jasper back home. A quick check over my shoulder confirmed what I already knew. Yep. The vehicle in the drive was definitely his. I recognized the Keep Whitewater Valley Clean sticker on the front bumper.

Maybe the doorbell was broken. I hadn't heard its sound from inside the house. This time, I knocked. No footsteps came from the other side of the door. No one peeked out from the narrow window to the side. I even tried the handle. If it was unlocked, I could always give a shout while staying on the porch. The handle didn't budge.

Shrugging, I looked at Jasper, who stared at the door. He gave a small mew, the sound so faint I thought maybe I'd imagined it. Was the little guy scared of something?

"Don't worry, Jasper. I'm sure your daddy is around here somewhere. Let me go check the side yard. He might be doing something there, okay?"

After I placed the carrier on the welcome mat, I hurried down the steps and along the front cement path, which ran parallel to the rose bushes beneath the large picture window. I rounded the corner, then stopped.

A pair of shiny black shoes were visible, toes pointed toward the grass. Another few steps allowed me to see more. Durbin was lying face down in the dirt of his vegetable garden. Had he fallen?

"Durbin!" I raced toward him, then jumped over a small azalea bush and a leafy fern to reach the side of the long garden.

I edged closer. He wasn't moving. Had he passed out? Grasping his shoulder, it took all my strength to turn him over. His face was ashen. His lips blue. Then I saw—

A small garden hoe protruded from his chest. The whole front of his previously spotless shirt was drenched in blood.

No...no! I knelt and pressed my fingers to the side of his neck. It took a few seconds for it to register. Durbin wasn't breathing. At all. He was dead.

My fingers wouldn't work right, so I fumbled the phone a few times before finally pulling it from my purse. I managed to punch out 9-1-1. The few seconds I waited for someone to answer seemed an eternity.

"Nine-one-one. What's your emergency?"

"Hi, um, this is Molly Stewart. I'm over at Durbin Haines's house. His address is—"

"Molly? Hi, It's Effie. Sure, I know Durbin's place. What's going on?"

Comforted when someone I knew was on the other end of the line, my shoulders drooped. "Something terrible has happened. He's d-dead. There's a garden tool stuck in his chest."

Her sharp intake of breath startled me. "How awful. Okay, Molly, I'll notify the sheriff. He'll be there pronto."

"Thanks, I...thanks." It sounded lame, but suddenly I didn't know what else to say. The whole situation was surreal. Horrifying.

"You hang in there. He's on the way. I'll stay on the line until help arrives."

I thanked her, then stood there, staring at nothing in particular. My brain grew sluggish as my thoughts trudged slowly across my mind. Was that my body's way of coping with the horrific sight I'd witnessed? Not wanting to acknowledge the truth of what had occurred?

Come on. Snap out of it. I didn't want the sheriff to think I was in some sort of trance when he arrived. I needed my wits about me if he asked questions. With determination, I forced myself to get it together and turned.

As I glanced away from my phone, something caught my eye. When I'd first discovered Durbin and flipped him over, I'd only briefly taken in his face—the deadly hoe had claimed my attention. Now, however, I had a chance to focus on him more clearly.

His hair, always so tidy it was almost plastered to his head—did he use a lot of hair spray? —was now mussed, as if a strong wind had tossed it to and fro, leaving it in a disarray of waves, spikes, and tangles. But today, there was no wind. Not even a leaf moved on his nearby maple tree. His bow tie—blue plaid today—sat askew and was partially untied.

When I'd seen him earlier in the day, he'd been his usual pristine self. While falling down, especially on a sharp object, could cause the blood on his shirt and the bluish coloring to his lips when he landed on his face and couldn't breathe, it wouldn't mess up his shellacked hair or have undone his tie.

As I edged closer, there was something else. The small garden hoe protruding from Durbin's chest had handles made for a left-handed person's use. I knew because I was left-handed and used lots of items from a left-hander's website. This tool was angled in such a way that it would be awkward for a right-hander to even be able to hold or use the tool properly. It was like a special club made for a left-handed golfer or left-handed scissors.

Durbin, however, was right-handed. He'd bought a right-handed grooming glove from me a few months before, making sure I got the correct one for him. He'd made a huge fuss about it when he originally received the wrong one.

I couldn't imagine Durbin, so persnickety about everything being just so, would use a tool not made specifically for his needs. Someone else had to have killed him.

Was a murderer living in Whitewater Valley?

Chapter Two

Sheriff Lawrence King showed up a few minutes later. I was waiting on the front steps with Jasper. He'd meowed from inside his carrier, so I'd gotten him out and cuddled him to my chest. Poor kitty. His person was gone. I so hoped Durbin's wife was close to Jasper too. It would help them both through the process of missing their family member.

The cat squirmed, wanting down. He was an indoor kitty and wasn't ever allowed outside unless Durbin had him on a leash. No way would I let him run around the corner and discover Durbin. After looking at the cat's sad eyes, somehow, I thought he already knew. Pressing him closer, I waited as the sheriff made his way from his car he'd parked at the curb.

"Molly? What's going on? Effie said something about a *death*?" His gray eyebrows remained lowered as he headed toward me.

The word *death* made my hands shake as I placed Jasper back in his carrier. The cat hissed and took a swipe at the closed carrier door, but there was no other choice. I needed to take the sheriff to see Durbin, and Jasper simply couldn't come. "Yes, Sheriff. I found Durbin. Um, his body. He's in the side yard." Just saying those words caused another wave of shock to course through me. Who had done this?

If possible, the sheriff's expression showed more alarm. He hustled behind me and stepped on the back of my shoes twice. It got my attention since the guy was so big. Like a hippo stepping on a squirrel. I moved aside and stopped so he could get the full picture of what I'd found.

He moved closer, then knelt beside the body. After donning some gloves, he pressed the fingers of one hand against Durbin's neck. "No pulse. Not

13

that I expected one with him in this sorry state." He removed his gloves, put them in his pocket, then called the town's mortician.

I took that moment to quietly check around the corner of the house. Jasper's eyes were closed. Good. Maybe he was taking a nap.

From behind me, the sheriff coughed.

I turned. He might have questions for me since I'd found Durbin. I headed back to the two men, one breathing, one not.

The sheriff ran his hand over his bur haircut. "All right. Let's start from the beginning. Tell me when you got here, what you saw, everything."

Crossing my arms over my chest, I tried to remain calm. I hadn't done anything wrong, but being questioned by the authorities always gave me hives. Like I was guilty of some ghastly crime I wasn't aware of. "Well, I'd spoken to Durbin this morning. We were both at the library's auction."

"Go on."

"He said he hoped he'd win the grooming session and—"

"What session?"

"I donated one for the auction," I said.

"Oh. Okay. Continue."

"Well, he did win."

"And..." He moved his large hand in a circle.

"He brought Jasper to my shop."

"I assume that's the cat on the front porch," said the sheriff.

"Yes. Um, I groomed Jasper."

The sheriff frowned. "Was Durbin with you the entire time?"

"No. Usually, he would be. I mean, he had a tendency to critique me while I worked on Jasper and—"

"Please stick to the facts, Molly."

"Sorry. Anyway, he got a text. Durbin, not Jasper."

The sheriff rolled his eyes.

Dumb, Molly. I dropped my arms from their crossed position, then clenched my hands together in front of my waist. I needed to calm down. "Durbin said he had to leave after he got the message and asked me to drop the cat off here."

"And that's the last time you saw him?"

"Yes."

"Then what happened?"

"When I got here, I tried the doorbell a few times and even knocked. No one answered. Which is weird because he'd said he'd be expecting me and would wait for me to bring Jasper back and...."

The sheriff gave me the same glazed look as before.

"I know," I said. "Stick to the facts."

He sighed.

I pointed toward the front of the house. "When no one answered, I left the cat on the porch and came around here to see if maybe Durbin was doing something in the yard. He was here. But wasn't doing anything. Uh, as you can see."

"Obviously. Did you touch the body?"

I sucked in a breath, remembering the blue color of his face, "I turned him over. Then checked for a pulse."

"What?"

"He was lying face down when I found him. I didn't know until then he was dead."

He studied the man in question, took out a small notebook, and jotted something down.

I craned my neck, hoping to make out what he'd written, but it wasn't legible, at least not to me. "Did you find some clues?" I asked.

"Only noted what I saw. Don't think I'd call them clues, just observations."

Maybe the sheriff hadn't caught on yet to the likelihood of this being murder. Otherwise, wouldn't he collect evidence? And act more agitated that a member of their town had been killed in broad daylight? "What I'm thinking is, Durbin was attacked. Maybe by someone he knew," I said.

"Why on earth would you think that?" He pointed down. "It's apparent to me poor Durbin slipped and fell on top of the garden implement. Accidents happen, don't they? Guess this was his unlucky day."

My head was shaking before he'd finished. "No. I don't think this was an accident. See how his hair is mussed? And his tie is halfway undone? When

15

was the last time you saw Durbin when his appearance wasn't perfect?"

"So what? He fell. Maybe it happened when he hit the ground."

"I don't believe that."

"Listen, let me do the police work, and you stick to making cats pretty, okay?"

Indignation burned in my chest. Yeah, okay, I did make cats pretty, but it was more than that. I took great pride in caring for the well-being of my furry clients and helping them feel and be their best. How dare he make it sound so trivial.

"Also, the tool he supposedly used was made for a left-hander," I added.

"I don't see your point."

"My point is Durbin is, was, right-handed. It would have been awkward for him to hold and use the tool. He is—was—so particular about tools and items he used. He'd made it abundantly clear he wanted me to get a right-handed grooming glove for him to help him care for Jasper. I remember because they sent a left-handed glove the first time, and he about had a cow, so I had to reorder. The man, as I'm sure you know, was persnickety." I pointed toward the metal hoe in Durbin's chest. "I can't imagine him having any use for that tool."

One eyebrow rose. "Anything else?"

I blinked. He wouldn't even consider my theory? "No. That's all. I really wish you'd reconsider that he may have been murdered. It's highly improbable this was an accident."

He held up his hand. "Enough. You need to let this go. Stick to your own line of work."

I held in a sigh. He wasn't going to change his mind. How was that fair to Durbin? Someone had done this to him. I just knew it. Since he'd once saved my life, I wanted to at least get him justice for having had his life taken away.

The sheriff tilted his head. "You said no one answered the door. No sign of his wife?"

I snapped out of my thoughts and focused on what he'd asked. "No. Wilma was nowhere to be seen."

"Did you try the door? See if it was unlocked?"

Heat rose on my face. "Well, yes. It was locked." Would I get scolded for trying to go into someone's house?

Yet, he didn't even address it. "Let me get her number from his phone." He bent down and searched Durbin's pockets. "You didn't, by any chance, take his phone, did you?"

I put my hands on my hips. "Of course not."

"Had to ask." His eyebrows drew together. "Strange. Most men carry a phone on them somewhere."

"He definitely had it earlier when he got the text."

"Would you happen to have his number since he's a client of yours?"

I nodded.

"Go ahead and try to call him. That way, if the phone got tossed someplace nearby, we'll hear it ring."

I did as asked, listening while, from my end, the call beeped over and over. Nothing was heard from Durbin's phone.

"Well, it was worth a try. Let me try a different way." He called the station. "Betsy, see if you can get Wilma Haines's number and connect me, will you? I'll wait."

Was I supposed to stay while he made the call? And what about Jasper? I couldn't leave him here alone on the front porch.

The sheriff tapped his toe as he listened to something on the other end. Finally, he lowered his phone. "Can't seem to reach her. I'd rather not leave this particular information in a message. Guess I'll have to track her down."

"Wait. What about Jasper?"

"Oh, the cat?" He stuffed his phone in his pocket. "I'll drop him off at the local shelter for now."

My chest constricted. "No."

He took a step back. "Excuse me?"

I pointed toward the front of the house. "You can't. He'll be scared. He won't understand what's happening."

"I doubt a cat will know the difference."

My hackles rose. This man was obviously not an animal lover. "Yes. He will. Cats are highly intelligent and sensitive. Believe me. I'm around enough of them to know."

"Then what do you suggest? *You* wanna take him?"

He was right. There was no other answer. I couldn't stand the thought of Jasper, afraid and lonely in a strange place. At least he was comfortable with me, after all the grooming sessions we'd shared. "Yes. I'll take him. At least until you locate Wilma." Hopefully, Jasper could be back in his own home soon.

"Whatever." Sheriff King flipped his hand. "One less thing I have to do." He glanced behind him toward Durbin's prone form, then back at me. He sighed. "Nothing more for you to do here. You can go. And don't even think about sticking your nose in police business. I mean it, Molly."

I didn't long to stay around poor Durbin, especially when the mortician came, but I hated having someone tell me what I could or couldn't do. Still, I had things to get to. First of all was to help Jasper. "Fine." The word came out sounding forced as I expelled a quick breath at the same time. I angled away from the sheriff in a hurry to go get the cat.

Jasper was awake again, staring at me with huge eyes.

"Okay, little one. You get to come with me." I picked up the carrier and headed to my van. Jasper meowed until we got inside. When I put my fingers through the holes in the metal door, he closed his eyes and purred.

Since he'd sneezed during his grooming session and I'd be taking him home to spend time with Percival, a trip to the vet was necessary to make sure he was healthy.

Our town veterinarian, Hank Chenoweth, was a couple years older than me and a super nice guy. We'd been acquaintances for years, as our work overlapped in the care of animals. Even though I liked him, and we were both single, we'd never been more than casual friends.

Veronica, however, had suggested more than once she thought he and I would make a cute couple. He was indeed cute, medium height with short dark-blond hair and brown eyes, but that didn't mean I was ready to be flung into something quite yet. After Veronica got married, she'd made it her mission to try to find someone for me. So far, though, I had found several

Mr. Wrongs.

I took the chance I might not have to wait too long if Jasper and I showed up without an appointment. It wasn't something I ordinarily did, but I needed to make sure the cat was healthy enough to take home today.

I pulled my van into the small lot and parked. Once I had my purse and Jasper's carrier, we went inside.

Luckily, they had just finished giving vaccinations to a beagle and had some time to see us. The receptionist, Andrea Evers, waved us on through to the back, where Hank waited.

"Hey, Molly. How are you?"

I set the carrier on the table in between us. "Usually, I'd answer *fine*. But today? Not a normal day."

"What's up?" He opened the cage door and snagged Jasper beneath the armpits then eased him out. "Hey, where's Percival? Is he okay?"

It warmed my heart his expression was alarm that perhaps something had happened to my cat. He genuinely cared for his patients, as I did my clients. "Percival's fine. This little guy is—"

"Wait. Isn't this Durbin's cat? Jasper?"

"Yes. Well, it was. He sneezed this morning, and I need to make sure he isn't sick and is up to date on his vaccinations, since I'll be taking him home to be around Percival."

"Now you really need to explain. Did Durbin give you his pet?"

"If only it were so simple."

His eyebrows rose.

"Durbin won a grooming session from me at the Library Auction," I said. "Okay."

"When I went to drop Jasper back at his house, Durbin wasn't there. Well, he was, but not really."

Hank studied me. "Did you forget to drink some coffee this morning? You're not making much sense." He put on his stethoscope and placed the metal piece at the end on the cat's chest.

"What happened was this. I found Durbin face down in his garden. And... he's dead."

Hank must have squeezed Jasper a little too tight because the cat gave a hiss. Looking down, Hank smoothed Jasper's fur. "Sorry." When Hank made eye contact with me, his eyes were opened wider. He hung the stethoscope back around his neck. "Did you say dead?"

"Yep."

He shook his head. "Wow. I...wow."

"Yeah, pretty much my reaction." I could still picture the blood. Durbin's bluish skin, the shocked expression frozen on his face. I forced myself to take a deep breath and try to relax. "Listen, Wilma hasn't been told yet, so don't tell people, okay?"

His eyes widened. "She doesn't know about Durbin?"

"Not as of a little while ago. The sheriff couldn't locate her."

"Glad I'm not the one to have to give her the news."

I made a face. "Same here."

"I won't say anything. What happened?" He leaned forward and studied the cat's eyes, ears, and mouth.

"The sheriff thinks he fell on a garden tool and died."

Hank watched me for a second. "You don't agree?"

I leaned closer. "My opinion? He was murdered."

Hank's expression of skepticism made me pull back. I crossed my arms and waited for him to reply.

He ran his hands over Jasper's sides and paws. "Don't take this wrong, but the sheriff is the professional. Why wouldn't you believe him?" Hank lifted Jasper's tail, earning him a long, low growl.

Would everyone who heard my theory react the same way and not believe me even though I'd been the one to find Durbin and had witnessed his change in appearance? "Because our never-a-hair-out-of-place acquaintance had exactly that."

"What do you mean?"

"His hair was all mussed up. Also, his tie was halfway undone. Have you ever seen him like that?"

"No, but I don't think it proves he was murdered," said Hank.

"No. It doesn't prove it. But, along with the fact he was right-handed and killed by a left-handed tool makes me think it wasn't an accident. You know how particular Durbin was about everything. He wouldn't have used the wrong tool. I wish the sheriff would at least consider the idea."

Hank picked up Jasper and placed him on the portable scale. "Jasper's weight is fine, and I don't see a thing wrong with him. Maybe allergies. He's up on his vaccinations. It's only been a few months since we did them, although you can check with Andrea out front for the exact date."

"Okay. Well, thanks for getting us in so fast to check him out. I'm only keeping him temporarily. As soon as the sheriff tracks down Wilma, I'll take Jasper to her."

Hank ran his hand over Jasper's fur. "And as for Wilma? I could be wrong, but I never got the impression she was fond of the cat. You might be looking at taking him on permanently."

As if Jasper understood us, he gazed at me with something in his eyes which could only be defined as hope.

I picked the cat up and cuddled him, then placed him back in his carrier. "I guess we'll find out soon. Thanks again."

"You're welcome. As for your murder theory…."

"Yeah?"

He shrugged.

I waited to see if he'd say more, but he didn't. He'd said earlier he didn't agree with me. The shrug confirmed he hadn't changed his mind. It irked me a little that he'd shut down my idea so quickly. But then, so had the sheriff.

When I reached the reception area, Andrea was waiting for me. "I checked Jasper's records for you."

I raised my eyebrows. Was she that good, or had she been listening?

"Sorry." She smiled. "Small office. Hard not to hear."

I understood since my business was housed in a small building as well, and Veronica always liked to know what was going on. "No problem. When was he vaccinated?"

"Three months ago. He's good to go."

"Good. Thanks. Do you have my invoice ready?"

She tapped her computer screen. "I can bill you, if you like."

"That'd be great. Thanks." I hadn't planned on a vet visit today, so having the payment delayed would help.

"Oh…" Andrea glanced over her shoulder toward the exam room and then back to me. "I'm sorry to hear about Durbin's passing. Even though I'm afraid I didn't have a high opinion of the guy."

My opinion of him had never been great either, but now I was curious. "Why?"

She motioned me closer. Her voice was low. "My brother, Ken, was cheated out of a lot of money by Durbin in a shady business deal." Andrea tilted her head. "Did I hear you say you think he was murdered?"

Oh boy. Andrea was one of the town's biggest gossips. News about my theory would be out in no time. "Yes, I think he was. Listen, please don't mention this to anyone, okay? Wilma hasn't even been told yet."

Her face fell. Had she hoped for details about blood and ickiness so she could tell everyone else who entered the building? I wasn't going there. It had been hard enough to see a garden implement in his chest. No way would I say more.

I gave her a wave and picked up Jasper's carrier from the counter. "Thanks again, Andrea."

Chapter Three

I phoned Veronica to see if she could take my next two appointments. I gave her only the bare facts about Durbin, that I'd found his body. She'd have enough shock to deal with that Durbin was dead. Any gory details would be too much right now.

My next call was to Russ. I told him about Durbin. He was shocked, of course, but was more concerned about me and how I was handling things. I told him I was fine. It was a fib, but I didn't want him to worry too much about me. Since Russ was in the middle of something at work when I called, I ended the conversation with a promise to fill him in completely at our upcoming lunch.

Then I headed home. Time to introduce Percival to Jasper. They'd met before, during grooming sessions, but this would be different. I wasn't too concerned. Percival spent so much time at Fabulous Felines and in my mobile grooming van, he didn't seem to have a problem with other cats.

This would hopefully be a formality of a reintroduction of the cats. Besides, as soon as the police located Wilma, she'd want the cat back, wouldn't she? Hank's words about her came back to me. That she didn't seem to like Jasper much. Surely, she'd want him now since Durbin was gone.

When I got to my house, I pulled into the garage and lifted Jasper from his carrier. He collapsed against my chest as if he'd had the worst sort of day. He had, even if he might not know how bad yet.

I held Jasper close with one hand and opened the door to my kitchen with the other. As usual, Percival was right there. He meowed, turned in circles, practically danced on his hind paws for me to hurry up and feed him, then cuddle him. Always in that order.

Jasper might be hungry too. It would be a good time to help them get acquainted with the thing cats loved most. Food.

As Jasper shifted in my arms, Percival stopped dancing and stared right at him. And hissed.

What? He'd never done that to other cats before. More often than not, he was too friendly, and sometimes, the other cats didn't like *him*. Maybe it was the surprise of having a cat in his own house. That was a first. Sure, that had to be the reason. It would take a little time, but he'd warm up. As soon as his belly was full, he'd be over his hissy fit.

Jasper struggled against me, wanting down. I obliged and set him a few feet away from Percival. Before Jasper's paws were even all the way on the wooden planks, Percival was there, right in his face.

Uh-oh.

"Percival! Stop that."

Jasper backed up until his rump hit the base of a cabinet door. His eyes were wide. My cat growled and crouched low to the floor.

"Oh no. Not gonna happen." After I grabbed Percival beneath his armpits, I carried him to his dish and poured in some dry food. He wouldn't even look at it. My groan was loud as I picked up Jasper, a bowl, and the bag of food, then headed to my bathroom. It looked like they'd have to be apart to eat. Not at all how I'd envisioned this going.

Feeding them separately at least cut down on the hisses. Once they were finished, I took Jasper to the litter box, which he immediately seemed to need, then cleaned it before Percival got there. Even though Percival would smell that another cat had been there, no sense in making him even madder than he already seemed to be.

I needed to head back to the shop, so I shut the cats in different parts of the house. When I'd first come home, I'd assumed it would go off without a hitch. What had I been thinking?

When I reached my shop, I was nearly to the door when I saw the sheriff. Why was he here?

"Sheriff? Something I can do for you?"

He rubbed his hand over his face. "Wanted to let you know I went over the evidence again, where you found Durbin."

Okay. Was he going to tell me a second time how I was wrong and Durbin's death had been an accident?

"I took into account his appearance. But especially about the left-handed tool used and him being right-handed. After looking at things more closely, and having gathered more information, I thought you should know I've changed my mind. I do think he might have been murdered."

My shoulders slumped in relief. Now, at least, Durbin might get some justice for whoever killed him. "Thanks for letting me know." Ready to get to work, I reached out for the door handle.

"There's more." His expression was dark, with lowered eyebrows and a frown.

What was going on? Something was way off about this. Sudden panic clawed at my throat. The reason he was here…. "Wait. You don't think I killed Durbin, since I was the one who reported the death?"

He shrugged. "You're a possible suspect, but not my number one suspect. My eye is on someone else."

"Oh." I let out a breath. While it made sense he might consider me a suspect since I'd found the poor man, relief swept through me that I wasn't his main one.

"Normally, I wouldn't give out this information, but since you found Durbin, and are connected to the case…."

"Connected? Sure, Durbin was my client and all, but—"

"You're connected because my main suspect is Russ Stewart."

Uncle Russ!

I was shocked the sheriff had revealed this information, but glad he had. Our town's usual crimes were minor compared to murder. And our sheriff had never been good at keeping things quiet, not a great quality in an authority figure. It looked like he was doing the same thing here.

"You can't be serious," I said. My uncle would never in a million years hurt anyone. He's the kind of person that, instead of killing spiders, captures them and releases them back into his yard."

"Listen, I happen to know that your uncle and the victim had a contentious relationship. Recently they had a major blowout about the library contract. So, it seems to me your uncle does indeed have a temper. That negates your silly spider-release story."

"It's not a story. He really is a kind, caring man. But everyone has people they don't get along with. Having an argument is way different than taking someone's life. Besides, my uncle was only defending himself during that argument. Durbin started the whole thing when he—"

He held up his hand. "I'm not going to go into any more of this with you. Your uncle had a motive to kill Durbin. And he's left-handed as well. It's now an official situation, so I'll be on my way." The sheriff turned and headed up the sidewalk.

My mouth dropped open. That was it? He dropped a bomb and sauntered away?

I glanced inside the front window of Fabulous Felines. Veronica stood just inside the door, ready to open it. I held up my finger in the *wait* signal. She nodded and walked back to the counter.

First, I had to call Russ.

The phone rang and rang. *Pick up, please,* I needed to speak to him, not leave a message. I was about to give up when he answered.

"Molly?"

"Russ! I just talked to Sheriff King. He said—"

"Yeah. I…know what he said. I've already spoken to him."

"What can I do to help?"

"There's nothing you can do, Molly. It's all a mistake, of course."

"I know you didn't kill him. You couldn't."

"You and I know it, but the sheriff has other ideas," said Russ.

"Why didn't you call me before I had to hear it from him?"

"I wanted to. But I needed to speak to my attorney first."

I frowned. "Yeah, you're right. I'm sorry."

"You did nothing wrong."

"Just sorry you're going through this. I know you don't think there's anything I can help you with, but I'm a Stewart, and you know what that means."

I heard him let out a long breath over the phone.. "It means you're stubborn, and you're not going to let the authorities handle this. Am I right?" he asked.

"That's right. Stewarts don't give up."

"Honey, I'm worried that if you get in the middle of things, you might get hurt. If Durbin was murdered, then there's a killer out there. Maybe even someone we know."

Right at the moment, I wasn't concerned about myself. If there was anything I could do to help clear my uncle, I'd gladly do it. "I'll be careful. I promise."

He sighed. "Molly, I…oh wait, I'm getting another call." He paused for a moment. "It's my attorney. I have to take this. Please be careful. I love you."

"Love you too." I ended the call and put the phone in my purse. There was one thing I was sure of. My uncle was innocent. No way was I going to sit idly by and let the sheriff arrest him for a crime he didn't commit.

I stepped inside the shop.

Veronica rushed toward me. "What happened?"

I tried to take a deep breath to relax, but my lungs felt like a hundred-pound cat sat on my chest and refused to budge.

She grabbed my upper arms. "Here, you need to sit down." She guided me to a grouping of chairs in the waiting area. Thankfully, no other people were in the shop, but, the way I felt, I wasn't sure I could have stayed on my feet even if there had been.

After hurrying to the back room and returning back to me, she handed me a bottle of water. I couldn't seem to drink it fast enough. Why was my mouth so dry? When the water was nearly gone, I set it on the floor.

Veronica dragged a chair closer to me and sat. "All right. You look like someone died."

I flinched.

"Oh, sorry. That was…" Her face reddened. "Does this have to do with Durbin's death?"

"Yeah."

"It's horrible you found him." She pointed to the front window. "I saw the sheriff. Did he have more questions for you about when you found, um, the body?"

The body. I shuddered. Not only because of poor Durbin. But also because one of my favorite people in the world was considered the main suspect in his death. I grabbed her hand and held on tight. "He said…." I shook my head, still having trouble believing it. "The sheriff said that I was a suspect and…."

"Oh no. I can see why you're so upset."

"But it's not that. See, he has set his sights mainly on one person."

"And that would be…."

"Uncle Russ."

Veronica squeezed my hand so hard I let out a squeak.

"Sorry." She released my hand and rubbed my shoulder instead. "How's Russ taking this?"

"I just talked to him. He's…it's just hard to wrap your mind around something like that. I didn't get to speak to him very long because he had to take a call from his attorney."

"Attorney. Now that's really getting serious," Veronica said.

"Very. That's why I told him I'm going to help him."

"But what can you do?"

"Do my own investigation."

"Wait, Molly. Do you even know how to—"

"I'll figure it out. How hard can it be?"

Veronica raised her eyebrows.

"Okay, so it won't be easy. Still, you and I both know that what we do for a living is checking out the smallest details in the cats we care for. Not only do we make them pretty, as the sheriff said…."

Veronica rolled her eyes.

"But think of all the times one of us has discovered something wrong with the cat that the owner hasn't noticed. Like the beginning of an ear infection. Or a tiny thorn in a cat's paw."

"That's true. But investigating a murder is way different."

I sat up straighter, my strength and determination returning. "It doesn't matter. I'm going to do it. For Russ."

Chapter Four

I f I was going to do my investigation right, I wanted to return to the scene of the crime. The shock of finding Durbin had been so overwhelming, I hadn't taken into consideration any more of the actual area surrounding the body. Also, I'd heard before that a person's spouse was generally considered a suspect in a murder.

The sheriff might consider Durbin's wife, Wilma, as one of his suspects, but I couldn't know for sure. However, it was worth checking out since the sheriff told me Russ was his main focus. The way the sheriff glared at me when he'd said it, I had a hunch he might not check into anyone else very closely or at all.

As I parked next to the curb, I glanced at the house. Wilma stood on her porch. Watching me.

Well, perfect. Now what? I couldn't drive away since she obviously saw me. She'd know it was me because of the great big letters spelling out Fabulous Felines on the side of the van. I'd, of course, give her my condolences, but we weren't close enough I'd automatically run right over to her house during a time like this. There had to be another plausible reason for me to show up. *Think, Molly.*

Well, of course. Jasper.

I got out and headed up the sidewalk to the driveway. Wilma's face was red. But it appeared to be more from anger than grief. Had something else happened to upset her? What could be worse than having lost her husband?

I hurried up the steps, trying to formulate some words of comfort. Maybe having Jasper back would help. "Wilma. I'm so sorry for your loss."

Her eyebrows lowered. "I heard you're the one who found him."

"Um, yes, I did. I—"

"The rat got what he deserved."

I gasped. "Excuse me?"

She stomped down the steps so fast, I almost stumbled as I tried to back down to the driveway. "He was a lowlife. Scum of the earth. I'm glad he's gone."

Tell me how you really feel, why don't you?

"Let me tell you something." She poked her finger in the air for emphasis. It was then I noticed the sharp edges of her nails. "Durbin Haines was bad enough in life. But you know what?"

I shook my head and snapped my mouth shut at the same time. How long had it hung open?

"My husband is still causing me trouble even though he's dead."

I swallowed hard. How could I get out of this awkward conversation? Of course, there was no way I could go check out the garden for clues now. The woman was so angry, she might use a garden tool to attack me with.

Durbin had mentioned she might have been the culprit who messed up Jasper's appearance to drive Durbin crazy, and that, of course, was just something spiteful one did to another. But could she have hated her husband enough to do him in?

She crossed her arms over her chest. "That man. He...well, first off, he was unfaithful."

My eyes widened. What in the world had I walked in on? "Um..."

"He was sleeping with his coworker. That awful Candi Jones."

Wow. So much more information than I'd come for. "Well..."

"And not only that, I found out from his lawyer he didn't leave me any money. He left it to her!" Wilma's face turned an alarming shade of red. Was she going to have some sort of breakdown? Was I going to have to dial nine-one-one twice in one day?

"Listen," I said, "can I get you something? Like maybe a glass of water? Or we could sit down on your porch."

Her eyes narrowed. She studied me as if she'd just noticed my presence.

"Why are you here, anyway?"

Now to use my excuse of Jasper. Although, it had lost some of its umph after the news of the coworker and Durbin's will. "I'm not sure if the sheriff told you, but I'd brought Jasper here after his grooming appointment, and that's when I found…." I pointed toward the corner of the house but lowered my hand when her expression turned even more threatening.

Wilma's eyes narrowed. "Blasted cat. Durbin was forever fawning over it, actually dressed it in little necktie things. Every single day. It drove me mad."

Maybe Wilma had been the one to mess up Jasper's fur and bandanas, just to get back at her husband. "I'm sorry. Really. Um, listen, Jasper is at my house. I can go get him and bring him—"

She sliced her hand through the air. "No way I want the mangy cat back. Not ever. I don't care what you do with it. Take it to a shelter, for all I care. Do not, under any circumstances, bring it here. I hate cats."

Wow. Guess Hank was right. Wilma really didn't like Durbin's pet. I eyed her. She still looked angry enough to bite me and obviously had no interest in Jasper. Plus, I wouldn't be able to snoop for clues while she stood there. "Okay, well…" I backed away slowly, hoping to make a clean getaway before she threw something at my head or chased after me. "I'm sorry for your loss."

Whatever she mumbled as I hurried away didn't sound like anything I wanted to hear, much less repeat to anyone.

After I scrambled into my van, I drove off faster than normal, wanting to be far away from the crazed, angry woman. I'd head home again. I needed to check in on the cats. Maybe Percival was over his tantrum; only one way to find out.

When I opened my kitchen door, Percival wasn't there. That was a first. The house was silent. Not good with two cats, who a little earlier weren't getting along. I set my purse on the counter, then tiptoed through the house. If they were in the midst of naps, I didn't want to wake them. The kitties needed their rest, especially after experiencing so much stress.

When I got to the top of the stairs, Percival was crouched in front of my bedroom door. I'd put Jasper in there before I left, so I assumed he was okay.

I frowned at my cat. "Percival, how did you get out of the kitchen without opposable thumbs? Have you been here terrifying Jasper the whole time?"

His expression was the cat version of a smirk, like he had indeed sat here, hissed at the door, and maybe even stuck his paw beneath the crack above the floorboards. I sat down and ran my hand over his back. At first, he stiffened, but as I stroked his fur, he relaxed and nuzzled my hand with his nose.

"I'm so sorry to put you through this. But Jasper...his dad is gone and his"—the word mom didn't sound right since she didn't even like him—"his dad's wife doesn't want him so... I'd hoped maybe you could find it in your heart to make some room for Jasper to stay here with us. What do you think?"

Percival closed his eyes, then opened them, a sign of feline contentment.

"Really? You'll do it?" I ran my fingers through the fur between his ears. "Thank you. You're such a good boy. Okay, I'm going to let Jasper out now." I turned the knob.

The cat in question sat so close to the door, I'd bet he'd been leaning against it.

"All right, you two. Why don't I get you some—"

Jasper stepped into the hall. Percival arched his back. The chase was on.

"Hey! I take it back. You're not being a good boy after all."

Well, wasn't that perfect. So much for the cats getting along. Since Wilma had made it clear she wanted no part of Durbin's cat, and I couldn't bear the thought of taking the little guy to the shelter, I apparently was now a two-cat owner.

I'd better get some supplies from the store because as mad as Percival was now, I could imagine his ire if he had to share a litter box, food dish, and kitty bed with the interloper. Also, I needed to stock up on catnip. Sometimes it took the edge off tense situations.

I was able to snag Percival from behind as he stalked the other cat by the side of my living room couch. He hissed and lashed his tail side to side, but I speed-walked with him to my guest room. Once he was inside, I tested the door to make sure he couldn't get out. There, that should do it.

The supermarket was a few blocks away. I'd been known to go by foot if I only needed one or two items, but today I was going for the big kitty haul. I'd purchase anything I could think of to help the current mayhem at my house.

I'd already placed litter, a litter box, and cat food in my cart when I rounded the corner. To my surprise, standing in the middle of the aisle, eyeing the toys, was Hank. I was still a little miffed about his comments at his office concerning Durbin. Right now, though, I needed his advice. *Swallow your pride. At least for a little bit.* "Hey, Hank."

He jerked, as if startled. "Oh, hey. I was just looking at...."

When I reached him, it was hard not to laugh. In front of him was a rack of pink fluffy feathered cat toys. Some even had sparkly fake gems that winked in the overhead fluorescent light. "Like pink, do we?"

His face turned precisely that color. "It's not for me. It's for Beatrice."

I tilted my head. "Don't remember you've ever mentioned anyone by that name. Is she pretty? Have you been seeing her long?"

"She's a cat."

I snorted. "Yeah, okay. Have a new fluffy love of your life now?"

"I got her a couple months ago from the shelter. She's really cute. A tortoiseshell. You'd love her."

Although it was obvious from the way he cared for Percival when he had his regular checkups that Hank liked cats, I'd never heard the guy gush about anything before.

"I'm sure I would love her. Anything to do with cats. You know me." I bit my lip. It made it sound like he and I were close. Like he'd automatically know what I liked and what I didn't. Wait, why was I so defensive? I did run a cat grooming salon, after all. Why did interacting with Hank outside his office make me nervous?

Hank grabbed a feather toy and stuffed it in his cart. After he gave them the once-over again, he grabbed another.

"Afraid there might be a run on the pink ones, and there won't be any left?"

He mumbled something I couldn't make out.

I stifled a laugh as I held up my hand. "I'm sorry. Really." I studied the toys in his cart. What could it hurt? I grabbed two, as well. "Listen, I do have a question to ask you."

"Oh, you didn't hurry over here to mock my choice of purchases?"

"Hey, I didn't even know you were in the store until—"

His smirk stopped me cold.

"Fine." I rolled my eyes. "I had it coming."

Hank took a fuzzy blue catnip mouse from a bin, studied it, then tossed it in his cart. "Okay, what did you want to ask me?"

"First of all, you were right about Wilma."

His shoulders slumped. "Sorry. I was hoping to be wrong. Will you keep Jasper, then?"

"Yeah, that's why I'm here. Need to stock up." I pointed to my cart. "I can't in good conscience take him to the shelter. I wouldn't be able to sleep at night thinking about him there."

He nodded. "I totally get it. Since Beatrice has come to with me, I couldn't imagine her back at the shelter."

I eyed the bin of fuzzy mice and scooped out two for my own cart. "So, yes, I'll keep him. That is, if you'll give me some advice on helping them get along. Because, right now, they aren't even trying."

He placed his hands on the push bar of his cart. "Not so uncommon with cats. Takes them a while to warm up sometimes."

"I know, but Percival is around different cats all the time at the salon and has never had a problem with them. Something about Jasper has set him off."

Hank tapped the cart with his fingers. "Might be nothing more than he's not used to another cat on his home turf."

I nodded. "I wondered that too."

"If you'd like, I can stop by soon and see what's up."

"Thanks. That'd be great. I can use any help you can give me. Maybe if—"

A scuffle and loud voices came from one aisle over. Was someone fighting? I glanced at Hank, who shrugged. He angled his head toward the main aisle in a *follow me* gesture. We left our carts and tiptoed to peek around the end cap, taking care not to be seen by the men.

Tom Peterson, a local construction manager, stood there, toe to toe, with Ricky Notts, the town's postman. Both had reddened faces and clenched fists.

Ricky's dark ponytail flipped against his back as he pushed into Tom. "How dare you say such a thing? I just heard the man's dead. Show a little respect."

"I'm glad he's dead. He was crooked all the way through. Besides, I have plans to win the bid to build the new library. At least now Durbin can't stand in my way anymore."

An older woman who'd started down the other end of their aisle caused a distraction in the testosterone cloud surrounding them. The anger between the two men fizzled as they stepped apart and went their own way. As Tom headed in our direction, we scurried back to our carts.

I pointed to the aisle where the two had nearly come to blows. "What Tom said sure sounded like an admission of guilt to me. He's glad Durbin is dead."

Hank shook his head. "That doesn't necessarily mean he was murdered."

I crossed my arms. "It doesn't mean he wasn't. Besides, the sheriff now thinks it may have been murder."

He nodded. "Oh, Okay, then."

"Okay, what?"

"I guess if the sheriff thinks it could be murder, then...."

"So, you believe him and not me."

His eyebrows lowered. "He is the professional, after all."

My former mirth at his choice of pink cat toys vanished. It was replaced by irritation. How dare he? Without another word, I pushed my cart past him and headed to the checkout.

Chapter Five

After talking—I mostly listened—to Wilma about her husband's
affair, I wanted to talk to Candi, who happened to be one of my
clients. It would be super convenient if she was due to bring in her
cat, Honey, so I could hopefully get some information about Durbin.

However, when I checked my schedule, she wasn't due for another two
weeks. I'd heard somewhere the longer a murderer got away with his crime,
the less chance of making the charges stick. Nope, that wouldn't work. I
needed to see Candi today.

Once Veronica was free after a cat's shampoo, blow dry, and brush, I pulled
her aside.

"Veronica, is there a way for us to see Candi Jones's cat today? I know she
isn't due yet, but I need to talk to her."

She brushed her short dark hair away from her face and watched me for
a few seconds. "You think you might get her to let something slip about
Durbin, and what happened?"

"Yeah, I'm hoping."

"After I finish this client, let me look at the schedule and see what I can
work out."

"Thanks. You're a gem."

"Yep, I know." Her dark eyes sparkled.

I'd been so blessed the day Veronica had answered a want ad for an assistant
position. She was forty-five, so she did tend to mother me since I was only
twenty-seven, but that was okay. She was also goofy and funny, which made
work all the more fun. The fact she believed my theory about Durbin gave

me the courage to continue to check for clues.

I waved my client James Larrabee closer, from the waiting area. His Persian, Minnie, had a tendency toward hissy fits. To be fair, not every cat liked having someone mess with their hair. I got that. I wasn't a fussy person, either. Guess I used more energy to make sure my clients were beautiful before worrying about myself. Maybe putting off my own appearance wasn't always a plus, though. What did Hank think when he looked at me?

Wait. Why did I even care? Was I starting to be influenced by Veronica's attempts to get us together? Plus, I was still annoyed about what he'd said in the grocery store.

I shoved aside the thought and got to work on Minnie, taking great care to be extra gentle and keep my voice low. By the end of the appointment, she didn't purr but had only hissed once when I placed a new ribbon around her neck. Win-win.

Minnie's dad smiled as I handed him the feline. "Thanks, Molly. You do such great work."

"Awww, thank you. I just wish it didn't seem so traumatic for Minnie to come in."

"Traumatic? Oh, no way. This is calm for her. You should see her after she's been at the vet's office. She growls the whole way home and into the next day until she settles down."

Hmmm. Better not tell Hank. Although, if this was Minnie's calm mode, I was sure he already knew.

Veronica came back a few minutes later. "It looks like Candi and Honey have a mobile appointment two weeks from today, and I don't see any holes in the schedule before then to slip her in."

"Shoot." I frowned. "Too long to wait."

She placed her hand on her hip. "I know you don't normally see your clients too late in the evening, but want me to call and see if she can see you tonight after hours?"

I nodded before she'd even finished. "Perfect. The sooner I find out more from Candi, the closer I might be to finding out who killed Durbin."

The rest of my day was packed. So much fur to groom, so little time. But I loved every second of it. Some people had made fun of me when I opened a grooming business for cats only. Those same people had since taken back their words. I was beyond blessed with the outpouring of support from clients who brought in their precious pets for my care. In doing so, I'd made new friends along the way, both of the human and fur-bearing kind.

Veronica had worked her magic with Candi, saying there'd been a conflict with the schedule, and I wanted to see Honey that evening. My assistant had a way with people as much as I did with cats. Her sense of humor and gentle manner put people at ease. She was the perfect person to make appointments and converse with pet parents. When at work, I had a tendency to try to do too many things at once, and sometimes my words tumbled out too fast, which confused the other person on the phone. I was better face-to-face.

Later, as I steered my van to Candi's house, I formulated questions I might ask to get her talking about Durbin. According to Wilma, Candi had been his mistress. Surely someone who'd spent so much time with the man would know something useful in the search for his killer.

When I pulled into Candi's drive, I was pleased to see the woman was already on her front porch with Honey in her arms as they waited for their appointment. Hopefully, she hadn't minded us moving her date up.

Candi, wearing a tight-fitting short dress to show off her curves, also wore a frown. As she marched down her front steps, she jiggled the light orange cat in her arms. On closer inspection, Honey was frowning too.

Maybe Candi wasn't so happy about the appointment.

Before I could even get out of the driver's seat, she met me at the van door. "Molly, what's going on? Why did you change our time? Honey isn't emotionally ready right now, but Veronica said it was important."

Hopefully, my shoulder shrug appeared nonchalant. "Oh…lots of things have come up lately. Wanted to make sure Honey didn't miss out on her grooming if I had to switch some things around."

Her face softened a little, and she nodded. "Oh. All right. I thought…"

"What?"

"No. It's nothing."

I waited for her to say more, but she'd clammed up. Would it have been useful to my search? Better get on with the grooming. Maybe she'd say something else, then. While having had Durbin look over my shoulder as I groomed Jasper had annoyed me, I usually didn't mind when clients hung around while I worked. Most of them were courteous and didn't try to give me pointers on my performance.

I opened the rear doors of my van, lowered the portable steps, and climbed in. Candi handed me Honey. After I waved Candi up, she joined us. Even though the van was an oversized one, it was a tight fit when one of the pet parents was there too. Often a parent stood right outside the vehicle, but close enough that they could observe their furry baby being pampered.

As I ran a brush through Honey's fur, I glanced at Candi, who wasn't even watching her pet, which was unusual. Her gaze had wandered out to the street. Normally, she seemed interested in anything to do with her cat. Was she fixated on recent events?

I cleared my throat, which snapped her back to the present. "Hey, thanks again for agreeing to let me see Honey early."

She ran her hand down her long blonde ponytail. "Oh, it's fine. Sorry if I came across a little moody before."

Maybe this was my chance. "No problem. Everyone's allowed a little mood change every so often." I smiled. "How've you been?"

Her deep sigh lasted a whole three seconds. "Not great, I'm afraid."

"I'm sorry to hear that. Anything I can do to help?"

She glanced at her hand, then curled her fingers into her palm. Her nail polish was chipped. Strange, I'd never seen the woman anything less than picture-perfect. Sort of like Durbin. When I eyed her face, I stiffened. Was she crying?

"Candi? Are you okay?"

As she wiped her fingertips beneath her eyes, she gave a wobbly smile. "I guess you've heard about Durbin."

Obviously, she hadn't heard who'd found the body. "Um, actually…"

Her mouth dropped open. "Oh! Wait. Did I hear you were there when he…" She rubbed her temples. "I've been so preoccupied with him, I've only half paid attention to what people around me have said."

I brushed Honey's fur a few more strokes, then gave her a chin scratch. Setting down the brush, I focused on Candi. "Unfortunately, yes, I was the one who found him in his garden."

She blinked, then shook her head as if to clear away cobwebs. "It had to be awful."

"It was. But you were his coworker. I'd guess it's difficult for you as well."

When she nodded, light reflected from new tears forming in her eyes. "Yes. Very."

I checked Honey's ears for anything out of the ordinary. "Were you and Durbin close?"

She gave a small gasp. "Close? What do you mean?"

"Only that since you worked together, you might have spent a lot of time with him."

"Oh."

I checked Honey's teeth but didn't say anything more to Candi. Maybe if I waited, she'd tell me more on her own.

Candi tapped her foot with increased frequency as more seconds ticked by. She huffed out a loud breath, then crossed her arms. "Well, if you must know, Durbin and I were…lovers."

I held still, trying not to show any reaction but mild surprise. "Really?"

"Yes. Since he's gone, I…I suppose it doesn't matter if the news gets out."

"I'm sorry for your loss. From what you've just told me, you must be suffering even more than if he'd been only a coworker."

"I loved him. I really did."

Love? Surprised, I must have squeezed the cat without realizing. She squawked and whipped her head around to give me a glare. "Oh, sorry, Honey." I petted her until she purred, apparently over being miffed.

Absorbed in apparent thoughts of Durbin, Candi hadn't seemed to notice. Wow, if it had happened at any other time, she might have glared at me for causing her baby any discomfort. Guess she truly had loved Durbin.

Candi sighed. "Sorry, Molly. Didn't mean to drag you into all this."

"It's okay. If you want to talk about it, I'll listen." A part of me did feel guilty since I'd maneuvered Honey's appointment for this very reason. However, if Candi did want to tell me anything further, it might give me valuable information to help Russ.

"Thanks. It does feel good to talk about him now. Not as if I could do so before. Not when Wilma always stuck her nose everywhere."

My first inclination was to say that Wilma had the right, since she was his wife. I clamped my lips together and checked Honey's eyes instead.

"Oh, Molly, my heart is broken."

As I took in her swollen tear-filled eyes, her quivering mouth, and her arms crossed protectively around her middle, I had to agree. "I'm sorry." And I was.

The poor girl. Even though she'd had an affair with a married man, she still obviously had cared deeply for him. Maybe the knowledge of him leaving her everything in his will would somehow soften the blow. But she might already have known. Only one way to find out. "Listen, I overheard something about Durbin. It's, well...."

"What? Tell me."

"I won't say how I found out, but I heard Durbin left everything to you in his will."

Her eyes widened, and her mouth dropped open. "What? He did? I..." She shook her head slowly. "Wow. Now I know he meant it when he said he loved me as much as I loved him. That he would go so far as to do that for me."

Question answered. She'd obviously had no idea. Next came the hard question, the one which would ruffle feathers. But I'd come this far, and Russ needed my help whether he'd admit it or not.

I finished up Honey, tied a bright pink bow around her neck, and gently handed her back to her mom.

Candi, usually so delighted with the results of her cat's grooming sessions, gave a barely perceptible smile and cuddled her cat against her chest. "Can you bill me, Molly? I didn't expect the session to be today, and I don't have the funds on me right now."

"No problem. I understand." Seeing as how I'd finagled the early appointment, I'd make sure Veronica sent an invoice for a discounted amount.

Candi eased down the stairs, and then I did likewise. Once again, on Candi's driveway, I faced her. "Listen, sorry if the information I told you about you being in Durbin's will upset you. Actually, I thought it might make you happier."

"I'm sure once it sinks in, it will. Right now, I can't get over the fact he's gone."

After a glance both ways to make sure no passersby could overhear, I stepped closer. "One thing to keep in mind, though."

"What?"

"The sheriff...he might want to question you. You know, since you'll inherit Durbin's money and all." I didn't know if the sheriff considered her a suspect or not. However, Candi couldn't know that. Maybe if I planted the seed of doubt, she'd tell me a little bit more.

Candi's eyes widened. She no longer appeared lost in thought or had a glazed expression. She watched me for a few seconds. "Do you really think he will?"

"I'm not sure what the sheriff's current thoughts are about the situation. Just to be on the safe side, you might want to have some answers ready in case he questions you."

She frowned. "But I didn't do anything."

"Of course not." I shrugged and left the rest unsaid.

"I suppose, just in case, I should at least think about it."

"That's all I'm saying." I scuffed my toe in a small patch of dirt on her crumbling paved drive. "For instance, he might ask if you have an alibi for the time of Durbin's death. You know, where you were at the time he died."

"Oh, well, that's easy." She nodded. "I was talking to Tom Peterson when it happened. He was giving me a quote for a shed I'd like to have built out back."

I tried to keep a frown from my face, but it didn't work. "You didn't want to have Durbin do it for you, since he was in the construction business too?"

She shook her head. "Didn't want to mix business and pleasure, so to speak. I'd been trying to come up with a way to explain to Durbin that I was hiring his competitor for a job." She sighed. "Guess now I won't have to worry about that. But about my alibi, I'll make sure the sheriff knows who I was with and why. If he asks."

Whether or not Sheriff King questioned Candi, it was good to know she had an alibi for the time of the murder. If nothing else, it helped out my investigation immensely.

Chapter Six

T
he day of Durbin's funeral showed up with appropriate weather—dark skies and drizzling rain. The turnout was bigger than I'd expected, since most people in town hadn't liked him all that much. Nevertheless, the man was visible in the community, so surely had many connections I'd never considered. Maybe they wanted to pay their respects or were just nosy. Probably the latter.

Although I had known Durbin my whole life, as had my family, Veronica and I also fit into the latter category. Our nosiness was for a good cause, though. Our hope was to discover some clues about Durbin or someone who showed up at the funeral who might answer some questions.

For instance, how many left-handed people, besides me, lived in Whitewater Valley? Statistically, only about ten percent of the world's population were lefties. It didn't leave a huge chance in a town our size. And since Durbin's murder weapon was made for a southpaw, that narrowed down the number of potential suspects.

And out of the many citizens who'd seemed to dislike the recently deceased, who hated him enough to do something about it?

Maybe something would catch my eye today and give me a direction to take to get those answers.

There was the usual hush surrounding the somber atmosphere. People milled about, having quiet conversations. A line of twenty or so people waited to speak to Wilma, who stood beside the casket. I didn't think there'd be much use in viewing the body, since I'd already seen him when he'd been newly deceased, but maybe I'd notice a helpful clue. Besides, small-town etiquette frowned on going to a funeral and not viewing the body. If someone didn't adhere to protocol, it would be noticed and talked about.

Veronica nudged me and tilted her head toward the line behind us. "Isn't that Buford Robbins? I thought he and Durbin had a falling out a while back."

When I stepped to the side to be able to see past the line of people, I agreed with her. Though the man stood with his back to us, and it was difficult to catch a glimpse with people shuffling around, it was indeed Buford, Durbin's nephew. I shrugged. "Guess any argument they had wouldn't matter now. He probably wanted to say his final goodbye."

Even with what I'd said, I still watched him. The guy was strange, always had been. He'd never owned a cat, so he had no reason to frequent my shop, yet once a month or so, he wandered into Fabulous Felines apparently to just hang out. I'd never said much about it, just figured he was lonely or bored, but on more than one occasion, the pet parents in the shop at the time watched him with narrowed eyes. As far as I knew, he'd never done anything nefarious or illegal, but something about him must have made others in town as wary as I was.

I kept an eye on him now. The man had a creepy quality about him which made me not want to turn my back on him. Probably harmless. Yet, with a murderer on the loose, I couldn't be too careful.

As I glanced behind me again, I studied him. He kept staring at his watch. Did he have an appointment to keep? It wouldn't be a job he had to return to. As far as I knew, he didn't work. He had some sort of disability that kept him from doing so. At least it was what he told people. From what I'd observed of him over the years, it wasn't visible. Maybe it was emotional, or mental. But those were just as real. Besides, asking someone about a disability was a faux pas of the highest order.

His agitation worsened as he tapped his black dress shoe in a rapid rhythm against the vinyl flooring. Those nearest him gave him stares and glares. He didn't appear to notice and added loud sighs to the mix. Nearby funeral attendees edged away from him, as if afraid he might do something either embarrassing or harmful. He was dressed as some of the other men, wearing a suit jacket.

However, he'd gone the distance and had on a tie and crisp white shirt as well. It wasn't out of the ordinary for Buford, as opposed to other guys in town, who only donned a jacket for funerals, weddings, and sometimes church. He wore a suit every single day of his life. I'd rather not know if he had just one or had several all the same color.

Veronica nudged me again. "Molly, look." I turned around. The line had moved quicker than I'd anticipated. How long had I watched Buford? If I didn't pay better attention to my surroundings, people might glare at me too.

I moved out of line again, this time to get a better look at Durbin's wife, Wilma. Black dress, black shoes, black gloves. Didn't see many women wearing gloves anymore, at least not anyone younger than my great-grandmother. I'd always found Wilma to be intimidating. Quite tall and broad-shouldered, with rarely a kind word for anyone.

Several minutes passed before we got to the small group of people standing up front. The first ones in line looked to be about Wilma and Durbin's age. Were they their siblings? The Haines never had children. Maybe it was why Durbin doted on Jasper so much.

When we finally reached Wilma, her expression was one of sorrow. Exactly what I would have expected from a grieving widow.

However, I knew different. The words she'd said to me about her husband convinced me she'd had no love for the man. Unlike Candi. Would she show up today? It was possible she had no idea Wilma knew of her affair with Durbin. If that were the case, Candi would show up and act as a concerned, caring coworker, there to offer her condolences.

While it was true I was there to find clues, and also knew Wilma's real feelings, I was nevertheless sorry about what had become of Durbin. No one deserved what happened to him.

I stepped closer to Wilma and held out my hand. "I'm so sorry for your loss."

She eyed it for a moment, then gave my hand a brief squeeze. "Thank you for coming."

Though she'd accepted my handshake, she didn't, however, make eye contact. Her gaze landed somewhere around my left ear. Did she regret her outburst at me at her house? Maybe she hadn't meant to reveal her actual feelings for her husband and was now embarrassed at what she'd told me.

When there seemed nothing else to say, I nodded and moved forward three additional steps, which put me squarely in front of Durbin's prone form. Just as he always had been, his appearance was spotless with no wrinkles, no smudges, and his hair smoothed down. His ever-present tie tack was there. That part changed daily, but he'd always worn one. Today's was large and mostly green. A bluegill fish, its teeth flashing, ready to chomp down on a dangling worm.

As I moved away, a glint of light from the casket caught my eye. I halted, causing Veronica to stumble into me.

I whispered "Sorry" to her but stayed put. "Check it out." I tried not to be obvious when I pointed down. Didn't want others to think I was being critical of Durbin's appearance.

"What?"

"His watch."

She squinted her eyes. Then widened them. "Oh…"

I took in the scene again. Durbin's watch, usually so well cared for it shined, now had a small scratch across the watch face. The scratch was surrounded by a tiny pink line. Paint? Nail polish? Hard to imagine Durbin would make use of either one. Could his watch have been defaced during the murder?

Though I tried to remember every detail from that awful day, nothing surfaced about his watch. The scratch might have been there, but I'd been so in shock I hadn't noticed. Could it have occurred afterward? Maybe by the mortician?

That made no sense, either. Wilma was almost as picky about her appearance as Durbin. Wouldn't she have caused a fuss and insisted they not put her husband's damaged watch on display? Maybe she'd been so distracted by the many details in planning the funeral she'd overlooked it.

For the third time, Veronica nudged me. "The line behind us is backed up."

I cringed as several people pointed at me. "Right. Let's move on."

We stepped a couple feet away and took spots along one wall to stand and people-watch.

Buford had reached the coffin and stared at his uncle. Was he feeling regret for their fallout? Sorry he hadn't made amends? As he bent over the casket, I tried to see what he was doing. A tall man stepped into my line of sight, blocking my view. I turned to Veronica. "Can you see what he's doing?"

She shook her head.

I tilted my head toward the casket. She nodded. I took slow steps to get a little closer. I needed to see what Buford was up to.

The rest of the line of people had stopped back by Wilma. She seemed to be speaking at length to the person nearest her, creating a logjam of mourners in the line. That left Buford the only one standing close to the casket.

When Buford straightened and stepped away, I eyed Durbin. What was different? He was...I let out a gasp.

Veronica's eyes widened, and she grabbed my arm. "What is it?"

"Look at his tie."

She whipped around and studied the scene, then looked back at me. "Where's his tie tack? It was the huge, gaudy one with the fish."

"That's what I'd like to know." Had Buford taken it from his uncle's body? Why? Had anyone else witnessed him standing for so long by his uncle's casket? But as I glanced around, there was no one else nearby. Those who'd already gone through the line had stepped away. And Wilma yakked away to the same person, leaving a line of impatient people still waiting to speak to her.

I checked around the room. No sign of Buford. Had he raced off after stealing from his uncle? Was he not even going to stay for the private family service following the viewing?

The line to see Wilma had lengthened and now snaked to the doorway. We'd been here long enough, as it wouldn't be long before someone wondered why we'd hung around, leaning against the wall. Time to go. I angled my head toward the entrance and Veronica nodded.

We said quiet hellos to several people on our way out and were nearly to the door when Candi stepped inside. She caught my eye and startled, like she was in shock. Maybe it really was shock, though, not at seeing me, but because of her circumstances. The man she'd loved had died and, in a few moments, she'd have to come face to face with the man's wife. Not an enviable situation. She wouldn't be able to show her emotions as she mourned, since she'd be in view of Wilma.

Candi avoided eye contact, much as Wilma had done. Not that I blamed her. She'd poured her heart out to me at the grooming session and maybe now regretted it. She raised her hand to her cheek and smoothed away tears. Today, her nail polish was red. At the grooming session, it had been white. I was sure she sometimes wore pink polish, like the color on the watch face because every time I saw her, the color was different. Was it possible she'd been the one to kill Durbin?

Her now free-flowing tears had me shaking my head. No. I didn't believe it. When she talked about Durbin, it was obvious she grieved for the man she loved.

When Veronica and I stepped outside, we both squinted against a ray of sunlight that worked its way through the clouds. At least it had stopped raining. Why did funerals seem to often take place in either rain or cold weather?

"Hey, Molly. Veronica."

We turned. Hank headed up the concrete ramp, which led to the front door. Right before he reached us, Veronica's phone buzzed.

She reached into her pocket to get it and checked the screen. "Sorry. I need to take this." She smiled and walked toward her car.

Hank rose on his toes to see over the crowd. "Looks busy in there."

"It is. Wasn't sure I'd see you here."

"Why not?" He frowned. "Jasper is my patient, after all."

"True. I didn't know if you'd be booked up with patients right now. I know it's not always easy to ask people to switch appointment times."

He shook his head. "Had Andrea reschedule a couple of them. They were fine with it since they planned on coming here today too. What about you? I happen to know he wasn't your favorite person. Just here to pay respects?"

This time I was the one not making eye contact. "Something like that."

Hank tapped his foot.. "What are you up to?"

I wrapped my arms around my middle. "What do you mean? Why would I be up to anything?"

"After you told me your...." He glanced around us and back to me "...theory about Durbin's death, I'd guess you're doing a little bit of sleuthing."

My noncommittal shrug obviously didn't pacify him because his eyebrows lowered.

He nudged my hand. "I'm concerned for you, that's all."

I eased my hand out of reach. "Why would you be?"

"I just don't want you to get hurt," he said.

"I'll be fine. Really."

Hank shook his head, like he wanted to disagree with me. He gave a shrug. "Okay, listen, I'm sorry I upset you at the grocery. I hadn't meant to. Honest." His brow furrowed, and his eyes watched me intently.

I believed him but was still a little miffed about what he'd said. Now wasn't the time to discuss it further, though. "It's okay. "Don't worry about it."

He gave a brief nod.

A few people trod up the ramp and stepped around us. Hank pointed toward the door. "I better get in there. Have a patient in an hour. And I'll be lucky to make it in time the way it is. See ya later?"

"Yep, see ya later."

Veronica leaned against the trunk of her car and put her phone in her purse. I'd parked next to her, so I headed over.

She pointed toward the building. "Hank have much to say?" Her eyes were wide, curious. And her lips quirked into a grin.

"He didn't ask me on a date, if that's what you thought."

She frowned. "I can always hope."

I hit the remote button on my key fob to unlock my van. "Why do you seem more excited to see me go on a date than I do?"

"Because you're too close to the situation."

"What situation is that?"

"You've had some bad experiences and don't want a repeat. I get it.

However, look at Jerome and me."

I smiled. "You sure did hit the jackpot with your husband."

Jerome was sweet and kind and treated Veronica like a queen. The fact she'd met him on a blind date was even more amazing. She'd been afraid she'd never meet anyone special, someone she'd want to spend her life with, but those two were a perfect pair.

Veronica put her hand on her hip. "Yes. I did hit the jackpot. I want the same for you."

"I'd love it too, but I'm not sure Hank thinks of me the same way I do him."

She grinned. "You've just solved half the problem."

"I have?" I narrowed my eyes.

When she gave me her wide grin, something was always up.

"You admitted you like him." She rubbed her hands together. "It makes my work even easier than I'd anticipated."

I rolled my eyes. "Oh boy. I've done it now, haven't I? Turned loose the side of you that won't rest until everyone else in the world is happily in love and settled."

"Not the whole world. Just you." She winked. "At least for now."

Chapter Seven

When my shop door opened the following morning, I didn't expect it to be Hank. Jasper hung over my shoulder like a sleepy sloth, so I kept my voice low. "Hey there. Don't you have furry patients to see this morning?"

Hank grinned. "Had a cancellation, so thought I'd stop by." He reached out and ran his fingers over Jasper's back, which caused the cat to sigh and purr all at once. "Any luck last night with these two?"

"I wish, but no. All three of us were up all night. Percival howled and chased Jasper all over the place. Jasper hissed and tried to climb up my leg. And me? Get me a black and white striped shirt, 'cause apparently, I'm now a cat referee."

"Aww, sorry to hear that. Where's Percival now?"

I pointed behind me to the side counter, where my cat had his back turned, his tail lashing side to side.

Hank leaned to the side to see the cat. "Pouting?"

"Yes. He's a champion at it. His whole body puffs up, and he huffs out these little indignant snorts."

"Have you tried having them spend time together with you there with them?"

I patted Jasper on the back. He gave a nearly silent mew, then went back to sleep.

"Tried. No luck."

"Did you try giving them treats? Or catnip?"

"Jasper seemed too nervous to eat much. Percival was plain mad. Even food, which usually works with him, isn't cutting it this time."

Hank rubbed his hand down his chin. "How about if you keep them separated in different rooms and let Percival sniff Jasper from under the door?"

"We tried that too. I'd been out of the house for a bit and had them in separate rooms. Percival somehow got out and was doing exactly what you said when I returned."

"And?"

I shook my head. "My cat lies."

His eyebrows rose. "Excuse me?"

"Well, I explained to him how Jasper was a sad homeless waif now,"—I lowered my voice and pointed to Jasper—, "and his dad wasn't coming back, and didn't Percival have it in his little heart to take in an orphan? Percival acted all sweet and compliant, so I opened the door. I thought it would all be okay. Then as soon as Jasper came out, Percival chased him down the stairs and all through the first floor. See? A furry little liar. You'd think you could trust your cat, if anyone, right?" I angled my head back to view Jasper. His eyes were still closed.

A kind of muffled snort came from Hank. I looked at him. He bit his lip, his nostrils flaring. Was he laughing at me?

I narrowed my eyes as I waited until he'd lost some of his mirth. "Anyway," I said, "I can't think of what else to do. Any help you give me would be greatly appreciated."

Being made fun of was never enjoyable, but I'd endure it this time if Hank could figure out some solution to the problem.

He reached toward me, his arms out. Startled, I thought he wanted to hug me. My heartbeat raced, and my body heated. However, my hopes were dashed when he eased Jasper from my shoulder and cuddled the cat to his chest.

I blinked a few times as I watched them together. My hopes were dashed? Where had that come from?

Veronica picked that moment to clear her throat from across the room. She wiggled her eyebrows up and down. How long had she stood there and watched us?

I gave her the best stink-eye I could manage, learned from my years of dealing with moody cats. It only made her smile and wink. Her hand motion from me to Hank and back had me shaking my head. Nope, she wasn't going to try to fix me up with a guy. Been there, regretted that.

When I refocused on Hank, he was watching me. He tilted his head. "No, what?"

"What?"

"You shook your head."

I eyed my assistant, who was trying so hard not to laugh, her eyes watered from the effort. "Uh...." I pointed to Jasper. "I just... I hope you don't have the same result I did, trying to get these two to at least act civil around each other."

"Oh, believe me, I'm not giving up. Percival is so friendly when I see him. Isn't he the same way with your other clients when he's here?"

I nodded. "Always. That's why it's so odd."

Hank rocked Jasper side to side, which caused the cat to close his eyes and smile. "I guess you've never taken other clients to your house before?"

"Well, no. I've never had a reason to." I placed one hand on my hip. "Do you think that's the problem?"

When Hank shrugged, the cat moved up then down but was so comfortable he didn't seem to mind in the least. "Could be. Cats can be territorial. So, even though he does fine when he's here...."

"And also has no problems when he's with me in my mobile van."

"Right," said Hank. "He does great, from what you've told me. But bring an interloper into his own house?" He let out a sigh, causing Jasper to give a kitty mumble and squish down in Hank's arms to get more comfortable..

I placed my hands on my hips. "Well, rats. I'd assumed this would go off without a hitch."

"You never know with cats. They're high-strung and can even hold grudges. And yes, can often lie." His mouth formed a one-sided smile, and he tilted his head in Percival's direction.

We both turned to watch Percival, who had changed positions and now faced us. He didn't exhibit his normal placid expression. There was no kitty smile. No squinty eyes. Just plain irritation.

Perfect. The world's friendliest cat wasn't having any of a new housemate.

Hank handed Jasper back to me. As Hank stepped closer, the same warmth as before encompassed my whole body, and my knees nearly buckled. *Get a hold of yourself, Molly! It's just Hank.*

He grabbed my shoulders. "Hey, you okay? Thought you might pass out or something."

It was definitely the *or something*. "Nope. Fine. Maybe I didn't eat enough today."

A loud snort came from Veronica, who'd witnessed me practically inhale an entire box of cheese crackers less than an hour ago.

Hank's eyebrows lowered as he studied me. "If you're sure you're all right."

"I'm sure. Thank you, though."

Hank pointed toward the chairs in my small waiting area. "Mind if we sit down a minute?"

What was going on? First, I thought he'd hug me, then my knees quivered, now he wanted to talk?

Veronica rushed over and took the sleepy Jasper from me. "Let me look after the little guy while you two talk in private." She gave an exaggerated wink.

No way Hank could have missed it. Veronica hurried across the floor, skirted around the counter, and headed into the back room. The door closed with a decisive click.

Since when did she care about my privacy?

I sat in a chair, and Hank took the one closest to me. I crossed my legs and made small circles with my hanging foot, a motion I did when nervous. "What's up?"

Hank leaned forward on his chair, hands clasped together on his knees. "I owe you an apology."

"You do?"

"I do. See...when you brought Jasper in to see me and told me your idea that Durbin had been murdered, I blew you off."

"Yeah. Kinda noticed."

"That's why I'm sorry." His shoulders slumped.

"It's okay. You have your opinion, and I have mine."

"True, but I didn't take time to listen to you. After you left, when I had time to think about our conversation, I was ashamed."

I touched his arm. "You don't have to…."

"You're a smart woman. Bright and intuitive. I could have at least listened to what you had to say before I formed an opinion you were wrong."

I blinked. Hadn't expected that. My face heated. He thought I was smart? Bright? Intuitive? While women liked being told they were beautiful, me included, I valued those other qualities so much more. "Thank you."

"You're welcome. Since we've gotten that out of the way, I'd like to hear your thoughts on what happened to Durbin."

"You would?" While I appreciated his apology, the fact he actually wanted to hear what I thought meant even more. I could use all the positive vibes from friends I could get.

He nodded. "If you have time. I know you're a busy person."

I smiled. "I have time. That is, if you don't have a Doberman or Persian impatiently tapping their paw at your office right now."

"Nope. I have at least thirty minutes before my next appointment. Besides, Andrea's good about sending me a text if it's a few minutes before someone is due and I'm not back yet."

"Okay. Great." I drummed my fingers on the arm of the chair, anxious to tell him things but also dreading going over the bad parts again. Still, I was grateful he was interested. "Well, of course, you know I found Durbin in his garden."

"Yes." He sat back and appeared to have settled in for however long it took to hear about my experience.

"I'd gone over to return Jasper after grooming him. Durbin had said he'd be there when we arrived. You know how punctual he always was."

"Always. Never even a minute late for appointments. Or anything, as far as I could tell."

I nodded. "Right, it seemed weird he wasn't impatiently tapping his toe on his porch when we got there. When no one answered the doorbell, I'd thought maybe he was out in his side yard."

Hank frowned. "And he was."

I closed my eyes briefly. "Yep. It was awful. I rounded the corner, and there he was. Face down. I…"

Hank grabbed my hand and gave it a gentle squeeze.

Warmth encompassed my fingers and hand and spread up my arm. "I turned him over, thinking he'd just fallen, but…his lips were blue. He wasn't breathing."

"I heard a rumor about a garden implement."

"Unfortunately, it was the murder weapon. Ghastly looking thing."

"Was there anything about it that was special? Seems an odd object to stab someone with. Yet, a person determined to kill someone might grab whatever was handy."

"Yeah, here's the thing. It seems hard to believe it was handy. I don't think he would have been using it out there. Durbin, so neat and tidy, wasn't one to leave tools around if, for some reason, it belonged to Wilma." I'd have to try to find out if, by chance, Wilma was left-handed. "See, Durbin was right-handed. I know because I'd had to order, then reorder the correct grooming glove to use on Jasper for him. He was so particular and adamant that I get him the glove as fast as humanly possible."

Hank nodded. "Yes. He was particular. When he brought Jasper to see me, he stood right at my shoulder and barely gave me room to examine the cat. Sometimes I'd suggest he go to the other side of the examining table so he could see what I was doing a little better. It usually worked. Durbin was all about whatever was in Jasper's best interest."

I gave a small smile and edged my hand from his, hoping it didn't seem rude. I'd enjoyed the sentiment, but the longer he held my hand, the more I liked it, way too much. "Sounds about right."

Hank looked at his now-empty hand. He frowned slightly. Was he disappointed I'd moved, or was it because we discussed a macabre subject?

"Since the sheriff is now mainly focusing on my uncle as the killer," I said, "I'm more intent than ever on doing my own investigation. The trouble is,

I'm getting scolded by him now when I do anything. Apparently, he thinks I should be in some sort of time-out before I cause him trouble. I'll admit, at the funeral Veronica and I people-watched, hoping for clues. We know Buford stole Durbin's tie tack right out of the casket."

"He stole his uncle's tie tack? How low. Sounds like he might be a suspect." He squeezed my hand again. "I'm sorry I didn't believe you before. But I believe you now. And I want to help. Who else do you suspect?"

"Well, Wilma looks awfully guilty. She flat-out told me she hadn't loved Durbin. That she actually hated him."

Hank's eyes widened.

"And do you know, she'd even gone to the trouble of messing up Jasper's appearance every day. Undid his little tie and mussed his fur. She said it was so funny to irritate Durbin. Also, because she intensely disliked Jasper."

"I'm sorry I was right when I said she'd never seemed enamored of the cat, but I'm so glad Jasper has a good, loving home with you."

"Thank you. Just wish they'd get along."

"They will. We'll help them. Once we figure out the key to help them to bond."

Chapter Eight

Whenever I met Russ for lunch at The Sandwich Shack, it was the highlight of my week. And though I was anxious to see him today, my stomach was in knots. Because this time, we wouldn't be shooting the breeze, teasing each other, or just catching up on our week. No, this time, our conversation would be serious. Being considered a suspect for murder was nothing to laugh about.

I arrived first and sat at our favorite table in the back with the large picture window overlooking a pond with a weathered dock surrounded by wildflowers of pink, yellow, and lavender. Lorna, the waitress, waved and pointed to a menu, but I held up my finger, telling her to give me a minute.

She smiled and nodded. Russ and I had been here so often, she wouldn't be surprised that I was waiting for him to meet me.

My hands fidgeted, so I grabbed a paper napkin from the dispenser and folded it into a square. Then again. I kept folding it until it was too small to try again. Where was Russ? Most times, he beat me to the restaurant, being a person who thought if someone wasn't early, he was late. I'd give him another minute, then text him a message.

It was only eleven-thirty, so the lunch crowd hadn't filtered in yet. But Whitewater Valley was small enough there weren't many restaurants, so The Sandwich Shack would be busy by the time we left.

I glanced down. Good grief. My mind must have been more preoccupied than I'd realized. Without noticing, I'd completely shredded the napkin into tiny bits. I brushed the pieces into my hand and placed them to the side of the table. Maybe when Lorna cleaned up later, she'd be too busy to wonder why I mutilated a perfectly innocent paper product.

"Sorry I'm late."

I jumped when Russ sat down across from me.

He frowned. "Hey, you okay?"

I placed my hand on my chest, hoping my heartbeat would slow to a normal rhythm. "Shouldn't I be asking you that?" I leaned closer, not wanting anyone to overhear. "Being accused of murder would make me a basket case." I was nearly there myself, and I wasn't even a main suspect.

He reached across the table and patted my other hand. "I was late because I was meeting again with my lawyer to discuss my possible case. I haven't been formally charged. Yet. But because of the way Sheriff King grilled me the other day, my attorney feels we need to be ready. So, yeah, I've been on edge."

"Only on edge?"

"All right. I'll admit it. I'm scared." He looked behind him and back. Knowing my uncle, he wouldn't want anyone to know he was anything but in control of whatever situation he was in. But the tables nearest us were still empty. That would make it easier to have our conversation without someone listening in.

The waitress came over and took our orders. Since we always knew what we wanted, we ordered food as well as drinks.

Russ tapped the table. "Now, about what you said on the phone the other day, I don't want you getting involved in anything to do with the investigation. Okay?"

I slid down a few inches in my seat.

Russ shook his head. "You already are, aren't you?"

"Um, yes." I wouldn't meet his gaze.

"Molly?"

I straightened in my seat. "Look, I can't sit still and not help you. You're my family."

"Yes, but—"

"Wouldn't you do the same for me?"

"You know I would. In a heartbeat."

"Exactly. So please, don't give me grief about doing something for someone I love."

Russ studied the table, his eyebrows lowered. "All right. But I still don't like it. You have to promise to be careful. I mean really careful."

I raised my hand. "I promise."

Lorna brought our drinks. "Food will be right up."

Russ' smile looked forced. "Thanks."

"You bet."

Once she was a few feet away, Russ leaned closer. "Though I'd like to, I can't very well go skulking around town hunting for clues."

"Hey, there's been no skulking." I smirked, hoping to lighten the mood. "Okay, maybe a little."

One side of his mouth rose in a smile. "Since you're already, um, looking into things, why don't you tell me if you've learned anything so far."

I took a sip of my drink, then set down the glass. "Well, as I'm sure you already know, Sheriff King has a couple reasons, at least, for suspecting you."

Russ nodded. "Unfortunately. That I had that argument with Durbin. And I'm left-handed."

I held up my left hand. "But you're in our special club, remember?"

"Of course, I remember. Just you and I being the only ones in the family to be southpaws."

"I've always liked that about us."

"Me too, kid."

Lorna brought our food, then left to check on another table.

Russ picked up his fish sandwich and took a couple of bites. He put it on the plate. "It's good, but I don't have much appetite."

"Makes sense, considering what's going on." I eyed my BLT. Truth be told, my appetite seemed to have vanished as well. "Okay, so I thought about who else might have wanted Durbin dead."

He spread his hands. "And who did you come up with?"

"For starters, Wilma."

"Yes, I agree. Spouses seem to be suspects. At least normally. Not sure why the sheriff has his sights set on me so fast when there are others who could have had motive."

"I went to see her and—"

"You did?" His eyes widened.

I shrugged. "It hadn't been my original plan. I wanted to check out the garden again for clues."

"So what happened?"

"When I got there, Wilma was standing on her porch."

"Oh great." He rolled his eyes. "So she saw you."

"Right. I didn't see any graceful way of leaving, just driving away after I'd already parked, and there she was."

He pushed his plate to the side. "Then what happened?"

"I wasn't sure what to say until I got up to her porch. At first, I gave my condolences."

"That was smart. Good reason to be there."

"And then, I mentioned Jasper."

"Jasper?" He frowned. "Do I know him?"

"He's Durbin's cat. I can't believe I forgot to tell you. With everything going on, I ended up with him. Wilma had no desire to even be around the poor little thing. And I sure wasn't going to take the sheriff's advice and take Jasper to the shelter."

His eyes widened. "No. Of course not." Russ loved animals as much as I did. He had two cats of his own and doted on them like the children he never had. Although he'd been previously married, he and his wife had never been able to become parents. Then, after they divorced and she left town, Russ adopted two precious cats.

"Ever since I brought Jasper home," I said, "I've been dealing with Percival's displeasure of having another feline in his domain."

"But he's so friendly. Seems to do great with other cats. Even mine."

"All true. But he's having none of a second one staying in the house. Then Hank told me…." Warmth ran up my cheeks.

"Hank Chenoweth? What about him?"

"Uh, he's trying to help me. With the cats. And for that matter, with your investigation."

Russ lifted one eyebrow. "Is that so?"

"Not you too." I waved my hand. "Don't even go there. Besides, you're getting off the subject."

"But that's more fun to talk about than what's happening to me."

"I know. And I'm so sorry you're going through this. That's why I'm helping you."

"Thank you, honey." He sighed. "Okay, what else have you found out about Durbin's murder?"

"Well, I overheard Tom Peterson and Ricky Notts arguing in the grocery about Durbin. Tom was glad he was dead. Said he wanted the library contract."

"That doesn't surprise me. Tom isn't trustworthy. Sounds like a good one to be on your suspect list."

"Oh, he definitely is." I wasn't going to add that when I'd overheard the men fighting, I'd been with Hank. It would only get Russ off the subject again. "Next, I spoke to Candi Jones."

"Why her? Oh wait, didn't she work for Durbin?"

"That's right. Apparently, they were having a fling."

He made a face. "Big age difference there."

"That's what I thought. But she insists they were in love."

"Do you believe her?"

I nodded. "Yeah, I do."

"Sounds like you've been busy with this. Anyone else?"

"Yeah, now get this. You wouldn't believe what Veronica and I saw at Durbin's funeral." I tilted my head. "Hey, I didn't see you there."

"Think about it. If word gets out I'm under suspicion for his murder, wouldn't it seem odd I went to the funeral? Besides, Durbin and I weren't friends, far from it. Probably wouldn't have attended the service anyway."

"I see your point." I fidgeted, and moved the tattered napkin pieces a little further away from me.

"So, what happened when you were there?"

"Veronica and I had gone through the line and stayed a bit to people-watch and when it was Buford's turn to view the body, he took something."

Russ blinked.. "He did?"

"You know how Durbin always wore those big tie tacks?"

He nodded.

"When Buford stepped away from the casket, Durbin's tie tack was gone."

"Wow, that takes a lot of nerve."

"Yeah. That was my reaction too." I took a sip of my drink, then set down the glass. "Sorry, but that's all I have to go on so far."

"Please don't be sorry. I'm impressed. And grateful."

I smiled. "It's what we Stewarts do. Take care of each other."

A sheen of tears shown in his eyes. "I'm so lucky to have you, Molly."

"Right back at you."

Chapter Nine

I'd hoped to see Jillian pop into my grooming shop. I had so much to tell her. She couldn't really talk on the phone much when she was at the library and got only thirty minutes for a lunch break. Some days, it was all I could do to contain myself until I could fill her in on things that had happened.

Unfortunately, the one who entered my shop was Buford. I let out a groan, hoping he hadn't noticed. At least once a month, the man showed up at Fabulous Felines. It made no sense. He didn't have a cat, actually no pets at all. He never bought items for someone else who might have had a cat. Why did he come here? Boredom? Curiosity? He never stayed long, just long enough to annoy me.

He edged around the perimeter as he studied everything on my shelves. The main focus for the shop was cat grooming, as well as pet boarding when the need arose, but I also kept a steady supply of all things cat-related a pet parent might want, treats, toys, leashes, home grooming supplies. However, Buford wouldn't have need of any of it. A few other people who sat in the waiting area watched him closely, suspiciously. I wasn't the only one who thought the guy was odd.

I shook my head. He'd been coming in here for such a long time now, it seemed too late to come out and ask why. I should have inquired about his interest from the start, once I found out he had no cat and didn't even seem to like them very much, but I couldn't. My small-town polite gene kicked in, which caused me to smile and nod when he reached my counter. "Hey, Buford."

His eyes lit up, like I'd given him a gift. Too bad some of the pet parents who frequented the place didn't feel the same when they came in. A few were downright argumentative at times, if they thought their fur baby didn't get the same amazing treatment as other cats they'd seen. Some pet parents were moody but had calm cats. Others were meek folks with hyper felines. Some, the double whammy, had over-excitable humans who owned cats who thought they should be treated like royalty.

Buford leaned against the counter I'd recently cleaned and placed both hands, palms down, on the otherwise sparkly glass. "Hey, Molly." He stood there, unblinking, like he'd made the first move in a game only he knew about, and waited for me to take my turn. What did he want?

Knowing I'd get the usual answer as every other time he'd come to visit, I asked anyway. "What can I do for you today?"

His shrug caused his bright blue tie to lift up, then down, a couple of inches. It was hard not to focus on the shiny decoration on his chest.

Wait. Was he wearing—

I squinted at his tie clip. The man had the audacity not only to steal his uncle's property while he lay prone in a casket, he even wore it out in public. The nerve! As if he taunted people and hoped someone would point it out so he could boast about having it when he shouldn't have.

Buford must not have noticed my scrutiny of his attire, because he gave me a wan smile, that, as always, creeped me out. "I'm just browsing. Thank you so much for asking."

It took me a second to remember I'd asked him a question about how I could help him. I still couldn't fathom why on earth he tromped around town wearing the tie tack. Normally, people wouldn't notice a man's attire so closely— not many men around here even owned a tie — but Durbin had an eclectic array of tie accessories, and it got people's attention because they were so unusual.

This one looked identical to what Durbin had been wearing at his funeral. There couldn't be two like it. Not when we'd all but seen him take it from his uncle's tie. There'd been no doubt. Durbin had been wearing it when Veronica and I had passed by the casket. Then shortly after, when his nephew had leaned over the casket and then stepped away, it was gone. What other explanation could there be?

My stare finally caught Buford's attention. He glanced down at his chest, then back up. His eyes sparkled as he rubbed his hands together. "Isn't it great?"

Not the word I would have used. Better might have been *theft, dishonest,* or *super creepy.* "Well, it's...."

He nodded, which caused a lock of hair to bounce around his eyebrow. He reached up, smoothing it back into submission. "Yeah, it's new. Just got it, in fact."

Just got it? He made it sound like he'd come from a shopping spree. Anger boiled in my chest, then rose to my face. If my cheeks were red, I didn't even care. Even though I was polite, and tried awfully hard to hold my tongue, no way was I going to let this pass. Buford was no more than a grave robber. Technically, Durbin hadn't been in a grave yet, still....

No longer concerned with the cleanliness of my counter, I mimicked his stance and placed my palms on the glass. "Now listen, here, Mister." My voice came out like a cat's hiss.

Buford's head jerked, and he blinked.

I pointed at his chest. "I will not let you parade around town wearing something you so obviously stole." Though I hadn't intended it, my voice had risen on the word *stole.* Four sets of eyes from other people in the shop locked onto me.

Well, perfect, Molly. Let's upset everyone and give them more than usual to gossip about.

Buford frowned. "What do you mean?"

My forced smile was for the benefit of my new audience, as I hoped to minimize the gossip which would no doubt come from today's interlude. I locked in on Buford once again but kept my voice barely above a whisper. "I know good and well you took it from Durbin while he was lying in his coffin."

His head shake was quick, exaggerated, as if trying to make his point as fast as he could. "No. I would never...." He peeked over his shoulder at two women who now stood and had edged closer. Had they hoped to catch the softened words I wanted to keep private?

I gave a small wave to Nanny Gates, who'd moved another six inches in our direction. "Hi, Nanny. Be right with you."

Her face fell, and she took a step back. "No problem. Take your time." She was a big-time gossip queen. She'd happily spread what she heard and make up the rest. It was what my business didn't need at the moment. When more people found out I was the one who'd discovered Durbin's body in his garden, I'd have more customers than I knew what to do with. Although, they wouldn't be here for my goods or services. They'd want the dirt. And not the kind found in a garden.

I leaned closer to Buford than I would have liked, hoping the nosy ladies wouldn't be able to read my lips. "I. Saw. You."

His already pale face whitened even more, and his mouth opened and closed, not unlike the fish his tie tack image was based on. His hand closed over it, as if trying to protect it. Did he think I might steal it from him? "You… you're wrong." His throat moved as he swallowed hard.

Steps sounded from behind me. Veronica sidled up and now stood on my right. "Everything all right here, kiddies? Need some help from Miss Veronica?"

Her normally teasing words fell flat. Anger at what Buford had done had taken over. If my face wasn't red by now, I'd have been shocked.

Veronica moved closer. A finger poked my shoulder. "Molly? You okay?"

Since she was here, might as well get her to back me up. She'd witnessed everything I had at the funeral calling. Without taking my eyes from Buford, I said, "Veronica, Buford, here, claims to have just bought this tie clip he has on. What do you think about that?" I turned my head toward her, interested in her take on the situation.

For the first time, her gaze lowered to his chest. She let out a long, loud gasp worthy of a soap opera actress. "It's…"

"Yeah, it is." I then watched Buford. "See, Veronica was with me when I saw you take it from your uncle. At his funeral. From the casket."

He glanced hopefully at her. Did he think she'd lie to protect him? Or that she hadn't seen him?

As she narrowed her eyes, Veronica frowned. "Oh, I was there, all right. Yes, I saw you bending over his body, admiring that." She pointed to the open-mouthed fish. "And when you straightened, it was gone."

Buford tilted his head, then his eyes widened. "Ah ha." He pointed at her. "Then you didn't actually see me take, did you?" He smiled, as if he'd already won the argument, like there'd be no way he could be accused on a technicality.

I turned back to Veronica, who was already eyeing me. While it was true we hadn't witnessed the actual theft, there was no doubt he'd done it. Durbin himself hadn't reached up to remove it, and no one else stood close enough at the time it went missing. It had to have been Buford. Especially with him standing here, proudly wearing the evidence. I caught Buford's eye again and huffed out a breath. "Listen, here, you can play the semantics game all you like, but the fact remains, you are a thief."

Someone let out a surprised squeak from somewhere near the door. Oops, must have raised my voice again. Had to quit doing that. The nosy ladies wouldn't need to read my lips for information if I practically yelled it.

Buford took a step back from the counter. "I don't think I like the way this conversation is headed. I can't believe you'd accused me of—" His hand reached up to touch the tie clip. "I loved my uncle. He...he gave me this. Before he died."

Veronica and I made eye contact, her eyebrow-raised expression probably mirrored my own. I shook my head at Buford. "It's not possible. We saw Durbin wearing it while he was lying there in his—"

The front door opened and closed. Yet another pet parent stood in the entrance. Was everyone going to show up way before their appointments today? Time to get this wacko out of the shop and tend to the people who were supposed to be here. I hated not being on time with my schedule, and Buford made that difficult.

His eyes watered. Was he crying? "My uncle loved me a lot. And I loved him. He gave me this extra special gift."

I crossed my arms. Veronica mirrored my stance. We gave him the double stink-eye.

Buford frowned, his hand protectively over the fish as if Veronica or I might try to take it from him now that he'd been found out. "I'll be leaving and taking my business elsewhere." He stormed across the floor, flung the door open, and rushed past the picture window down the sidewalk.

Veronica let out a snort. "If everyone's business they brought to us was like Buford's, we'd be broke."

Chapter Ten

Still miffed about my interaction with Buford, I took a short break to get a caffeine fix for Veronica and me once we'd caught up with taking care of the pet parents who'd stopped in. Carrie's Coffee was only a block away, but the short walk helped relieve some of my irritation. Buford sure had some nerve. To take his uncle's tie tack was terrible, and then to wear it and lie about how he'd gotten it was unbelievable. Did he live in a dream world where people didn't notice the things he did out in public?

I reached for the door and tugged, only to come face to face with someone who was exiting the shop.

It was Buford. Again.

He almost stumbled but caught himself and his coffee before a major mishap occurred. I jumped back to avoid getting dowsed with his coffee and allowed him to pass. Why did I have to see him twice in such a short time? My plan had been to say nothing, because what more could I add to our recent unpleasant conversation? Yet, Buford had other plans.

He stood in the doorway, not having left enough room for me to step inside the building. Why wouldn't he go away and take his weirdness with him? "Listen, Molly. I want you to know I forgive you for what you said in Fabulous Felines. I realize you didn't know what you were saying."

Had I heard right? He'd come in there dressed in stolen goods, and, when called out on it, thought I'd somehow made it up. "Excuse me?"

"That's right. I forgive you. I don't know why you'd say I took my uncle's tie clip. Maybe you're just having a rough day? Anyway, I hope it gets better for you." The same creepy smile followed, and he scurried away from me down the cracked sidewalk. A young couple stepped out of his way, then stared after him for a few seconds.

My mouth hung open—for how long? —and I snapped it closed. Good grief. The man was a loon. More determined now than ever to get to the bottom of all this, I entered the coffee shop, intending to grab a couple drinks and go. I needed to discuss this latest wrinkle with Veronica. If she hadn't been with me to see what Buford had done at the funeral, maybe I'd doubt what I'd seen. But she'd been there too, witnessing the exact same event. No, Buford had stolen the tie tack, and acted like he hadn't. What was he trying to prove?

I stepped to the line of people who waited for their orders at the counter. As I stood in line, there was whispering from my right. And meowing. I angled around.

In a back corner sat Florence and Lottie. Their cats, Helga and Eleanor, were also there, who sat in seats beside their humans. Both cats were of the hairless sphinx variety, so the ladies kept them dressed in sweaters and booties year-round. Each cat lapped up a small dish of milk.

Though it wasn't customary for people to take their pets inside every public place in town, Carrie made an exception for the ladies. They weren't harming anyone, and I knew for a fact both cats were exceptionally well-behaved, even if sometimes moody. Florence and Lottie told people the reason they took their cats everywhere was they were emotional support pets, but the women had confided in me, they said it so their cats could get out of the house once in a while to see the sights.

I couldn't hold back a smile. There weren't many sights to see in Whitewater Valley, but to a house cat, maybe it was like a catnip amusement park, with the occasional saucer of milk.

As soon as I placed my order, I made my way around a few other tables to reach them. "Hey, ladies. Everyone doing okay?" I reached down and scratched Eleanor between the ears. The cat smiled, but Helga gave me a glare. I knew better than to show favoritism, so I petted her as well.

Lottie winked. "We're marvelous. We'd offer you a seat, but as you can see"—she waved her hand around to her friend and their companions— "our party is full up."

"No problem. I need to head back to my shop in a minute anyway." The ladies somehow always knew the latest happenings in town. Maybe because they spent an inordinate amount of time hanging around establishments like this one and at some point or another, encountered every member of town to overhear—eavesdrop—on pertinent conversations. If I waited long enough, they'd spill what they knew.

Lottie motioned me closer. "Did you see Buford Haines just going out?"

"Yes. I did." I wouldn't tell them about my oh so recent run-in with him in my shop. They'd know soon enough.

She rapped her knuckle on the table. "Well, I have it on good authority that some things he told people aren't exactly true."

"Really?" Maybe they'd already heard about what happened. News did travel at the speed of sound in this little place.

She caught Florence's eye, then nodded. They weren't related, but were as close as sisters, with a built-in code of eyebrow raises, nods, and winks. "That's right. Have you heard him say how much he loved and admired his uncle?"

"Sure have."

Florence shook her head, wisps of short white hair moving slightly. "It's a lie. He's always despised him."

My eyebrows rose. And no, it wasn't a signal to the ladies. It was news to me if Buford hadn't cared for his uncle, at least on some strange level. Buford was so odd, far be it from me to understand the workings of his mind as to what might be considered love for a family member. Yes, he'd stolen from the man, but I assumed maybe they'd been close in years past when Buford was growing up. The fact it wasn't true might add a new angle to the whole mystery surrounding Durbin's demise.

"You see, we" —Florence pointed to Lottie and then herself — "happen to know things about Buford that most might not." Her eyes sparkled. She obviously enjoyed knowing juicy tidbits before others.

I took a step closer. "Do tell."

Her eyes lit up, seeming glad I was interested. "Well, Lottie and I know

Durbin's family quite well from way back. Durbin's dad went to school with us."

Lottie nodded, dislodging a lock of short silver hair from behind her ear. "That's right."

I tilted my head. "How interesting."

Florence's eyes crinkled at the corners. "We thought so too. His father ate glue on a regular basis. Not saying it's why Buford turned out so odd, but who really knows for sure?"

While the glue theory might be intriguing, if not disgusting, I had other things to find out first. "So why do you think Buford lied about his uncle?"

"I'm getting to that." She waved her hand at me.

I cringed, sometimes forgetting Florence was a former elementary teacher who still thought of everyone younger than herself as a wayward puppy who needed a smack on the nose for leaving something unpleasant on the carpet.

"For years now," she said, "Durbin had promised Buford a prominent, well-paying place in his construction business way up in management. Not doing manual labor, of course."

"Of course." No, I couldn't imagine Buford, in his dress clothes and tie, bent over a pile of dirt with a shovel.

"Buford tells people he has a disability, but it's because he's lazy. When his uncle said he could be in management, Buford assumed he could sit around and do nothing."

How sad that Buford had invented an illness to get out of work.

Lottie poked Florence in the arm. "Go on. Tell Molly the rest."

Florence rolled her eyes at her friend, but her expression was one of fondness, not irritation. Apparently, people of her own age escaped her teacher-mode treatment. "Yes, well, anyway, after years of waiting for his uncle to make good on his promise, Buford was sorely disappointed when Durbin reneged on the whole affair. He'd hoped for a job on easy street, but Durbin changed his mind."

I shook my head. Though Buford wasn't my favorite person, it still seemed a cruel thing to do, especially to a family member. After I'd waited what seemed an appropriate amount of time for Florence to add more, I took the chance her silence meant she'd finished and I wouldn't get scolded again. "Do you happen to know when all this took place? When Buford found out he wouldn't get what he'd been promised?"

"Of course, dear. It was the week before Durbin died."

It was a rather good reason to want revenge on someone. Buford might have snapped when he found out he wouldn't get what he'd been promised. He was now officially on my list of suspects for Durbin's murder.

Lottie squinted toward the front picture window behind me. I turned around just in time to see Wilma stroll past the shop. When I returned my focus to the ladies, they were winking furiously at one another like Morse Code with false eyelashes.

Now what? Learning about Buford was huge. Was there anything else?

Carrie called out my name with my orders. Rats. I wanted to know what the ladies knew. I rushed to pay for my coffees and hurried back to their table.

Lottie grinned. "I thought you might like to know something else."

With a coffee cup in each hand, I said, "Yes, I would." Being a tad late to the shop might be worth it if I discovered useful information. Veronica would love to hear the news as well.

Lottie clasped her hands together on the table. "Apparently, Wilma Haines has been a bad girl."

Bad girl, as in something illegal? Or as from her friend's former-teacher perspective, as in she talked in class or chewed gum.

Florence leaned forward. "Let me tell this one."

"Very well." Lottie sighed.

Florence sat up straighter in her seat, which caused her chair to squeak loudly. Helga and Eleanor simultaneously whipped their hat-covered heads in her direction and gave her the stink-eye for the interruption of their enjoyment of their treats. She gave each cat a wink. "Sorry, girls. My mistake."

The cats returned their attention to the dairy delights, again ignoring the rest of us.

"Anyway," said Florence, "Wilma, who'd been so weepy at her husband's funeral, hadn't even liked the man."

Was that all? I knew that from my recent encounter with her on her porch. Nothing new there.

"Say the rest." Lottie stirred her what now had to be cold tea.

"I'll get there. As I was saying, our Wilma had been up to something nefarious."

I straightened. Nefarious had definite possibilities. Maybe worse than being a bad girl.

Leaning closer, she glanced both ways before saying, "She's been spending time with a lawyer from out of town. They're having a wild sex affair."

Lottie gasped. "You didn't need to say it like that."

Florence shrugged. "I'm sure Molly knows about the birds and bees." Raising her gaze to me, her eyes widened. "Don't you, dear? Or have I spilled the beans about a subject you weren't aware of?"

I bit my lip and tried hard not to laugh. "No. I think I heard about all it somewhere along the line."

Lottie let out a breath. "Oh. Good. I was afraid I'd scarred you for life."

"Not to worry. It's all fine."

As I said goodbye and headed toward the door, my face heated. Why did talk about a wild sex affair make me think of Hank?

Thankfully, the brisk breeze outside cooled me off before I got back to my shop. Now I could think clearly about what I'd learned about Buford and Wilma. More reasons to keep them on my list of suspects.

Chapter Eleven

Back at Fabulous Felines, I was glad to see Jasper asleep in a basket on the front counter. Instead of bringing both cats to the shop or leaving them stuck together at home, I now alternated the days they'd be here. Hopefully, soon, they'd get along. I'd tried so many ways to get them not to fight, but so far, Percival wasn't having it. I still couldn't understand why he was so stubborn about Jasper when he'd never balked at being around other cats before.

I'd just handed Veronica her coffee and was ready to fill her in on the latest when Candi stormed into the building. What in the world? Since I'd recently talked to her and groomed her cat, I couldn't imagine why she'd need to see me again so soon.

She glanced left and right, then hurried toward us. "Molly, there's something I need to tell you."

I waited a few seconds, but nothing else happened. "Um, all right."

Candi stared at Veronica, then back at me. "It's personal."

Veronica's eyes widened. She struck a dramatic pose with the back of her hand pressed over her forehead. "I know when I'm not wanted," and sauntered to the back room.

Candi gasped. "Oh, I didn't mean to upset...."

I waved my hand. "You didn't. She's kidding."

With a glance toward the back area for a few seconds, Candi must have accepted my explanation because then she focused squarely on me. "I'm glad you don't have any customers right now."

I wasn't so glad, since pet parents paid my bills, but kept it to myself.

I'd rushed back to the shop only to discover my pet parent had called to reschedule. "You said you needed to tell me something?"

"Yes." She cleared her throat. "Since you and I had the talk… you know… while you were grooming Honey, I realized it helped me out to have someone to vent to. I hope you don't mind."

Normally, I wouldn't be thrilled to be someone's sounding board, someone who I wasn't close to, but in this case, I welcomed it. Whatever she told me might get me closer to the truth of who killed Durbin. "I don't mind. You can tell me anything."

Candi let out a sigh ending in a tiny whimper. "Thank you so much. You have no idea how…. Well, anyway, what I have to say is about Wilma."

"Go on."

"That woman…she's having an affair. Do you believe it?"

It wasn't my job to point out Candi had done the exact same thing with Wilma's husband. I also didn't want to spill the beans I already knew about Wilma. It was more important to keep Candi talking. "Wow. What a surprise."

"I know. Who would have thought anyone would want to do that with a woman who looks like her."

Ouch. Now we were being extra catty, which was saying something considering where we stood. I shrugged and tried to remain noncommittal, because anything I said in return would be flung to the far corners of Whitewater Valley in record time.

"But it's not even the whole reason I'm here."

That got my attention. Just when I thought I already knew what she'd say. This might be interesting, and useful. I nodded.

"Wilma is sleeping with a sleazy lawyer who told her she might get some money from Durbin's death after all."

"Wait, aren't you supposed to get—"

"Yeah, from what you told me. By the way, you never said how you heard that."

"I…."

Jasper had woken up from his nap and sat a few inches away as he stared at me. *Thanks, little dude, for the interruption.* I patted him on the head. "This is Jasper."

Candi barely flicked a glance at him.

I ran my hand down his back. He gazed up at me with adoration. I smiled back, then asked Candi, "Do you recognize him?"

Her eyebrows lowered. "Should I?"

"He was Durbin's."

She squinted and took a closer look. "Oh. Right. But I was never at Durbin's house, so hadn't met him. I do remember a picture of his cat on his desk at work. Why do you have him?"

Yes, why indeed? "It just seemed to work out that way. Um, since I run a cat grooming shop and all."

"Oh, like people bring their unwanted pets to you?"

I cringed at unwanted and pets in the same sentence. "Something like that." People didn't normally dump their animals here. Fabulous Felines attracted dedicated pet parents who, yes, I'll say it, spoiled their furry babies. Not that there was anything wrong with it. Time to get Candi back on track. "Um, you said Wilma might get some money?"

Candi blinked, as if trying to get her thoughts back in the right order in her head. "Oh yeah. Right. This guy, Al Swartz, said there were some jewels which weren't included in his will for some reason."

"I see."

"Wanna know what I think?"

More than you know. "Of course."

"I believe Wilma now has an excellent motive to have killed my poor sweet Durbin. That is, if his death turns out not to have been an accident."

Ah, now we were to the crux of why she made her mad dash in here. "But you, of course, have your alibi with Tom, so you don't need to worry about getting in trouble."

"Right." She tilted her head. "You know, it's funny. The sheriff hasn't approached me yet with any questions."

And he wasn't likely to. But Candi sure didn't need that particular information. "Hmmm. Well, sometimes local authorities take their time, but it doesn't mean you shouldn't be ready."

"Ready?"

"You know, with your alibi. The reason you couldn't have killed Durbin. If it comes to that, of course."

"Sure. Of course." She gave Jasper a pat on the head, which earned her a muffled purr. "I knew, of course."

"Knew what?"

"About the jewels," said Candi.

"Oh? From Wilma's lawyer?"

"No. I don't know him."

"Then how?"

She leaned closer, even though we were alone. Did she think Jasper might repeat it to Wilma somehow? "Well, as you know, Durbin and I worked together."

"Right." No doubt it's how they hooked up in the first place.

"I'm his—was—his secretary." Her eyes glistened. Would she cry? I reached beneath my counter and retrieved a box of tissues. Candi grabbed one and dabbed at her eyes. "Thanks."

"No problem."

"Anyway, it was part of my job to file all his documents. I have to skim them to know where they belong in the cabinet."

"Makes sense."

"I didn't realize that one wasn't work-related. Honest." She held up her hand.

I made eye contact. Was she afraid I'd try to get her in trouble for doing something wrong at her job? "Of course not. Anyone might have done the same."

She let out a breath. "Yes, you're probably right."

Candi knew the jewels weren't in the will, yet hadn't known she would be the recipient of everything else Durbin would leave behind. At first, it raised a red flag. But the more I examined it, the two documents might not even have been together when she went to file. Maybe Durbin's will wasn't even kept at his office. Who knew? People often protected important items in a safe or with their bank's safe deposit boxes.

This girl was tightly wound, but could I blame her? She'd lost the person she was in love with and maybe her job in one fell swoop. I reached out and touched her hand briefly. "I'm sorry for all you've gone through." Now it seemed selfish of me to make her think the sheriff would come talk to her when I didn't know for a fact he would. All because I tried to figure out who'd killed Durbin. While it was true finding out the killer's identity might benefit Candi with some kind of closure, I'd gone about it in an underhanded way. "Listen. The more I think about it, the less I think the sheriff will question you."

Her eyes widened. "Really? You don't think he will?"

I shook my head.

"Why not? I mean, not that I looked forward to it or anything, but you'd seemed so sure."

"Maybe I've watched too many crime shows lately. Thinking the authorities wait around every corner ready to pounce on unsuspecting people." I winked.

She gave a brief smile. "I get it. I've been known to binge-watch shows too. Thanks for putting my mind at ease." Candi dabbed her eyes again, then tossed the tissue in a nearby wastebasket. With a glance at her watch, she grimaced. "Oh, I need to run back to work."

My eyes widened. "Um, I'd thought with Durbin...."

She let out a breath. "He had a partner, Frank Veerk, who recently signed on with him. He's my new boss now. It's sad, though."

"What is?"

"From day one, they never got along. They'd argue in Durbin's office. So much so, I couldn't figure out why he would want the guy for his partner. Sometimes their arguments got loud. I'd never heard Durbin raise his voice like that before." She shrugged. "Maybe Frank's the guilty party in his death." She shook her head. "Now you've got me doing it. Thinking everyone is a suspect."

"Sorry to put those thoughts in your head."

"No, it's okay. I appreciate you listening to me vent my troubles."

"Anytime, Candi." I meant it. Seeing how upset my talk of the sheriff had made her caused a pang of guilt to sliver up my middle.

She waved as she left the shop.

Rapid footsteps approached from behind. Veronica now stood beside me. "That girl doesn't seem remotely sorry she slept with someone else's husband. And your comment about watching too many crime dramas? If she only knew how hooked you are on some of them."

"Hey, you were listening?"

"Of course. Not much to do back there with no furry client at the moment. Well, let's face it. The walls are thin."

"You're shameless."

"Thank you."

Chapter Twelve

I had a light morning the next day at the grooming shop and hoped to catch up on stocking some shelves and ordering supplies. While I sat at the front counter, my stack of paperwork and laptop were positioned in front of me.

Someone rattled the doorknob. Had a pet parent gotten their time wrong again? With a sigh, I waited until the door opened. In stormed Sheriff King. He frowned.

I placed my paperwork on my keyboard, then slid my laptop to one side. The man wasn't here for advice about a cat, since he didn't even seem to like them. "Hi, Sheriff. How can I help you?"

He glanced around the empty room and gave a nod. Was he glad no one else was around? I didn't like the thought of that. Might mean he had something not so nice to say to me. I wasn't in the mood for his attitude. Hopefully, he'd have his say and go, soon.

When he reached my counter, he stood, arms at his sides, like a soldier who reported for duty. What was he up to? After clearing his throat, he fixed narrowed eyes on me. "Listen, Molly. I've heard some things about you, things I don't like."

"And what might that be?"

"According to Mrs. Long, who lives right across the street from Wilma Haines, you were seen arguing with her the other day on her front porch."

I shook my head. "It's not true."

"You weren't at her house?"

"Well, I was, but—"

He held his hands out, palms up. "What did you think you were up to fighting with someone right out in the open where anyone could see you? It's a respectable neighborhood. Surprised I didn't get more than the one call."

I held up my hand. "Now, wait a minute. Yes, I was there."

"What was your reason for doing so?"

I couldn't very well tell him I'd hoped to snoop in their garden for clues. "I… I offered my condolences." That much was true. Even though she hadn't appreciated my sentiment since she loathed her husband, I had indeed given her my thoughts.

He shrugged. "Since when do offering condolences result in raised voices and nearly coming to blows?"

My mouth dropped open. I snapped it closed and shook my head. "There were no blows. Nothing of the sort. Maybe Mrs. Long needs her glasses updated, because if she says it's what she saw, she's wrong."

"Why don't you tell me what you think happened?" Sheriff King crossed his arms.

"It's not what I think. It's what really went on."

"Well, I'm waiting." The sound of his impatient foot tapped out a quick beat could be heard from the floor on the other side of the counter.

Think, Molly. "I…." A movement to my left caught my eye. Jasper had risen from where he'd finished his nap, gave me a sleepy look, then turned in a circle for another sleep cycle. I pointed to him. "I told Wilma I had Durbin's cat. Remember when you'd wanted to take him to a shelter, and I'd taken him instead? I offered to bring him to Wilma."

"Then why is he"—he tilted his head toward the cat— "still here?"

My mouth turned down at the corners at the memory of her refusal to have anything to do with Jasper, at how she hadn't cared what I did with Durbin's cat as long as she didn't have to deal with him. I leaned closer. "Because she said she didn't want him." I kept my voice low.

"Why are you whispering? There's no one else here."

I jerked my head toward Jasper.

The sheriff made a face. "What? I don't know what you're doing. Is it some sort of code?"

"Because he might overhear, and I don't want his feelings to be hurt."

He blinked, then stared at me. "His... wait, are you telling me you think that"—he pointed— "has feelings?"

My eyes widened as anger coursed through me. How dare he say such a thing? "Of course, he does. All cats do. Not that you'd ever know."

"Might want to adjust your tone, missy." He raised one eyebrow. "I am the law."

If he wanted to arrest me for caring about cats' feelings, then he could go right ahead. "All right, Sheriff. You've had your say. I do have work to do after all." My gaze flicked to the door and back. Would he take the hint and leave me alone?

"Don't see anybody sitting in your waiting room."

"That's not all we do here." I touched my laptop.

With a wave of his hand at my computer, as if it was meaningless, he then focused his beady eyes right on me. "You've explained about Wilma. I guess I'll have to take your explanation at face value."

I let out a breath. Maybe he'd leave me alone now.

"But...."

Oh no. What else? I crossed my arms. Why had I thought I could have a quiet, peaceful morning without drama from someone interrupting me?

Sheriff King knocked his fist on the counter, which startled Jasper, who woke and hissed. The sheriff gave the cat a disparaging look, but Jasper gave it right back. As if chastised, the man took a step to the left, moving a little farther from the feline. Was it possible he was afraid of cats?

I eyed the sheriff. "What else did you need to say?"

He gave Jasper one more glance, then looked at me. "What I want to say is this. While you arguing—"

I opened my mouth to speak.

He held up his hand. "Supposedly arguing with Wilma might have been an issue. The other thing I need to speak to you about is more serious."

Serious? I didn't like the sound of that. I grasped my hands together on the countertop. Hopefully, I appeared calm. *Breathe deep, Molly.* How bad could it be?

"According to several folks, you caused an upheaval at Durbin's funeral calling."

"What? No, I didn't. Upheaval implies doing something outrageous, like smacking someone or doing a jig in front of the casket."

He raised his eyebrows.

"Of course, I didn't do any of that. I think, once again, you've gotten false information about me."

"Well, let's just see, shall we? Someone told me you and your assistant, Veronica, spent an inordinate amount of time standing in front of the casket when there was a line of people behind you who waited to pay their respects."

"It wasn't an inordinate amount. Anyway, I fail to see how it's a punishable offense. Isn't that one reason people go to funerals? To pay their respects?"

Rapid footsteps sounded from behind me. Veronica popped up next to me, wearing a silly grin. "Did I hear my name mentioned? Someone need to see my pretty face?"

I stared at her. She'd been eavesdropping again. Veronica blinked at me, all innocence and light, and shrugged.

Sheriff King shook his head. "Veronica, this is a private conversation between Molly and me."

She smirked. "Oh, come on, Sheriff, I know the real reason you came into Fabulous Felines."

"You do, huh. What would that be?"

She reached beneath the counter and pulled out a fuzzy pink cat toy shaped like a smiling mouse.

His shoulders stiffened. "Woman, what are you talking about?"

She shook it at him, which made the little bell inside the mouse jingle. "We all know you are an Ailurophile."

His eyes widened. "Excuse me?"

"It means a lover of cats."

His face reddened, and a vein popped out on the side of his neck. "That is a lie. Take it back!"

He was so vehement, both Veronica and I took a step away from the counter. After a look of disgust for the toy, he stood up straighter and smoothed wrinkles from the front of his shirt. "Why don't we stop all this nonsense and get back to our conversation, Molly. And Veronica?"

"Yes?" She batted her eyelashes as if he was going to ask her on a date.

"I think you should leave."

Beneath the counter, Veronica brushed her shoe against mine. She wanted to stay? When she got in one of her obstinate moods, there was no swaying her. "It's okay, Sheriff. I don't mind if my assistant is here. As a matter of fact, I think she should stay for the conversation."

She nodded. "That's right. Since I was with Molly at the funeral, anything you say to her, you can say to me too."

"Very well. Other people told me you two were watching people."

I eyed Veronica, then him. "So? Aren't people allowed to look at other people? Or is it some new law that recently went into effect. Don't you ever look at people?"

"Not just watching. They said you stood there a long time to see what other people were doing."

Veronica tapped her fingernail on the counter. "Wait a second. If we watched other people, then what were those folks who said we looked at others doing to us? Hmmm?"

I grinned. "Veronica has a point. How is what they said we did different from them watching us, uh, watch other people?"

The sheriff gave a low growl. Jasper jumped from his basket, trotted over to me, and then sat right in front of the sheriff. The cat stared at him and swished his tail.

Sheriff King backed away slowly, hands raised in a defensive position. "You ladies just…." He backed away even more. "You mind what you do from now on." He turned and nearly ran from the room.

Now to send Russ a text to tell him Sheriff King was still giving me trouble.

Chapter Thirteen

Twice a year, Paula's Pastries had an outdoor bake sale. No one missed it. No one. Her delectable baked goodies were to die for. She quadrupled her normal daily number of pies, scones, cakes, and tarts and lowered her prices for the day. People had been known to take vacation days from work to stand in line for a chance at some extra treats.

I was no exception. Veronica always marked off the mornings of the bake sales so both of us could go. It worked out well, because none of our pet parents wanted to miss either, so wouldn't have made appointments anyway.

At my house, Jasper and Percival had still been at it. They hissed and growled whenever in the same room, so the early part of my morning had been spent trying to calm them down. Had it been a mistake to bring Jasper home?

No. The thought of taking the cat to the shelter made me nearly ill. Maybe I could find him another home? Even the notion made me sad. I was already attached to the little guy, and since he'd lost his dad, I didn't have the heart to make him lose yet another home.

I rushed to the bake sale as soon as I'd gotten the two little guys somewhat settled in separate rooms, only to find a line already snaked down the sidewalk toward Evan's Photography Studio. As I glanced around, I didn't see Veronica. Surely, she hadn't forgotten it was today. The lady lived for sugar, and gossip, and teasing me. My face reddened as I remembered her comments about Hank. Did my assistant believe she could push two people together just because it was what she wanted?

A sound like air leaking from an old tire caught my attention. I turned.

Veronica and her husband Jerome were about ten people behind me. She once again gave the *psst* sound and waved furiously, like she hadn't seen me in a month. I laughed. With her goofy sense of humor and sunny disposition, Veronica always made my days brighter. That was, if I could get her to stop her quest of matching me up with someone.

I waved at her and Jerome until a slight nudge from right behind me pushed me forward. Agnes Temple stood directly behind me now. When had she snuck up there? As I eyed the line in front of me, which had moved forward without my notice, I grimaced. "Sorry." A few steps forward had me caught up with the line.

A low mumble came from Agnes, but I ignored her. It wasn't as if being a couple of feet behind the others would cause Agnes to lose her place in line. But since Pastry Day was one of the most exciting things to happen in Whitewater Valley, people went a little crazy.

I sighed. Too bad it wasn't the most exciting thing to happen. Durbin's murder had eclipsed anything that had ever, and probably would ever, happen in town. The memory of when the sheriff had scolded me about the funeral made me twitch. He'd treated me like some rotten little kid who hadn't followed directions in class. However, his reaction to Jasper had been interesting when he'd backed away from the cat.

A few people who must have stood in line while it was still dark were the first to purchase items from Paula. One woman placed her wrapped purchase in her large purse, but the man with her unwrapped his and took a huge bite. His expression rivaled any self-respecting cat's after the first intoxicating whiff of catnip kicked in.

My stomach growled, as did Agnes' behind me. I held in my laugh. She would be mortified if she knew I'd heard that. Better not to upset her further since I'd held up the line before.

Someone must have spoken to the first couple who'd bought their treats, because they paused, stepped closer together, and smiled. I leaned around someone in front of me. Ah...Evan Lakes was taking their photo. Had Paula asked him to cover her event for publicity?

Yeah right. As if Paula needed any help to get townspeople to come to her bake sales. The couple strolled to one of the many picnic tables Paula had set out to the side of her building where people could enjoy their treats in the sunny, crisp morning air. There was still a large number of people in front of me. If they all stayed and took seats after getting their food, there might not be a place for me to sit.

Good grief. Could I sound any more like an elementary girl who hoped not to be left standing in the lunchroom?

"Hey, Molly."

I turned. Hank passed by, giving me a wave. "Hey." I waved back. Catching Veronica's eye, I groaned. She'd witnessed the encounter and was no doubt planning our future wedding. With a roll of my eyes, I faced front, groaning again when I had to catch up to the line. If I scurried forward, maybe Agnes wouldn't growl at me a second time. Didn't I get enough of it from a few of my snootier cat clients on a bad fur day?

Ken Evers passed by me, heading for the back of the line. Andrea's words about her brother and Durbin having cheated him floated across my mind. Couldn't a deal gone bad, especially if it cost Ken a lot of money, be a good motive for murder? The little I'd known of Ken, he'd always seemed like a decent guy, but who knew what would make someone crack and attack another person with a scary garden implement?

As I turned my head back toward the front, I gasped. When had Buford appeared? He now stood so close to me, I could smell his overpowering citrus aftershave. I couldn't back up without the risk of another bump into Agnes. Besides, I didn't want to leave, because I'd lose my place in line. I held in a sigh. "Hey, Buford. What's up?"

"Up? Oh, nothing. Wanted to wish you a good morning."

Why did he stand so close? Did he want me to invite him to cut in line and stand beside me? Nope. Not gonna happen. "Um, okay. Good morning."

"You too." He smiled.

What was he up to? Someone a couple of people back snickered. Oh great. Would rumors now start that Buford liked me or something? Hoping not to sound too rude, I tilted my head to my left and said, "I think the end of the line starts back there."

He blinked. "I know."

Why was he still here? The line edged forward, so I followed. I let out a sigh when Buford remained where he was. "Well," I gave another wave, "uh, good to see you."

"Same here." The sound of his footsteps was covered by the early morning chatter of people as they wished each other good morning and caught up on the latest news. Someone mentioned Durbin's name, but I couldn't tell who. How many people already knew I'd been the one to find him in his garden?

At least Buford had moved on. What a strange guy. I was glad he hadn't worn his uncle's tie tack. Maybe he saw how dumb it was to parade around town in something his relative had been wearing as he'd lain in his casket.

A few people greeted someone as he or she passed by. I craned my neck to see. It was the sheriff. I didn't want him to see me in case he'd feel the need to give me the riot act again about the funeral, but there wasn't a convenient place to hide right now. I crossed my arms and waited until he reached me.

"Good morning, Molly."

"Hi."

"Behaving ourselves, are we?"

Someone behind me laughed. How dare the sheriff say that? My face heated, but I lowered my arms and stood up taller. "Well, I'm certainly on my best behavior. How about you?"

His mouth dropped open, then snapped shut. He narrowed his eyes but didn't answer. Then he rushed on by me. I didn't normally go out of my way to embarrass people, but he'd started it. Would people who'd heard his question now wonder if I'd been up to something illegal?

My phone buzzed. I dug it out of my purse and checked the screen. A text from Jillian with a request to get her a blueberry popover. I texted her a thumbs-up. Hopefully, it meant she'd show up soon, and we could have a chat.

A few minutes of people-watching later, I'd finally reached the table Paula had set up in front of her building. Her daughter, Danae, ran in and out of the front door as Paula instructed her on what needed to be replenished on the table.

"Good morning, Molly. How are you?"

"I'm great. Looks like a booming business for you."

Paula grinned. "Yeah. It warms my heart how much people love what I bake."

"Are you kidding? I've listened to people's stomachs growl now for twenty minutes while standing in line."

From behind me, someone cleared their throat. Probably Agnes.

I pointed toward a group of people having their photo taken at one of the tables. "Great to see Evan here taking pictures."

She nodded. "Definitely. He asked if he could. What could I say? Free advertising. I'd have been crazy to turn it down." She glanced behind me at what had to be, by now, a long line. "What can I get you today?"

"I'd like a box of apple tarts." I could freeze what was left over. Who was I kidding? They wouldn't last that long. "And a box of blueberry popovers."

She laughed as she packaged the items. "I guess your stomach is growling too?"

I patted it. "It is. But some of it is for Jillian." We traded money for pastries. "Enjoy."

"Believe me, I will." I headed to the left of the line, indeed long, and faced the table area. They were all full. I groaned. Now what?

"Molly!"

Florence and Lottie were tucked away at the back table with, of course, Eleanor and Helga. Lottie waved me over.

I had hoped for some private time with Jillian if she showed up, but I always enjoyed time with the ladies. "Thank you." I sat in one of the three remaining chairs. "I hope Jillian can join us." Reaching out, I petted first Eleanor, who ducked her head for the attention, then Helga, who ignored me as she ate her small piece of cheese danish.

Lottie gave me a big grin. She was so small, I could only see her head and shoulders above the tall table. "Wonderful. Jillian is one of my favorite people."

"Mine too."

Florence, taller than Lottie by several inches, bent down as she elbowed her friend. "Go on. Tell her why you like the librarian so much."

Lottie looked both ways, then lowered her head, like she was about to spill state secrets. "She gets me books."

Hmmm. She was a librarian, after all. "Oh. How nice."

"No, I mean... books."

"What she's trying to say is, Jillian gets her books about...." Florence waggled her eyebrows.

"Oh...I see."

"Do you, dear?" She turned to Lottie. "Maybe she doesn't really see."

"No. I do. Honest," I said.

Lottie's eyes focused squarely on me. "Have you read Heaving Bosoms?"

"No."

"Oh, but you must."

Having this conversation with someone my grandmother's age was a little uncomfortable. "I... Gee, I'm really busy."

Florence leaned closer. "But surely you don't work every hour of every day. You could sneak off in that little shop of yours and take a break, couldn't you?"

Lottie elbowed her friend. "Maybe she doesn't want to read it. Maybe—"

"Hey, all." Jillian stepped around me to sit in another empty chair. "How is everyone?"

Lottie pointed her fork at me. "I was just telling Molly about, you know."

Jillian tilted her head. "Er...about..."

"The. Book."

"Ah. Yes. The book." answered Jillian.

At least if the ladies insisted on a discussion of some sexy romance, I had Jillian here as a buffer.

Florence poked Lottie on the arm. "Look at the time. If we don't get to the grocery right away, all the fresh pineapple will be gone."

"Oh, you're right. We need it to make our mixed drinks in the evening. Helps us sleep. Medicinal, you know." The ladies threw their trash away in a nearby can, then scooped up their respective cats. "Come along, kitties." She winked at me and Jillian. "See you girls later."

Jillian and I waved and successfully waited until they were well out of earshot before giggling. I shook my head. "When we have girls' night out, can we label the drinks medicinal too?"

Jillian shrugged. "I don't see why not."

I unwrapped my apple tart and took a bite. "So good."

Jillian did the same with hers. "Almost as good as...." Her eyebrows rose and lowered a few times.

"Oh my gosh. Have you been reading 'Heaving Bosoms'?"

She shrugged. "I gave it a try. Honestly, it was a little over the top with writhing bodies and moaning."

A woman at the table beside us stared for a few seconds, then went back to her cherry pie.

Jillian leaned closer and kept her voice low. "Have you read it?"

I shook my head. "No. Not my choice of reading material. Besides, I didn't want Percival to get a hold of it and read it. He's too young for that stuff. Might warp his furry little mind."

She snorted. "True. But speaking of romance...." She tilted her head to something behind me. Hank stood beside a far table as he spoke to Ricky.

"What, you too? I get enough of it from Veronica."

She wiggled her eyebrows again. "He's cute. Hunky Hank."

"Sure. He's gorgeous," I said.

"Well then?"

"If you're so interested, maybe you should date him." Wait, why did I say that? If she ended up dating Hank, it would bother me. A lot.

"Hank is terrific." Jillian waved her hand. "But I like my men more cerebral."

Even though I was relieved she hadn't taken my suggestions seriously, I felt the need to defend the guy. "Hey, Hank is smart."

She nibbled on a small bite of her pastry, then swallowed the bite. "I know. But I kind of doubt he's the type to sit around and discuss the meaning of literature for hours on end."

Jillian had a point.

"Besides," she said, "you and Hank already have a love of animals in common."

Another point. However, since I had no clue if Hank even found me at all attractive, I wouldn't jump into a situation and get my hopes up as I had in the past. I was one disastrous date away from spending my life as a hermit as it was. I shrugged. "I have too much going on now to worry about dating." I dusted some crumbs from my hands. "You usually sample the new books that come into the library, right? But you didn't read the whole romance?"

"Not really my genre. You know me. I like mysteries, like you do."

"Then maybe you can help me out with Durbin's," I said.

She leaned forward, so I did the same. "I've given it some thought, Molly."

"I'd love to hear your theories. Add to that the fact that Veronica and I are certain that Buford took his uncle's fish tie tack right off of his body while he was in his casket."

Jillian grimaced. "That's morbid. Buford is one weird guy."

"Agreed."

A shout from near the end of the line had both me and Jillian turning to our right. Ken pushed Buford, who stumbled backwards, but didn't fall. Ken, a much bigger man, had the advantage of height and strength.

The crowd of people moved aside to get out of the men's way. People pointed and stared. Someone got out their cell phone. Would the fight end up on the Internet? It wasn't exactly the publicity our little town wanted to have.

I clenched my hands together as first one man, then the other, swung his fist. Would someone be seriously hurt? Maybe the person who'd gotten out their cell phone wasn't filming the fight but had called the sheriff. The caller might not know Sheriff King was already here in the crowd. "I wonder what's up with them. I don't know Ken very well, but as for Buford, he's been acting weirder than usual."

Jillian pointed toward Buford. "Considering his uncle just passed away, and he had stolen something from the poor man from his casket, maybe that's a good place to start checking out the mystery of his death."

"Good idea."

She glanced down at my cell phone that sat next to me on the table.

"What? I didn't hear it ring."

"No, but shouldn't you update your uncle on today's scuttlebutt?"

I picked up the phone. "Definitely. Lots to fill him in on."

Chapter Fourteen

A couple of my clients had mentioned they'd love to have portraits done of their pets. While they'd been hopeful I'd be qualified for the job, they'd have been sadly mistaken. Although most people had cell phones and routinely took photos of things they found interesting, I had a photography glitch. No matter how I tried to steady my hand to capture an image for posterity, my hand always seemed to move just enough that whatever I'd hope to capture looked like a fuzzy cloud as it zipped across the screen.

However, our local photographer might fill the bill. When I entered Evan's studio, he stood on a step ladder, placing a photo in his front window. I got a glimpse of it before he turned it to face the sidewalk. It was of Lottie and Florence, each feeding her cat bites of pastry. Adorable.

When he saw me, he smiled, his blue eyes creased at the corners. "Hey, Molly. How are you?"

"I'm good. Wow, what a great shot." I pointed to the photo.

"Thanks. I got a bunch from the bake sale. Besides drawing attention to my window, I thought maybe Paula might like a couple for her wall as well, of people as they enjoyed her wares."

"Great idea."

He stepped down, and the sun glinted through the window to his blond hair. He picked up a stack of a dozen or so pictures. "Here's some more. What do you think?"

As I quickly flipped through the images, I grinned. So many happy expressions. Who wouldn't have when sampling delicious sugary delights?

"These are awesome." I set them down on the window seat.

Evan beamed. "Why, thank you. Though I'm always glad to see you, it's probably not why you stopped by."

"Actually, some of my clients have asked about having photos done of their cats."

"Oh?" His eyes lit up. "I'd be all over it. Wonder why I never thought of it."

"Don't feel bad. I hadn't either. But when more than one person brought it up, it sounded like a wonderful idea." And they definitely wouldn't be happy with my feeble attempts at photos of their cats. They'd end up with a bunch of pictures of either white, black, gray, or orange fur. Not something they'd want to hang on their walls.

"I agree. What were you thinking in terms of how to go about it?"

I glanced at the pictures in the window. "Maybe have some fliers up in my shop about you and your work. A couple samples of animal photos if you have some."

He rubbed his chin. "I do. Not sitting pet portraits, but of wildlife around my property. Do you think that would work?"

"It would be perfect."

"Would you want to split the commissions I get since it was your idea?" he asked.

I waved my hand. "No. Just wanted to see if I could arrange it to please my pet parents."

"That doesn't seem fair." His eyebrows lowered. "Surely, we can work out a deal."

"Honestly, hadn't thought about it." I smiled.

"Let's see how it goes, then we can decide later."

I shrugged. "Sure. Thanks. I think my clients will love this. One thing, though. Sometimes cats cooperate, and sometimes they don't." I happened to know Evan was a dog lover and had a couple at his house. Most dogs tended to be more obedient than unpredictable cats.

Evan laughed. "I may not have any cats, but I sure know how moody they can be."

I raised my eyebrows. "Have some experience, then?"

99

"My grandmother had two elderly cats who were picky and particular about every little thing. They only liked to be petted by her. I tried a few times when I was little but got hissed at for my trouble. When one took a paw swipe at me, I decided maybe dogs would be a better choice."

"Most cats aren't like that. Honestly."

He held up his hand. "Oh, I know. I do like cats. Now. Just have a fondness for dogs, is all."

"And it's wonderful. I'm all about any animals. They're all great. Except skunks. I don't have anything against them personally. I'm sure some are quite nice. But...."

He made a face. "Right. Don't want to get too close. Not even to take a picture." He tilted his head. "Sounds like we both like the idea of me doing some pet portraits. I'll look forward to this. Hopefully, there will be lots of your pet parents who'd like to participate."

"I think this will be great."

He rubbed his hands together. "Can't wait to get started."

"Same here." Evan was so talented. He was bound to make people happy with whatever photos he took of their fur babies.

"Say, I have some pictures in the back room of wildlife I took a month or so ago when I was out hiking. I could get them for you to hang in your shop. That is, if you're ready to start spreading the word this soon?"

"Absolutely. Sooner, the better."

"Great. Let me go get them. May take me a few. I have to locate them first."

"No problem. I'll wait."

"Feel free to take a look around while I'm gone."

I picked up the stack of photos to take a closer look. It was good to see everyone as they enjoyed themselves. It was one reason I loved our small town. Not as much pretense or busyness as one would find in a big city. Slower pace and down-to-earth people.

I took longer to study each photo than I had before. There was one with Eleanor and Helga as they slurped their kitty snacks. This one was so close up, even their tiny eyebrow whiskers were visible.

The next one showed Veronica and Jerome as they shared a laugh. Those two sure were in love. My friend certainly deserved to be treated like a queen. Because of that, and her love for me, she wanted me to find someone like Jerome. Not that I'd complain about it, not at all. However, the chances seemed low since my dating experiences hadn't been enjoyable.

Evan had gotten a cute shot of Paula and her daughter, arms around each other, smiling. It was so cool to see family members who liked being together, unlike Durbin and Buford. But it made me think of Russ. We'd always been close. He'd done so much for me my whole life. Now maybe I could do something to help him.

Next was a picture of Jillian and me at the table. It was just two of us, so must have been after Florence and Lottie had rushed off to grocery shop. Jillian and I leaned toward each other. Were we whispering? I smiled. Probably about the book, which had the ladies all excited. The one they thought I should read. I shook my head. No way I wanted to read it. I wouldn't turn down a good who-done-it, though. Maybe if I read one now, it could put me in the right frame of mind to figure out the happenings in Whitewater Valley.

In the background of the last photo, I could make out Buford and Ken. They stood close together, obviously in deep discussion. From their cross expressions, it wasn't going well. I squinted and held the photo closer. Buford held out an item in his hand. Was it a small package? It didn't look like something they'd have purchased from Paula. It was square, wrapped in thick brown paper, more like a parcel to be mailed. Was he the giver or the receiver? Hard to tell.

Seemed an odd place to stand there and do that, with all the others around them, enjoying their day.

Odd? Well, it was Buford, after all. Nothing he did was commonplace or even understandable. Those two men weren't friends. In fact, I couldn't remember them together except when they'd fought at the bake sale.

What could've been so important they'd had such serious expressions in the photo when they talked? Maybe they were in on a scheme together. Could it be one which had something to do with Durbin's murder? I still had Buford on my suspect list. Should I also include Ken? Because so many people had waited for a place to sit that morning, Jillian and I had vacated our table before the sheriff had gotten wind of the fight, so I hadn't heard if they'd been arrested or just scolded. Having been the recipient of his public scolding, even that wouldn't be enjoyable.

Footsteps approached from the back room. I set the pastry shop photos back down. Evan headed over and waved a stack of glossy prints. "Here you go. Sorry you had to wait."

"No problem. It wasn't so long." I took the offered pictures and checked out each one. One was of a fox and her kit next to a row of bushes. Another was a fawn as she nibbled on grass, and the last two were each of a dog, the first, a dalmatian with a stick in his mouth, and the second, a black Labrador, who splashed in a pond.

Evan crossed his arms over his chest. "What do you think? Will those work for your wall?"

I smiled. "These are amazing. I love them. I'll get them placed on my wall later on today, along with a flier about your shop. Do you have a business card I could use for reference?"

"Absolutely." He stepped to a nearby desk, retrieved a few, and handed them to me. "I put a few extra in there in case someone else wanted one." He tapped the photos. "Sorry, there aren't any cats. Hopefully, none of your pet parents will be put off by the dogs."

"No, they won't. Lots of my clients have both cats and dogs. Maybe they can envision what their cat might look like in a portrait from seeing these."

"Or..." He raised his eyebrows.

"What?"

"You have a cat, right?"

"Yes, I have Percival. And now, I also have Jasper. He was..." I bit my lip.

Evan frowned. "What's wrong?"

"Jasper was Durbin's cat. I ended up with him."

His face fell. "Oh, right. Heard you'd found poor Durbin."

Guess word was getting around town. Surprising more people hadn't rushed up to me to ask all sorts of questions. "Yes, I did find him, unfortunately."

"I'm so sorry. It had to be awful."

"It was." Every time I thought about my discovery of Durbin, it was another hit to my gut. The poor man. I took a deep breath and let it out. Since I didn't want to discuss any of the details, I held up the stack of photos. "Anyway, what were you going to say before?"

He watched me for a few seconds with a concerned expression. He shrugged. "I thought maybe if you wanted, I could do a sample portrait of your cat you could use to show your clients. It would be free of charge, of course."

"Wow, that's so generous."

"Or both cats." He held up his hands and formed a square with his fingers, as if picturing the scene. "That would work too."

I sighed. "Unfortunately, it wouldn't. I have trouble getting them not to fight all the time. Still working on it, though."

"Sorry to hear that." He rubbed his chin. "Well, how about you choose one of them and we'll set a time up."

The possibility of having the cats' photos brightened my mood. Hopefully, by the time we did it, the cats might consider being in the same place without hisses or growls. "It sounds great. I think this will work out well. Maybe you better look out. Once the pet parents discover they can get custom photos of their babies, you might be super busy."

He grinned. "We can hope."

Chapter Fifteen

Although Hank did his best to help with Jasper and Percival, they continued to fight. There had to be something I could do to help them. I wouldn't give up Jasper, so I had to come up with a plan to help Percival deal with a new family member. If only Wilma had loved and wanted Durbin's cat. They might have been a comfort to each other.

Yet, after she'd talked about Jasper in hateful terms, there was no way I would push her to take the cat back. Even if she relented, Jasper wouldn't be in a loving environment. Nope, not a good situation for anyone.

I headed to the library, hoping to see Jillian. While I'd love to sit and chat, I knew she wouldn't have the luxury. Maybe there was a book I could find on cat behavior that would solve my problem. I'd read some articles online but had already tried most of their suggestions.

I reached the area in front of the library and had to maneuver around orange cones and warning signs. Guess the library construction had already started. That was fast. I'd never heard the total pledges from the auction, but it must have been a good amount, along with townspeople with deep pockets who all hoped the new wing would be named after them. Unfortunately, Russ hadn't won the bid for the contract. I'd heard Ken Evers had turned in the lowest bid and won the contract, but under the circumstances, how important would it have been for Russ to gain a work contract when he was under suspicion of murder?

After I climbed the wide front steps at the main entrance, I pushed open the heavy oak door and entered. It took a few seconds for my eyes to adjust to the darker interior. As always, there was a general hush, the universally accepted atmosphere for libraries everywhere.

When my boots sounded loud against the marble floor, I cringed. Hopefully, they'd put carpeting in the new wing so people wouldn't feel the need to tiptoe upon entering. As I reached the first counter, I heard a "Pssst!" from behind me. When I turned, I grinned.

Jillian speed-walked toward me, somehow without a sound against the floor. Almost as if she floated instead of stepped. With a glance down, I saw why. Sneakers. Was it something they learned to do in librarian training? I nearly laughed, but pressed my lips closed.

Jillian sidled up to me. "Hey, what's a cat groomer doing in a library? Want something to read to the kitties?"

"That's not a bad idea. Maybe it would work to help calm Percival and Jasper."

She frowned. "Awww. Still not getting along?"

"Nope. I came in to find a book on cat behavior. Maybe it will give me an idea what to do."

Jillian crossed her arms. "I thought Hank was helping you with your kitty project."

"He is. I mean, he's trying. But those cats aren't cooperating."

"In the meantime, you get to spend time with the cute vet. I'd say win-win, right?"

I put my hands on my hips. "Why does everyone try to fix me up with Hank? I like him, but I don't know if he even finds me attractive."

"Oh, I don't think it's an issue. You're gorgeous."

"You have to say so. You're my best friend."

"No, I don't have to say that. And yes, you are gorgeous. Now," she put her hand on her hip, "You need a book on cat behavior, right?"

"Yes."

"Okay, let's go over to—"

A light patter of footsteps came from my right. Jillian's assistant, Valene Day, hurried over. "Jillian, I need your help. One of the more unruly boys hung toilet paper all over the children's section again. Please hurry. It's an emergency." Even though they spoke in hushed tones, Valene flapped her arms in exasperation.

I understood my friend well. Her expression said *I'd love to roll my eyes,* but she refrained since she was at work. "Okay. Be right there."

When Valene had left, I lowered my eyebrows. "She needs you to help her remove toilet paper?"

"Yeah. You know how tiny she is. She's too short to reach it if it was tossed up high on the shelves and too weak to retrieve the ladder from the storage area. If you can wait a bit, I can show you where those books are."

Jillian had enough to deal with on a regular day with picky patrons. Having to help her assistant, probably pretty often, with tasks made more work for her. "No, just point me in the right direction. I'm sure I can find something on my own."

"If you're sure." She placed her hands on my shoulders and pivoted me around. "Nonfiction. Animals. See the sign beside the fourth aisle on the left?"

I spotted the sign, then looked at her over my shoulder and nodded. "Got it. Thanks. Have fun."

"Oh, sure." This time with Valene gone, Jillian did roll her eyes.

As I attempted to stay quiet, I edged over to the nonfiction section. A couple of women sat in upholstered chairs by a large picture window, reading what looked to be romance novels —a shirtless man clenched a fainting woman. Good grief. I couldn't read the title from here. Was it the book the ladies had been so enthused about and had wanted me to read? I cringed. Not my genre, at all.

Even though romances weren't my favorite books to read, picturing the guy and girl on the book cover drove my thoughts straight to Hank. Perfect. Now I was doing it too. Was it because those closest to me kept making the suggestion Hank and I would be a good couple?

I shook my head and rounded the corner of nonfiction, deeper into the abyss of narrow and thick-spined books which stood neatly in columns on shelf after shelf. I found the animal section easily enough. Nevertheless, it might take longer than I'd thought to locate the cat books. Who knew there were so many tomes about kangaroos, buffalo, hyenas, and badgers?

With a sigh, I headed past more books on gorillas, giraffes, and elephants before coming to the domestic animal section. Ah, that was more like it. Rabbits, parrots, dogs... and finally, cats, animals I could identify with.

However, the number of books on felines alone was overwhelming. Books about breeds, cat shelters, feeding, and care. The next aisle was a little more eclectic. *Teach Your Cat to Paint. Is Your Cat from Another Planet? Is Your Feline Trying to Kill You? Training Your Feline to be a Therapy Cat.* Had Lottie and Florence read this? I smiled. Guess they wouldn't need to since the therapy label for their cats was a farce.

I checked my watch. Shoot. I needed to get back to the grooming salon soon. I didn't want my next client to have to wait for me. As I was about to give up and head out of the library, a small section caught my eye near the end of the last aisle. Behavioral Problems with Cats. I blew out a breath. Finally, books that might shed some light on why my cats wouldn't stop fighting. Hopefully, one of the books would tell me something I hadn't already tried.

I chose three that had promise and pulled them from the shelf. Maybe Jillian was finished helping Valene with the emergency toilet paper situation and would be able to talk for a minute while she checked out my books.

A thud came from the aisle next to me. Had someone tossed a book on the floor? If it was a patron, the librarians would frown on it. Jillian had the expression down pat. Occasionally, I'd been the recipient of her librarian disapproval if I'd said or done anything she didn't agree with.

I peeked over copies of *Interesting Facts about Cats,* and *I Know My Cat Loves Me* to see through the shelves. Two men faced each other. One was Ken, his face red, his fists clutched at his sides. The other man, I wasn't sure. He turned his head to the side, so I got a better look. Maybe in his forties, bald, heavyset. I didn't recognize him, though. Whoever he was, the way his shoulders were tensed beneath his shirt, he didn't appear to be any happier than Ken. What was going on?

The other man poked Ken in the chest, twice. "This is not what we'd agreed on."

"That's how it is, Frank. Deal with it."

"You'd said with Durbin out of the way, we had a deal."

Ken shrugged. "Sorry, man. Things have changed."

With Durbin out of the way? My mouth dropped open. Glad I was able to hold in my gasp, since I'd rather the two volatile men didn't know I'd overheard. Had one of them been responsible for killing Durbin so he wouldn't win the bid on the construction project? The library wing was the biggest event to happen around here in an awfully long time. No doubt several contractors had wanted it. Had it been enough to kill for?

The name Ken had called the other guy—Frank. Could it be who Candi had mentioned when she'd said she now worked for Durbin's new partner? Why would two men from competing construction firms have a deal together?

Andrea had mentioned in Hank's office that her brother had been in a bad business deal where he'd been rooked by Durbin, so it made sense he might want Durbin out of the way. What about the other guy? Did he have something against the recently deceased as well?

I stood still, desperate not to sneeze, cough, or otherwise make some bodily noise that would alert the men to my presence. An intense itch danced up the back of my neck where the pesky tag inside my collar chafed my skin. *Not now. Can not scratch.* Because that would involve setting down the three books still clutched to my chest, which might make a noise.

My teeth clenched together as I forced myself not to think itchy thoughts. I counted to one hundred in my head to distract myself.

From across the shelves, Frank said, "Don't even think about trying to double-cross me. You won't get away with it."

Ken chuckled. "Too late. Already done." Another thud— had one man shoved the other against a shelf? —and then Ken rushed by the end of my aisle, followed closely by Frank. I let out a breath, set the books down on a nearby wooden bench, and finally relieved the itchy skin on my neck. Now I understood why Percival sometimes scratched his neck with his hind foot, even though his collar didn't have a tag that said 'wash in cold water, hang to dry' on the inside.

I waited a few more seconds. Maybe the men would be gone when I emerged from the cat section. As I checked around the edge of a sack of books yet to be shelved, I was glad to see no sign of the argumentative contractors.

After I retrieved my books, I tiptoed as soundlessly as possible across the wooden planks which led back to the front desk. Jillian was back and waved at me to come to her station. "Did you find something useful?"

I shrugged and placed the three books on the counter in a stack. "I hope so. I'll try to read some tonight when I get home." I eyed my friend. "Hey," I pointed to Jillian's hair. "Looks like you have an adornment besides your usual barrette."

"What?" She frowned and reached up to the left side of her hair and came in contact with a small tuft of toilet paper. She tugged it out and tossed it in the trash. "Thanks for the heads up."

"No problem." I smiled. "You'd do the same. At least, I think you would."

"You think so?" She gave an evil laugh, which earned her a shush and glare from an older woman who stood in line to check out. Jillian widened her eyes at me, then bit her lip, a sure sign she held in a giggle.

I turned to the woman who stood behind me, as she tapped her foot in a staccato rhythm against the floor. Guess making the sound was okay, but laughing wasn't? "Ma'am, I'm not quite ready to check out yet. Why don't you go ahead of me?"

The woman blinked. "Oh, well, thank you. It's nice to know there are some polite people still in the world." As she stepped up next to me, Jillian gave me a wink. She had to deal with ill-tempered patrons as much as I did moody cats and pet parents.

Once the woman had left and taken her huffiness with her, Jillian scooted my books closer to her. "I guess you're ready to check out now?"

"Yep. Good to know I'm not the only person who has to deal with cantankerous people every day."

She waved her hand. "That was nothing. Try being the sole librarian on duty when the new Romance Book of the Month is released, and there aren't enough copies to go around. You think you're the only one who deals with catfights? Think again."

I laughed. "Doesn't sound fun." I glanced behind me, then back. "Listen, I just overheard something interesting."

"You listened to ladies discuss the newest romance novel again? Their descriptions can be quite colorful. Perks up a person's imagination if you know what I mean."

"Ha, no. But I heard Ken and some man named Frank arguing back there close to the cat section."

Jillian glanced in that direction and back to me. "Really? What did they say?"

"They were talking about Ken winning the bid for the new wing."

"Yeah, that's right. Heard he'd boasted about it to someone in town the other day. How the project would make him rich."

I pointed my thumb to where I'd been by the aisles. "Well, he and the other guy, who Ken called Frank, disagreed on some deal they supposedly had. The other man was in his forties, bald."

"Oh, probably Frank Veerk. Yeah, I think he's fairly new to town. Don't know much about him except he's in a construction firm. The one Durbin had been at."

"Well, they did mention Durbin, and how since he was out of the way, it made things easier."

Her eyes widened. "That is interesting. I hadn't heard any gossip about any deals going on. I'll have to keep my ears open for more. Librarians hear more than bartenders in small towns, you know." She glanced behind me as someone rustled a bag or sack. Another person waited to see Jillian. Guess I'd have to wait until later to talk to her more.

Jillian placed my checked-out books on the counter. "Good luck with those. Hope they help you. Hey, I need to run. I have a board meeting."

Jillian's assistant materialized out of nowhere, ready to check out the patron next in line.

"Thanks. See ya later," I said. After Jillian stepped away, I sent Russ an update. He replied with a smiley face and the words, "Be Careful!"

I frowned. If only Sheriff King would focus on the real killer instead of my sweet uncle.

Chapter Sixteen

I'd just finished a mobile grooming visit. Percival sat in the passenger seat, paws pressed against the side window.

"Lots to see out there, buddy?" He'd done great with the two cats we'd seen. What was the deal with Jasper? Something would happen soon to make them be friends. It had to.

The van lurched, then sputtered.

What? No.... It coughed a few times. I was in the downtown area, right in front of the jewelry store. Thankfully, I was able to edge it to the curb before it conked out completely. Spreading my hands wide, I glared at the dashboard. "Really? So close to where we live? You couldn't have traveled six more blocks?" Although, it might not have made so much difference since I knew nothing about vehicles except how to put gas in the tank. I'd need to call someone to tow it and fix it either way.

Still, it would have been nice to have gotten Percival home before taking on the challenge. I reached over and rubbed the cat beneath the chin. His cheeks crunched up in a kitty grin. That was more like it. More like the friendly cat he'd always been.

At least before Durbin died and Jasper joined our family.

"You know, Percival, I'm not giving up. Jasper has no other place to go. Besides, I know deep down you like him. Didn't you prove that all those times you were there when I groomed him?"

My cat winked.

"What? You mean you really do like him? Then why all the commotion and hisses when you're together? You make this harder on Mama than it has to be."

He ignored me and gave his front paw a couple of licks.

"I know you can hear me. Don't act like you don't."

He stopped, mid-lick, tongue stuck out, eyes narrowed.

"Well, that was rude." With a sigh, I glanced around where we were parked. The sooner I got help with the van, the sooner we could get out of there.

I pulled out my phone from my purse and called Ollie Smith. He was the only mechanic in town. At least his rates weren't through the roof, with no competition for his services.

Someone picked up on the other end, but all I heard was a loud grind. Was there a problem with my phone? "Hello?" I shouted. "Anybody there?"

"Yeah, Ollie here."

I covered my other ear to hopefully hear him better. "Oh, hey. Can hardly hear you."

"Sorry. Hey Ernie! Cut the engine for a few, will ya?"

I jumped. Too loud! I pulled the phone away for a second but put it back when I heard his voice again.

"Who is this, by the way?" Thankfully, the loud background noise was gone.

"It's Molly Stewart."

"Oh, hey. Got a problem with your van? Needs fixing?"

"Yep. It coughed and wheezed a few times then died in front of Jennifer's Jewelry Shop."

"Coughed and wheezed. That doesn't sound good."

His diagnosis of my vehicle over the phone left a lot to be desired. "Yes, well, it's not going anywhere now. Wondered if you could tow it in and have a look?"

"Sure."

My shoulders slumped as I relaxed.

"But it will be a while."

"Oh. Um, how long is a while?"

"Let's see... Got a truck, car, and a motorcycle in line before you."

I held in a sigh. It wasn't his fault he was busy, and I called at the last minute needing help. "Okay. Well, we'll be here when you're ready."

"We? If someone else is there, can't they give you a lift home?"

I glanced at Percival, who stared out the window at a tuft of grass blowing in the wind and wagged his long tail like a dog. "It won't work. He doesn't own a car, and even if he did, he couldn't see over the steering wheel, and his legs won't reach the pedals."

A few seconds of silence, then, "Huh?"

"It's my cat."

He chuckled. "Ah. Should have known a cat lady like yourself would make a cat joke."

I smiled. "Right. Okay, so whenever you can get here, that'd be great. Thank you."

"You bet. You two"—he chuckled again— "sit tight."

I pressed end on the call and rolled my eyes.. How would we entertain ourselves for that long? We could trudge home and come back later, but I didn't want to go off and leave the van here for that long. It was too valuable a business commodity for something bad to happen to it. Under normal circumstances, I might have called Russ for help, but not now. He had so much to deal with. No, I'd handle it myself.

At least if I was here and the sheriff came by, I could explain why I hadn't moved my van. Plus, I was protective, okay, overprotective of my ride since I used it for business. Without it, my business would be cut in half. So many of my clients only wanted to use my mobile option, so they wouldn't have to take their pets away from their homes.

With so long of a wait, it would be more tolerable to spend the time out on the sidewalk in the sunny weather. Percival pawed at the window, a sure sign he wouldn't be happy sitting in the van if I wasn't with him.

"All right, little man. We'll have a mini adventure for a bit." I reached into the cubby between the seats and pulled out his harness and leash. He didn't love it, but tolerated it if he wanted to be outside rather than in. Once I had him in his purple harness, I put my phone in my pocket in case Ollie called back, picked Percival up, and we exited the van. He wiggled like a little furry worm until I placed him on the sidewalk and immediately tugged at his leash to sniff every inch of concrete and every blade of grass.

"Slow down there, little guy. We have to stay here by the van."

When a stray cloud passed over and let in the sun again, my cat stopped, lifted his face to the warmth, and sighed. Cats always did that, sat in the sun. Maybe there was something to it. As I stood still, I closed my eyes and raised my face, warming with the sun's rays.

"You know, Percival, I think you're right. This feels wonderful."

The cuff of my jeans pressed against my ankle as he pawed at my leg. Was he done enjoying the sunbeam already? Usually, it was a long process that ended with him in a semi-comatose state, totally sun-drunk.

"Oh, come on. I'm just now getting the hang of this cat sunbeam thing. Give me a little more time, will ya?"

This time, he didn't paw my leg, but gave it a good whack. The hiss which followed forced my eyes open. Even though I glanced down away from the bright rays, it took me a few seconds to focus on my cat. But he didn't face me. He stood rigid, fur puffed out, and stared at something way above him. What....

My gaze traveled from my cat to a pair of shoes, then upward to a tall body and face with a frown.

Wilma Haines. Well, it explained Percival's hiss. He might not have heard what she'd said about her dislike of felines in general, but cats always knew.

She narrowed her eyes. "What in the name of insanity do you think you're doing out here in public for anyone to see?"

"Uh...." I glanced behind me, embarrassed to see Ricky Notts standing close by, mailbag in hand. Well, great. Wilma might tell a few people willing to listen that Molly the loon liked to stand out on the sidewalk with her eyes closed as she talked to her cat. But Ricky would make it his mission to personally inform every single household on his route of my latest antics.

What I did wasn't odd, strange, or wrong. However, others might think so. It took everything in me not to roll my eyes. I faced Wilma. "If you must know, my van broke down." I pointed to my right. "And Ollie Smith said it would be a while before he could get here. And Percival"—I pointed down—"wanted some fresh air and sunshine, so I—"

She shook her head. "Enough of that. It's ridiculous. Not only have you blocked the path of other people trying to get past, but you talked to …it." Her shiny pink fingernail polish caught the sun's rays and gave a small flash of light. Pink? Could it be the shade from Durbin's watch?

Wilma, so agitated at her apparent distaste of having to deal with my public insanity, flung both hands around. An object flew out of one hand and smacked to the sidewalk. "Oh! And after, I just paid to have that repaired!"

She bent to retrieve whatever it was, but Percival was closer, and quicker. After he batted it around for a second, he shoved it with his paw toward my shoe.

Wilma held out her hand. "Here, give me that."

I crouched low and gave Percival a congratulatory pat on the head for his catch, which earned me a purr. When I reached down to pick up the item, I gasped. It was Durbin's watch! Why was it here, instead of on her husband's wrist?

I got to my feet, then held my hand toward Wilma, but didn't open my hand. She glared at my fingers. Was she planning to pry them open? She was a large, strong-looking woman and probably could. "Wilma, what on earth?" I opened my hand a little so I could take a better look at the watch. The scratch I'd noticed when Durbin had it on during his calling was almost gone. A tiny hint of pink remained at the edge of the crystal. She must have just come from the jeweler after having the scratch removed.

"Give it to me. It's mine," she spat out.

"I thought it was Durbin's. He was wearing it in his casket, after all."

Behind me, a gasp was followed by a thud against the sidewalk. Had Ricky dropped his heavy mailbag? I didn't bother to look, still locked eye-to-eye with Durbin's widow.

Wilma stood up even taller. I was sure it was meant to intimidate me. It did, a little bit. Still, not enough for me to give up the watch yet. I curled my fingers around the cool metal. "Listen," I said, "I'll give it back, but first, I want to know why you removed it from your husband's wrist."

"What right do you have to even ask? He was my husband."

While that was true, she hadn't even cared for him at all. "Seems like I heard you say lots of not very complimentary things about your husband not so long ago."

Her face reddened. "That's none of your business."

"Then why did you tell me? I didn't ask you to."

"Guess I had a weak moment. Big mistake to tell you anything. One I won't repeat."

After a glance behind me—yep, Ricky was still there and his mailbag, with several envelopes now scattered around, while he sat on the sidewalk—I faced Wilma, mirrored her stance, and stood up to my full height. It was laughable since she towered over me by several inches. Nevertheless, it gave me a tiny bit of courage. "You may not have intended to say those things to me, but you did. So, I know how much you didn't like your husband. I believe you'd even said you hated him."

Wilma's hands balled into fists at her sides. Did she plan to punch me? My heartbeat sped up, but I forced myself to take a deep breath. She wouldn't. Not with a witness watching, who, if I wasn't mistaken, had moved at least a foot closer to us while we'd talked. "How dare you say such things? They're all lies!"

"You're the one who said them."

Her fists relaxed, but her stormy expression remained. "Fine. I'll tell you what happened. Then you will give me back the watch." She stomped her large foot, the sound a crack against the hard surface.

I stood my ground and waited.

She avoided eye contact and focused on my left ear while she spoke. "I was standing beside the casket, and...the mortician was about ready to close the lid for the last time." She rubbed her eyes, but they were dry. Were those pretend tears? "I just knew Durbin wouldn't like to be buried in a less-than-perfect state. I wouldn't have wanted him to have been upset if he'd known. So, I had the mortician remove Durbin's watch. That's it. End of story."

"It seems hard to believe after all you said about him the other day."

"Maybe I had a moment of...grief. Yes, that's it. I grieved, and it came out as anger. It does happen, you know." She planted one hand on her hip.

116

I'd get no further with the current line of conversation, so I switched gears. "I noticed on the watch the jeweler was able to get most of the pink color out of the crystal. Not all." My gaze dropped to her left hand, specifically to her pointed pink fingernails. "Gee, looks like the same color you've got on your nails."

Wilma stiffened, then as if an afterthought, shoved her hands into her pants pockets. "How dare you. I would never be caught dead with such a cheap brand of polish."

Caught dead. Did she realize the significance of what she'd said? Her husband had nearly been buried with that exact color on his watch.

I put one hand on my hip, the watch still clutched in the other hand. "Looks the same to me. How can you be so sure?"

Her mouth formed a smirk. "It doesn't surprise me you wouldn't be able to tell the difference between dirt cheap and high quality." She eyed me down to my shoes, then back up. "Since you obviously know nothing about fashion."

My mouth dropped open. "Hey! Just because I don't have a trillion dollars to spend on frivolities doesn't mean I don't try to look nice."

Wilma shook her head. "My dear, cat hair is not an acceptable accessory. Ever."

I opened my mouth to retort. It might have been something clever and scathing, but I'd never know. Because right then, Percival stood on his hind legs, took a swipe at Wilma's pant leg, and hissed so long and so loud, Wilma would have a kitty spit spot on her pants for at least a week.

She screamed, then tried to kick Percival. However, he was quicker and jumped aside, so her shoe connected with nothing but air. "Oh! What a hateful, disgusting furball!" Another hiss, then a growl from Percival, had Wilma backing away. "Just...give me my watch. And I'll be on my way."

Fine by me. Time to get rid of the wicked woman. I tossed the watch to her. She caught it, but barely, snatching it out of the air by the end of the band. Wilma made a sound first to me, then to my cat, which sounded an awful lot like Percival's hiss, turned on her heel, and marched down the sidewalk.

I huffed out a breath and turned, startled to see Ricky still standing there. He crouched down and gathered the strewn mail, then stuffed it into his bag. "Guess I'll get back to my route now."

"Yep. Show's over."

He hurried across the street, then sprinted down the opposite sidewalk. Had he finally realized he was now running late to make his deliveries?

I bent down and scooped up Percival. "Thanks for having my back, little dude. That chick is some kind of scary."

Percival bumped his head to my chin and purred.

Chapter Seventeen

After Wilma stormed away and Ricky remembered he had a job to do, Percival and I hung out inside the van for the remainder of our wait. It seemed easier than standing there, having to explain to someone else why we were loitering on the sidewalk, doing nothing productive with our day.

A loud squeak and rattle preceded Ollie's truck rounding the corner and heading toward us. I frowned. Maybe he didn't have time to repair his own truck.

The cobblers' children have no shoes.

I climbed out of my van, grabbed my purse, and Percival then waited at the curb. Percival's eyes were huge as the large truck backed up to the front of the mobile van. When gears screeched as the winch lowered to attach to the jeep, the cat pressed his face onto my chest and burrowed into my shirt. I didn't blame him. It was super loud.

The van looked sad and dejected as it came to rest behind the truck. I hoped it wouldn't take too long to fix. It was my livelihood, after all. Also, that it wouldn't cost too much. No, I couldn't worry about it now. Whatever the price, I needed my van in working order.

Ollie stepped around to us, a clipboard now in his hand. "Sign here."

I took the clipboard from him, an awkward move as Percival was smack in the middle of the process. "What am I signing?"

"You're giving me permission to diagnose your van and do needed repairs."

Diagnose. Well, I sure didn't know the first things about anything mechanical. Besides, Ollie was the only one around who did. What choice did I have? I scratched my signature on the bottom line and handed it back to him.

"Okay, ready to go? I can give you a lift back to your home or salon, or you can come with me, your choice."

Since my appointments were finished early for the day, I opted to go to the garage. Even though I knew nothing about what he might be doing to my van, I'd feel better being there to give the van moral support. Not that I'd say as much to Ollie. "We'll go with you if it's okay."

He eyed Percival, then lowered his eyebrows. Oh no. Did he have a thing against cats? "I guess it's all right," he said. "Not sure Management would agree with having an animal on board, but we'll give it a try."

"Management? I thought you owned the garage. Then that would be you."

He shrugged. "Yep. Guess it would. All right. Get in."

I shook my head, reminding myself I had no other alternative. I tried to climb into the van while still holding Percival. It didn't go well. He balked at climbing in ahead of me, and I couldn't very well get in first and leave him on the sidewalk.

Before I could stop him, Percival climbed up my chest, onto my shoulder, and clawed his way onto my head.

It seemed the only way I was going to get both of us in the truck at the same time. Trying not to make eye contact with Ollie, I reached up to the handle right inside the door and hoisted us up, trying not to cringe at the decades of grime on the passenger seat.

From the driver's seat, I heard, "Nice hat."

Ignoring him, I plopped down and reached to my right for the seat belt. It wasn't there.

Turning to Ollie, who was grinning, I pointed my thumb behind me. "No belt?"

"Sorry. Haven't had the time. It's not far to the garage. Hold on tight. You'll be fine." He then proceeded to fasten his seat belt and start the engine.

This had to be in violation of more than one traffic law, but again, I had no choice. Placing one hand on Percival, still on my head, and the other clinging to the side of my seat, I took a deep breath and let it out.

We bumped and screeched through the streets of town, finally arriving at the garage. Ernie Price, Ollie's assistant was there, standing outside of a large, open garage door. He waited until Ollie waved, then gave a salute and waved his arms, air traffic controller style, until Ollie had backed us all the way into the building.

Percival was still on my head, but had repositioned to turn around, which involved sharp claws sticking and poking my scalp every time he tried to get comfortable.

Glad one of us was.

Hopefully, he wasn't drawing blood. Didn't want to have to explain that to anyone. Wearing my cat like a helmet was bad enough.

After Ollie had backed us in, taking forever to reverse and go forward numerous times to get it exactly right, Percival and I were permitted to exit the truck.

Surely once we were out of the vehicle, my cat would allow me to hold him again.

No such luck.

I reached up to grasp him, but he dug in even more.

"Ouch, not so deep, little guy."

Ollie rounded the truck and approached us. "Hat giving you trouble, is it?" His grin was wide.

I rolled my eyes. "He's just a little scared to be in here. Loud noises, big machinery, and all."

He nodded. "Sure. Guess I'm used to it by now. Doesn't bother me. Okay, well, you and your hairpiece can wait over there"—he pointed to a few old metal chairs against a back wall— "and I'll see what we're up against."

Rather than address his lame attempt at another joke at my expense, I headed toward the tiny, grimy waiting area.

I would have rather stood while I waited, but standing upright with the ten-pound weight on my head was hurting my neck and back. Plus, Percival didn't seem to have plans to vacate my head any time soon. Eyeing the five chairs and choosing the one which appeared to have the least amount of filth, I sat down.

Ollie got to work right away on my van. He lifted the hood and leaned over, peering inside as if searching for a secret magic kingdom hidden in its depths. Whatever the problem, I hoped he'd be able to fix it soon. Otherwise, there'd be major rearranging to do on my schedule. Veronica prided herself on keeping a tight ship with the salon appointments. I didn't want to be the one to inform her we'd have to shift everybody around if things didn't go well here.

Trying to relax, I leaned against the back of the chair. My neck muscles were sore from supporting my tubby cat's weight. When I'd settled, there was a warm vibration coming from above.

My cat was purring. Was the crazy guy asleep? On my head?

A commotion came from the small glass-enclosed office near the front of the garage. Ernie was shaking his head. Who else was in there? Ollie was still looking at the front of my van.

I angled a few inches to my left in order to see better, earning me another claw poke in my scalp. Ken was the other person with Ernie. Judging by the redness of his face, he was angry. The fact that he waved his arms around like a frustrated chicken reinforced it. What was he doing?

Ernie rushed out of the office, grabbed Ollie, and they hurried back to Ken.

I frowned. Now, wait a second. I'd been here first and needed my van fixed. I wanted to march over and say exactly that, but doing so with a cat on my head might negate some of the oomph from my argument. Having them laugh at my headwear wouldn't help me get my point across in a serious manner.

Leaning forward and placing my hands on my knees, I strained to hear their words.

Ken stopped waving his hands but was pointing his finger awfully close to Ollie's face. "You said you'd have it today. I was counting on it. Now you've ruined everything."

"Hey, now. I never promised any such thing. I said I'd try. It's all anyone can do."

"You better do more than try. I need it. Right now."

"I have a business to run." Ollie pointed toward me, sitting on my uncomfortable metal chair. I tried to slump down, but Percival growled.

Ken glanced out at me, narrowed his eyes, and glared. What did I do? He turned his head back to the other two men. "I don't care about your so-called business. This place is a rat trap. Surprised it hasn't fallen down on its own by now."

"Now, hold on, Ken. I don't take to people coming into my business, saying insulting things like that. "

I had to side with Ollie on this one. Though his place was grimy and disorganized, it was his business and source of income. Whenever people made comments about Fabulous Felines that were mean or disrespectful, it got my dander up too.

Ken poked Ollie in the chest, causing the other man's face to redden. "You do what you said. Do it soon. Or else." He stormed out of the office but didn't leave. Instead, he made a beeline right toward me.

What? Why would Ken come over here?

Claws dug deep into my scalp. I winced, ready to reach up to grab Percival, but he was too fast. He leaped to the floor, puffed up to twice his normal size, and planted himself directly in front of me. When Ken reached us, my cat crouched down and hissed.

He was trying to protect me!

Ken glared at Percival. I grabbed my cat and tugged him closer, afraid the angry man might kick him or something even worse. After pulling the cat onto my lap, I eyed Ken. "What's going on?" I didn't expect him to tell me what happened in the office but why he'd stomped toward me like an angry rhino. I'd never said more than hello to the man. While it was true I saw his sister often in Hank's office, Ken was barely more than a stranger to me.

He crossed his arms, making him appear all the more menacing. Whatever happened in the office must have ticked him off royally. "It would be in your best interest to mind your own business."

I thought I had been. I hadn't moved closer to the office to try to hear them better. It had to count for something. "Not sure what you mean. I'm here to get my vehicle fixed." I pointed toward my mobile van. Ken wouldn't be able to discount it was mine since it had my shop's name painted proudly across both sides and the back door.

"Never you mind whatever you overheard from in there."

I shook my head. "I'm just sitting here. Me and my cat."

He scowled. "Yeah, your mangy cat."

"Hey!" I covered Percival's ears, though I was sure he'd already heard. "How dare you come over here and say that?"

He stepped closer, his expression so menacing I scrunched down, causing Percival to give me a kick.

Pointing right at my face, he said, "You keep out of my way, you hear? Whatever you heard us say, you go on and forget. Wouldn't go well for you if I hear you've been spreading rumors about me." His gaze lowered to Percival. "And as for your cat, keep a close eye on him. Be a real pity if something happened to him."

I gasped, wanting to retort, but so shocked nothing would come out. Percival had no such problem. The long, low growl he gave in Ken's direction said more than I ever could have.

"You remember what I said." Ken's jaw muscles tightened, showing ridges beneath his cheeks. He turned and stomped away, giving a quick glance into the office where Ollie and Ernie still stood. Maybe they were afraid to come out until he'd gone. Not that I blamed them.

Ollie stuck his head out of the doorway, looked both ways, then tiptoed out, as if Ken might be waiting behind my van to leap out at him. Ernie followed, giving me a head nod, and hurried toward my van. Maybe now I'd get it fixed.

I cuddled Percival close. "Thanks for protecting me." I thought of Wilma on the sidewalk. "Guess it's the second time today you've done that. And sorry, dude, we may be here a while. Might as well try to get comfortable."

Percival heaved a huge sigh, then turned in a circle and closed his eyes.

Chapter Eighteen

Unfortunately, Ollie had to order parts for my mobile van, and I wouldn't have it back until the next day. Veronica got to work rescheduling people. I offered to help make calls, but she said I wasn't particularly good at it and she'd take care of it. She pointed out that if I had to do it, I'd cave, give everyone what they wanted, and we'd end up with thirty people all on one day.

She was right. I'd better stick to the in-person one on one with my clients and their parents. I trusted Veronica, and she'd do a good job calming everyone down when they discovered their babies might have to wait a little longer for their groomings.

Since I wouldn't be out using my van, Percival couldn't go along either. I'd felt bad Jasper might not have been getting much attention lately, so I left Percival at home for the day. Yes, I'd pay for it later, but I was trying to be fair to my two babies until they started playing nice.

I'd seen Durbin use a leash with Jasper in the past, so had purchased one for him in case we needed it. He didn't seem to mind wearing it, in fact, happily trotted along beside me as we walked the few blocks from my house to the shop.

We passed Carrie, gave her a wave—well, I did, Jasper just smiled—as she stood inside her front window cleaning the glass. Paula, speaking to Evan, gave us a wink as we passed by. Evan called out, "Hi, you two." I turned and waved, then made the rest of the way to Fabulous Felines.

Veronica had opened up the shop today. She had her monthly appointment with Pearl Sills, a woman who insisted her black and white cat Fluffy needed to have her grooming done early in the day before any other cats were around in the shop. Bless Veronica's heart, she dutifully came in early every time to give her client and pet parent the special care they demanded.

When I opened the door, I allowed Jasper to proceed me, then stepped inside. Veronica was tidying up from her appointment. I'd waited long enough to come in, hoping we wouldn't run into Pearl, since she didn't like her cat around any others.

When Veronica spotted me, she dropped her cleaning cloth, reached for something beneath the counter, and raced toward me.

What in the world?

She thrust the piece of paper she'd been holding right in front of me to read. A chill shot through my body as I scanned the words:

Mind your own business. Or you and your cat will be sorry.

I met her gaze, sure my eyes must have been as wide as hers. Maybe I was in shock for a minute because I couldn't seem to move. Veronica knelt beside me and removed Jasper's harness. He ran to the nearest low shelf to stand on his hind legs and sniff everything in sight.

She stood and slid out the leash still clutched in my hand. "Molly, are you okay?" After setting the leash on the counter, she got a nearby chair, angled it behind me, and pressed my shoulders until I sat.

I looked up at her. "The note was—"

"Yeah, I know. I found it right after Pearl left. It was stuck in our mailbox."

"Mailbox? You don't think Ricky—"

She shook her head. "No, I really don't. He's a gossip and a snoop, but he's harmless."

Once I was able to gather my thoughts into some form of clarity, I had to agree. Whoever had done it had used our box for convenience and anonymity. "You didn't happen to see anyone hanging around out there this morning?"

"Sorry, doll. Was too busy with Fluffy. You know how picky Pearl is with her cat's appearance."

"Yeah, I do know. Of course, you wouldn't have had the chance."

"Wish I would have. I have no idea who might have left this. I was getting ready to call the sheriff when—"

I held up my hand. "Don't."

"Why not? You've been threatened, and he needs to know."

"We know why someone left the note. It was from the murderer, and since Sheriff King seems intent on Russ being the killer, I can't see him doing much about this note. Besides, the way he's been watching me lately, I'd end up with another scolding. I've had quite enough of those."

She nodded. "I see your point. So, what should we do?"

I got up from the chair, then moved it back to its proper place. "We keep our eyes and ears open. And…" I pointed to Jasper. "Keep the kitties safe."

"The note threatened your cat. I take it that meant only Percival."

"Whoever it was might not know the difference. I could keep both cats at home, but they don't do so well together yet." I said.

"I still think you shouldn't leave either of them at your house when you're not there. At least until we find out who is behind all of this."

I eyed Jasper, who was batting around a catnip toy he'd grabbed from the shelf. "But the cats don't—"

She touched my shoulder. "We'll work it out. I'll help you. It's a small shop, but somehow, we'll keep them apart, or at least keep an eye on them."

Relief swept through me. I hadn't wanted to leave either one alone after getting a threat, but until Veronica offered help, I didn't see how it would work. I gave her a hug. "Thank you."

"No problem. It's what assistants do."

"No, it's what friends do."

She grinned. "That too."

I stepped away and went to pick up Jasper. I'd have time for a cuddle with him before Alan Wilkes and his marmalade cat, Kirby, arrived for their appointment. Facing Veronica again, I said, "You know who I think left that note?"

"Well, after what you'd told me happened at the garage, I'd say Ken."

"Yep. Not proof positive, of course, but he did threaten Percival right in front of me. We'll have to keep our eye on him."

"Since Ken's sister works for Hank, maybe she would be a way to get the latest scoop on him."

"Oh, I don't think I could ask Andrea to watch her brother for any illegal actions. What if she's not aware of what he's been up to? Could you imagine her reaction if I started accusing Ken of something and she didn't agree?"

"No, I meant talk to Hank."

"Stop trying to fix us up, please. I don't think he sees me that way."

Veronica's hands landed on her hips. "Hold on. If you'd just listen. What I meant was, tell him what happened with Ken's threat and have him keep his ears open for anything Andrea might say about her brother."

"Oh. Sorry. Yeah, your suggestion might work."

"Didn't mean to scold you and sound like the sheriff. Look, I understand you're scared about this note and about a murder in town. I'm scared too. We're in this together, though, right?"

I smiled. "Right.

Chapter Nineteen

Evan and I had decided on a day to try for a cat portrait. Hoping beyond hope, I put the cats in separate carriers and took them to the photography studio. Lugging them in at once wasn't possible, so I took first Percival, then Jasper. I figured if I'd left Percival in the van for a second longer than the minute and a half it took me to take in Jasper and set him down, Percival would be extra pouty. Although, lately, he'd been that way anyway.

Once I had both cats inside the studio, Evan came out from the back to greet us. He smiled when he saw two carriers. "Decided to try both for a picture?"

"We'll see. Guess I was feeling optimistic this morning. Mind helping me with them?"

"No problem."

I reached in and got Jasper out, and handed him to Evan.

"Aww, so this was Durbin's cat, huh?" He held the cat close, causing Jasper to erupt in a huge purr.

"I guess you really do like cats," I said.

"Sure. Just can't have one because of my dogs."

"Yeah, it might not work out too well. Although having two cats together hasn't been all rosy either."

He frowned. "Well, let's see what we can accomplish today."

I got Percival out of his carrier. He squirmed to get down. "Evan, mind if Percival takes a look around your shop for a minute? Might calm him down some."

"No problem. When Florence and Lottie have come in over the years, they always have their cats with them."

"I don't think they go anywhere without them."

"You know," he said, "I've heard the cats are actually sisters from the same litter."

"Really? If I didn't know better, I'd think the ladies were too. Not from a litter. Well, you know."

He laughed. "Yeah, I know. They really are close, those two."

"Speaking of the ladies, I got to sit with them at the pastry sale."

"They're a hoot." He patted Jasper's side.

I grinned. "Yep. Never a dull moment."

I had Evan place Jasper on the floor so he could investigate like Percival was. Speaking of Percival, where was he?

I frowned. "Is there anything the cats could get into that would be harmful or cause a problem for your photography?"

He shook his head. "The door is closed to the dark room. Everything is fine."

Knowing Percival, he might figure out a way to open the door and snoop. Maybe he'd be on good behavior since we weren't at home. Crossing my fingers, I went to look for him. Being a cat, he seemed to know I wanted to find him at the moment. So, right then was when he decided to hide.

Wonderful.

"Evan, so sorry about this. I know you have appointments to keep."

"No worries. I have a couple of hours before a family of four comes in for their yearly portrait. We'll find Percival. The shop isn't that big." Evan made an "A-ha" sound from behind a counter.

"Did you find him?"

He waved me over to where he stood and pointed down.

My cat was curled up on a jacket I'd seen Evan wear before, stashed on a shelf beneath the counter.

My eyes widened. "Most people didn't love having someone else's pet distribute hair on their clothing. I'm so sorry." I reached down and picked up my cat, who yawned and snuggled against my chest.

Evan laughed. "With two dogs? Are you kidding? They're huge and shed more hair than your tiny cats ever could. Don't worry about it."

Relieved, my shoulders slumped. "Thanks. I'd hate for the photography session to start out in a bad way."

"Nothing bad about it. Ready to give it a try with both of them?"

I placed my sleepy cat on the floor.

Though I'd started the morning with some optimism, now doubts crept in. But I was determined to at least try. "Yeah, we'll see how it goes." I headed to a chair near the front picture window where I'd stashed my purse. Inside I had a secret weapon. Hopefully, it would work. I drew out a plastic container and shook it. Percival came running.

Jasper, being a new resident in my home, had no clue of the delicacy I held in my hand.

Evan's eyebrows rose. "What'cha got there?"

"Catnip. Not just any catnip. It's a special blend I ordered that's supposed to be high potency. I'm hoping it's strong enough to get Percival to relax around Jasper. At least long enough for a photo."

He grinned. "I say let's give it a try."

I poured some out on the floor, and Percival dove into the pile, wallowing and closing his eyes in apparent ecstasy.

"Wow. Have never seen a cat with catnip before. Do they all do that?"

"Most. Some cats, though, don't seem to be affected as much as others. Not sure about Jasper."

I poured out another pile several feet away from Percival. Jasper, who sat across the room, didn't react at first. Then, he lifted his chin as his tiny nostrils flared.

It was working!

I crouched down next to the catnip heap and held out my cat. "Come here, Jasper. Check out what Mama has for you."

Something in my heart melted, referring to myself as his mama. Made me think of Durbin. He would have liked seeing his cat enjoy a special treat.

Jasper trotted to me and rubbed his face against my fingers. It lasted three seconds. His head lowered to the herb, and he sniffed it, then pawed at it, and finally, flopped down on top of the pile and rolled on his back from side to side.

Evan crept closer, his steps nearly silent. Was he afraid he'd scare Jasper away?

"Don't worry," I said, "they're pretty much drunk. I don't think they'd notice much going on around them."

"How long does the drunk effect last?"

"It varies. Not too long, so we'll want to try to photo soon."

Evan pointed over his shoulder. "I have things almost ready to go whenever you think it's time."

I nodded. "Let's give them another minute to, for lack of a better word, absorb more of the catnip and then try."

Evan hurried off toward the back, and a door opened then closed. After another minute, he was back. "All right, I have it all set to go in the next room. Want me to get one of the cats?"

"Yeah, if you could pick up Jasper, I'll get Percival."

I glanced at Evan, who gently gathered up Jasper. The cat flopped in his arms like a wet rag. At least one of the felines was relaxed. When I reached for Percival, he gave me a slight growl. Maybe this wouldn't work. But I got a little catnip on my fingers and placed it right under his nose. He sighed and calmed, so I picked him up.

When we were all in the room, Evan closed the door. He handed me a soft cloth. "Looks like they're both covered in catnip. Might want to brush some off. That is, unless you want it part of the picture."

I grinned. "Good idea." Jasper's fur looked clean, so Evan must have already used the cloth. I rubbed Percival's fur.

Once both cats were presentable, I stepped toward a table lined with a thick, soft blanket. Evan placed Jasper on it, and he immediately curled up in a ball. Was he going to sleep through the photo session? Maybe it was for the best. It would be preferable to having a picture with the cats' claws extended and teeth bared.

Now to see how Percival reacted.

I carried him to the table. The closer he got to Jasper, the more his body stiffened. "Come on, little one. This catnip is super strong. You should be relaxed by now." Slowly, I placed Percival on the table. He was still two feet away from Jasper.

Evan shook his head. "No, that won't do. We need them close together if you want a group shot."

"Yeah, I do want that. Hope this works."

I nudged Percival closer. He balked, legs stiffening.

Now what?

Evan held up his hand for me to wait. He was gone a few seconds and returned, his fist closed. "Let's try this." He spread more catnip right beside Jasper, who was still conked out. Then we waited.

Percival, at first, didn't seem to notice or care. A few seconds later, he stretched, sniffed, and took a tentative step toward the other cat. He got a few inches away and sniffed again. A loud purr rumbled from his chest. He crouched down, sniffed Jasper, sniffed the catnip, and snuggled right next to his nemesis.

"It's working," I whispered. Clasping my hands together in front of me, I watched as with practiced care, Evan repositioned the cats, a tail nudged here, a paw edged closer there. The effect was wonderful. My two cats appeared to be in feline heaven, both smiling, eyes closed and completely relaxed.

Evan tilted his head at me, indicating the right side of the room.

"Huh?"

He pointed his thumb in that direction. Laughing, he said, "I'm okay with you being in the picture, but thought you wanted just the cats."

"Oh!" Like a dunce, I was still standing beside the table. Scurrying out of view, I reached the opposite wall. "Is this okay?"

"Perfect." Evan's camera, already pointed toward the middle of the table, made a whirring noise as he moved some dials and buttons. Click after click sounded as my cats snoozed away. I couldn't believe we were actually getting a picture of my two cats together.

After a while, Evan took a step back. "I think that should do it. Just in time, too."

I looked at the table. Percival stirred and opened one eye. He stretched out his front legs, then the back. He pushed up to a sitting position and licked one paw, his eyes still partially closed. Was this the post-catnip hangover stage?

Jasper was still out, seeming not to care what happened around him, but Percival's eyes flew open, and he glanced down at his own feet. His gaze traveled the short distance to Jasper's face. He blinked, opened his mouth...

And hissed.

Groaning, I ran to get him and picked him up. "Time to visit your carrier again. Maybe you can take another nap."

Evan picked up Jasper, who was starting to stir. Once I had Percival settled, Evan handed me the other cat, who I nudged into his own carrier. Both cats settled down and seemed to give in to sleep again. They'd be okay for a bit.

Sighing, I faced Evan. "Well, it worked for a while."

He tilted his head. "Hey, cheer up. I'm confident we got some awesome shots."

I touched his arm. "Oh, I don't mean the pictures. I have no doubt they will be gorgeous."

"Then what?"

"Well, I thought when they seemed happy lying so close to each other, they'd gotten over being enemies. Then Percival hissed."

"Oh, yeah. Sorry."

"Not your fault. At least now I know there's a way for them to get along. Even if it means for a short time and they require inebriation. Can't depend on doing it all the time."

"No, guess not." He pointed to the front room. "Like a cup of coffee for a bit while the cats sleep it off?"

"Yeah, sounds good. Thanks."

Once we were seated at a small table near his front window, I relaxed. I hadn't realized how tense I'd been trying to get the cats calm enough for the picture. I took a sip of the coffee and set it down. "Thank you so much for taking their pictures. If nothing else, I'll have a wonderful photo of them being happy together for a little while."

"Don't worry. I think it will happen for you. May just take time."

"You sound like Hank. That's what he said."

His eyebrows rose. "You know, since you mention Hank, I remembered a rumor I'd heard."

"What rumor?"

"That you and he were…."

"What? No."

He smiled. "Guess I should know better than to l listen to the ladies."

I smiled. "I do like Hank. Just not sure…."

"I see. Well, from what I've seen, I think he likes you too."

"Now you sound like Jillian," I said.

He let out a sigh. "Yeah. Jillian."

I sat up straight. What was this? "Hey, do you like Jillian?"

His face reddened. "Um, sure. Who wouldn't? I mean, she's nice. And smart. And pretty and…."

Smirking, I couldn't help it. I now had a way to get Jillian to stop trying to fix me up with Hank. Now when she brought it up, I'd mention Evan. Although I had to admit, now that I thought about it, those two might make a really good pair.

Evan shifted in his seat and glanced away. Better let him off the hook, at least for now.

"Hey, I sure do appreciate you going to all this trouble to get a photo of my feuding cats."

"It was nothing. Ever tried getting a huge family of seven with two toddlers and a crying baby to all sit still and smile at the same time? Hey, maybe I could borrow your catnip for their next session."

I laughed. "Now that I'd like to see." I nudged my coffee cup a few inches away on the table. "Listen, changing the subject, I loved those photos you took of the pastry sale."

"Thanks. Paula did too. She has some copies in her shop right now."

"I haven't been in there for a couple of days. Have to check them out. I've been wondering, when you were taking photographs, did anything stick out to you?"

"What do you mean?"

I shrugged, trying to sound nonchalant. "Oh, did anyone do anything weird or out of line?"

His eyebrows lowered.

"Just, you know how crazy some of our townspeople can be. Always looking for a new story, I guess."

He smiled. "That's for sure. Never dull around here. Well, let me think. It was super crowded."

I nodded, then took a sip of my coffee.

"David and Donna White insisted on a picture with them holding their newborn twins. I couldn't say no. It was a great shot."

"I don't think I saw one with them."

"When you were here before, I didn't have them all printed out yet. Let me show you." He walked across the room and grabbed something from a drawer in a cupboard. "Here they are. See what you think."

As he sat back down, I flipped through them. There were the ones from before. The next ones were new. Agnes Temple, talking with Betsy Jones. Danae, laughing with Florence and Lottie as she petted one of the cats.

The last one in the stack was of Buford and Ken. I tapped the photo. "Looks like they were deep in a conversation here."

"Yeah, that was before they ended up having an argument."

I pulled the picture closer and squinted. It was the one I'd seen before of them with the parcel.

"See something interesting?"

Maybe Evan would have an idea of what they were up to. Hanging around for the whole time of the pastry sale, he might have caught conversations I'd missed. "Looks like they're exchanging something here."

He shrugged. "Can't tell. The package is too small. I'm afraid even if I blew up the image, it would be blurred. Don't think we could get any better detail on it. Why? Do you think it's important?"

"It might be." Whatever was in the package might yield some clues. Even more intriguing, was Ken giving something to Buford, or was it the other way around?

Chapter Twenty

Since Durbin had been killed with a left-handed tool, I needed to find out who in our little town was a southpaw besides Russ and me. I wanted to start with Wilma, since it happened at her house, and I'd heard from her own lips how much she'd hated her husband.

I couldn't come right out and ask her which hand she used. Well, I could, but as mad as she tended to get, I might come away with bloody stumps for fingers if she decided to bite me. And those fingernails. Truly scary, like a cat's recently sharpened claws. Didn't want to end up on the wrong end of those.

When Wilma went to have her nails done, which I'd heard was a frequent occurrence, she might let down her hair, so to speak, and jabber on about this and that. Or perhaps something would come up about which hand she used. I could imagine her wanting her dominant hand to have extra care for some reason, but what did I know? I'd never had a manicure in my life. For all I knew, the technician would use a chain saw and whitewash.

Maybe I could also find out something about her or the murder that would help me out. I needed to be in the nail salon at the same time she was, but to do so, I'd have to know the time of her next appointment.

A quick call to the local nail salon gave me the answer. Annie Bates, the owner, was a client of mine. Annie loved bringing her cat in to see me. She always said she'd come every week if I had the openings because her gray-striped cat Kiki always looked so elegant after her wash, dry, and fluff. I had something I thought might entice her to tell me what I needed to know.

After offering her a free grooming session for her cat in exchange for some information, I was told Wilma would be in this evening at six o'clock.

My grooming schedule had been full. Three mobile visits and several in the salon. I was worn out and wanted to go home, but I couldn't miss this chance to see what Wilma might chatter about to her nail tech.

I arrived a few minutes after six, hoping Wilma might already be seated when I got there, because sitting next to her in the waiting area wasn't what I had in mind. I'd have to force conversation and hope she didn't think it was suspicious I was there since I had never been before.

If things went as I hoped, I wanted to slide in the front door and hover near Wilma, hidden around a corner or something. Annie didn't know what I had planned, but since she was so excited about the prospect of an extra session—free, at that—I didn't think she'd say much to me hanging around.

As I entered the salon, I glanced at the wooden plank flooring and floor-to-ceiling picture window. It was an attractive place, with several nail stations set up, each one bearing the name of the nail tech who worked there, along with individual personal touches like family pictures, vases of flowers, or signs and plaques with encouraging sayings. Most stations were empty, but maybe not all the techs took appointments in the evenings.

I spied Wilma sitting in the far corner booth, her back to me. She was indeed spouting off about something, but I couldn't quite catch all her words. I needed to get closer. Annie appeared from around the corner and spotted me. She gave me a thumbs up, even though she hadn't been told my plans. Guess she didn't care as long as she got what she wanted. It worked out well for me. She left again, heading into the back part of the area. Maybe she had an office somewhere back there.

Now was my chance to overhear something useful from Durbin's widow.

After crossing the floor, I was almost to the other side of the partition from where Wilma sat. If I stood right there, she wouldn't be able to see me, but I could hear whatever it was she said.

Footsteps came from behind me. "Excuse me!"

I jumped and turned. A young woman, maybe late teens, stood there, hands on hips, wearing a frown on her pretty face. Her name tag said Trixie. I opened my mouth, but it took two tries to get any words out. "Oh, uh, hi."

My heartbeat slowed back down to a normal rhythm. I loathed being snuck up on. Yet wasn't it the same thing I planned to do to Wilma? No, listening to what she said wouldn't frighten her. Besides, it was for a good cause of finding who killed her husband.

"Do you have an appointment?" The girl eyed me.

"Me? Um, no."

"I'm afraid you need an appointment to have your nails done. No walk-ins." She pointed toward the back wall, where a sign told me exactly that.

I shook my head. "No, I don't need to have my nails done." The reason I'd never once had a manicure, especially not a pedicure, was I was extremely ticklish. Even the thought of someone rubbing their fingers on my sensitive skin made me squirm. The most I ever did was trim my own nails. In a pinch, I even used the cat nail trimmers from my own salon. Weird, but true. Hey, I was practical, if nothing else. If it was good enough for my clients, it had better be good enough for me too.

She stepped closer. "If you don't want a manicure, why are you here?"

I chewed my lip. Hmm. Good question. One I hadn't anticipated having to answer since Annie was okay with me coming in. "Well, I...."

She sighed. "Listen, we always tell customers they need an appointment, but—" she glanced down at my hands— "I can see you're in desperate need of emergency fingernail assistance."

"What? No." I curled my fingers into my palms, hoping to hide the monstrosities on the ends of my fingers. It had never bothered me much, but being in here, with all the photos of beautiful people with perfect hands and nails, I didn't want the nail professional to see mine. Thankfully, the cats didn't care about my nails or hands, as long as I petted them a lot and scratched beneath their chins.

"It's okay. Don't be shy." She looked both ways, as if expecting someone to catch her doing something illegal, then back to me. "I won't tell if you won't. I have an opening right now. It's your lucky day."

Lucky, try terrifying. "Um, See, I don't...I've never had...." I waved my hand toward the nearest booth.

She raised her eyebrow. "Oh, I see. A first-timer. Well, I'll be gentle." She giggled. Taking me by the arm, she led me to the very booth I was hoping to hide in. What was happening?

My mouth refused to work when I tried to protest. All that came out was a squeak.

She smiled. "Don't be afraid. I'm good at this. Have been out of my training for three weeks now."

Three whole weeks?

My stomach clenched. Not only would I be ticklish, but I also had someone with minimal experience. Would my fingernails even be attached to my fingers by the time she was finished?

I pushed myself up from the chair, but she placed her hands on my shoulders. "Now, now, it won't take long, and you'll enjoy it. I promise."

How could I get out of the situation without either angering the inexperienced tech or causing her to cry? There had to be something, though. I couldn't sit and let her—

Wilma's voice rose from the next booth, saying something about Durbin.

Taking a calming breath, I forced myself to remain in the chair, steeling myself for what was to come for my poor fingernails. If I wanted to hear what Wilma was saying, it looked like this was my only chance.

I barely noticed as Trixie got out several items and set them on the short table between us, because Wilma was talking again. I leaned to the side a little, hoping to catch every word.

Trixie touched my hand. "I need you to hold still, please."

"Oh, sorry."

She winked. "Like I said, don't worry about a thing. I know what I'm doing."

I gave her a nod but kept my focus on the next booth.

Wilma let out an exaggerated sigh. "You know, Lydia, I don't understand people in this town."

"What do you mean?" asked the manicurist.

"They all want to know how I'm doing after Durbin's death."

"Well, they just care about you," said Lydia.

"I don't think that is the reason."

"Why not? Why do you think they ask?"

"These are people who don't speak to me very often," said Wilma.

"It's a small town. People are caring."

"People are nosy. Take that Molly Stewart, for example."

My face heated. Why was she talking about me?

Trixie squeezed my hand. "Miss? Are you all right? Your face is red."

"Fine," I whispered. Wilma didn't know I was here yet, and I didn't want her to find out by hearing my voice.

"What? I can't hear you."

I cleared my throat. "Uh, sore throat, can't talk...much." I added a sort of wheeze to my speech. Would it keep Wilma from recognizing it was me?

She narrowed her eyes. "You seemed fine when you arrived. Besides, you haven't been here very long."

"That's it...it's a weird thing...comes on suddenly."

Trixie studied me for a few seconds, then tugged my hand closer. "Your nails are a fright. What did you do to them?"

I studied my hands. They looked like they always did. I kept them clean and trimmed. What more did I need?

"It looks like you've been using your nails to climb up a rock wall. They're all nicked and so short. I've never seen anyone who didn't have longer nails with no polish." She made a tsk sound. "What do you do for a living, anyway?"

"I'm a cat groomer."

"You'd think someone who works with cats would want to have long claws like they do." She blinked, then shrugged and continued to use an emery board on my nails. She repositioned her hand, her fingers tickling mine.

I let out a loud "Ah!"

"What happened? Did I hurt you? Oh, dear. Not again...."

Not again? How many people had she injured in the span of three weeks? "No, you didn't hurt me. It's okay."

"You're sure?" She sniffed, like she might cry.

Perfect. If she started wailing, it would get Wilma's attention. The last thing I needed was for her to come around the partition to see what was going on. "I promise. It didn't hurt."

"Oh, that's good. Well, let's keep going then." She continued to buff my nails with the emery board. How long did it take to do that to ten tiny fingernails? They were so short, she could barely get the board across each nail. Surely, she was almost done, but what did I know, since I'd never had it done before. However, I wanted to stay here as long as Wilma did to listen to whatever else she might say, so I forced myself to hold still.

It would tickle again, I knew it. I'd have to find some other way than letting out a laugh, squeak, or squawk when it happened. I gave Trixie an encouraging smile and focused again on Wilma.

From the next booth, Lydia said, "What color will you want today, Wilma? Want to change it up a little? I have midnight blue, orange citrus, and forest green that we just got in. It's retro."

"No, let's stick with the pink I've had before. It goes with most of my outfits."

Pink! I was convinced it was what had been on Durbin's watch face, but had it come from Wilma? Candi? Or someone else?

Lydia sounded disappointed as she said, "If you're sure."

"I am. Now, what was I saying?"

I edged toward the booth again. *Yes, what were you saying?*

"Well, that girl, Molly, she keeps asking me questions. Do you know she had the audacity to come to my house right after I discovered Durbin had died? Right up to my porch."

I slid down in my seat a little. How was I to have known she'd be standing there that day? I'd just wanted to search her garden for clues.

"Hey," Trixie tugged on my hand. "Please remain still."

"Oh, sure. Sorry."

She reached for a bottle of something and poured a little into a small cup. Then, she rubbed what looked like oil or lotion on my fingernails, fingers, and up my palm.

Oh, dear. My palm. So ticklish! Must not laugh. I tapped my shoe furiously on the floor, hoping to concentrate on the sound and not what was happening.

Trixie lowered her eyebrows. "What's that noise?"

I cleared my throat. "Um, have a tune stuck in my head. Tapping out the beat with my foot. On the floor. The beat."

She shook her head. "Okay."

Wilma went on. "I don't know what she's up to, but I wish she'd leave me alone. Isn't a woman allowed to grieve in private?"

Lydia made some sort of mmm-hmm noise of agreement.

"Durbin was the love of my life, you know," whined Wilma.

What? She'd hated him. I choked, then coughed. My breath stopped somewhere in my throat. Why couldn't I stop coughing?

Trixie jumped up, ran to the end of the room, and returned with a cup of water. Thrusting it at me, she said, "Here."

I downed it, then set the cup down.

My garbled "Thanks" sounded like it came from a frog with a sinus infection.

She narrowed her eyes. "Are you sure your throat thing isn't catching?"

"I'm positive. Honest. I'm not sick, just…." I touched my throat. "Have this thing."

"Well, you can keep your thing. I'd rather not have it."

I forced a laugh. "Don't worry. You're safe." Glancing down at my hands, I wasn't sure I was safe though. My skin was red in places, and globs of lotion sat in little pools in others. If she hadn't said she'd been here for three weeks, I might have thought I was her first client ever.

Trixie had a tight grip on my hand and was studying my nails with a look of determination. That couldn't be good. What was she planning? Paint yellow happy faces on them? Or the blue background and gold stars of the Indiana state flag?

Wilma said something I couldn't make out, then went on to discuss the flowers in her yard. A conversation about her daises and lilies wouldn't help me. I needed her to say something about Durbin, his murder.. My ears perked up when Lydia said the word *cat*.

Wilma let out a harrumph. "That sorry creature? No, I didn't keep it. He'd been Durbin's pride and joy. Let me tell you, I took great delight in messing with its appearance every day."

"What do you mean?" asked Lydia.

"Well, as soon as Durbin would leave for work, I'd undo its silly little bow tie my husband insisted on giving it and then would rub the cat's fur backwards, so it looked like it had pillow hair." Her laugh came out as a snort. "The look on Durbin's face was priceless when he'd see it. Made the times the cat scratched me almost worth it."

I clenched my teeth. Durbin had been right in saying Wilma had been doing that to Jasper on purpose. The witch.

My hand was tugged toward Trixie. "Did you call me a witch?"

"What? No, of course not."

"Well, I heard you say it."

"Um," I tapped my foot again. "The song stuck in my head. It's about a witch."

Her eyes widened, then she shook her head. "If you say so." She mumbled something about the customer always being right.

Wilma laughed. "I was able to pawn off the wicked feline on the nosy cat groomer. How perfect! Now she's stuck with the little furball, and I didn't have to bother with him."

My insides boiled. What an evil woman.

Trixie's hand tightened on mine. "Hey, did you just call me—"

"Nope. Song again."

Trixie sighed. "All right."

I concentrated on the next booth again.

Lydia, at least I assumed it was her, made a scraping noise. "What about your nephew? How's he handling all this?"

"Buford is not my nephew. He's Durbin's. What a piece of work. He's crazy, I tell you. Always hanging around. Wanting handouts. What a loser. With Durbin gone, though, at least I won't have to deal with him anymore."

While it was true Buford wasn't my favorite, it still didn't sound like a nice thing to say about her nephew, even though it was relationship by marriage.

Another sound came from the booth. Like scooting something made of glass across the table. Was it a bottle of polish? I vaguely wondered if Trixie would want to paint mine, but I'd tell her no when it came to that point. With my job, polish wouldn't last long, so what was the point?

Suddenly, a chair screeched across the wooden floor from the next booth. Then another. Oh no. Were they finished with the appointment? Wilma was getting ready to leave. My original intention was to have hidden out near her booth, listen to her conversation and then follow her out of the shop to wherever she'd gone next. That wasn't going to happen. I was stuck until Trixie was finished. Clenching my jaws together,, I tried to remain still and not fidget, giggle, or squeak.

Wilma sailed past my booth, still talking to Lydia. Neither of them ever looked in my direction. "Thanks. I'll see you in four weeks for my next appointment?"

"Sure thing, Wilma."

From where I sat, I could see them standing beside the front counter and a cash register. Wilma reached into her purse—they must use something to quick-dry the nail polish on customers' hands—and drew out a checkbook.

Holding my breath, I waited until she got out a pen and wrote out the check.

With her left hand.

I let out a sigh. At least there was someone on my suspect list I knew for sure was a lefty. That put her even higher on my roster. While it was extra incriminating if she used her own left-handed garden tool to kill her husband in their own garden, it might have been a crime of passion, something done in the heat of the moment.

It was still murder. If Wilma was the killer, she thought she was getting away with it. I couldn't let that happen.

I slumped down in my chair.. At least it had been worth sitting here enduring the torture of a manicure to discover Wilma was left-handed. It was a major clue.

Eyeing my nails, I groaned. Because while I'd been paying attention to Wilma, I hadn't kept an eye on what Trixie had been doing. My nails, now long and fake, were neon green with little decals of yellow pineapples all over them.

Okay, it had almost been worth it.

Chapter Twenty-One

It was time for the weekly grooming sessions for Eleanor and Helga. Since their humans lived next door to each other, I parked in one or the other's driveways to do both groomings at the same time. And, of course, I always changed up whose driveway we used every time. Couldn't show favoritism, or the ladies might get upset with me.

Percival was my assistant for the day. I'd left Jasper with Veronica in the shop. She assured me it wouldn't be a problem since Jasper had a fondness for an incredibly soft blanket Veronica had placed on a corner shelf to nap on. Sometimes he wouldn't surface for hours.

My cat rode shotgun, nose pressed to the side window as he took in all the amazing and unbelievable sights of exotic Whitewater Valley. I smiled, glad Percival was enjoying the day. I hated what he'd been through trying to adjust to Jasper living with us. Yet, I honestly didn't have a better solution, and taking the poor kitty to the shelter was not an option.

When we reached our destination, I parked in Florence's drive. Both women were standing on their porches, waiting to see where I'd end up. Once I'd parked, they both descended their nearly identical front steps holding their cats. I got out of the van and met them at the back doors. I had a remote to open them from inside, so I didn't have to do it manually unless I wanted to.

"Good day, ladies."

They both smiled.

"And how are the girls today?"

Florence waved Helga's paw at me. When Lottie noticed, she did the same with Eleanor's paw.

Gee, no competition there.

I waited while they both handed me their cats, something we did every week—by now, I was rather good at holding one in each arm—and the ladies hurried to their garages. Florence came back with two folding chairs and Lottie with two glasses full of something pink and fruity looking.

Florence narrowed her eyes at her neighbor. "Did you remember to add the vodka this time? Last visit, they were a little weak."

"Of course, I did." She rolled her eyes and looked at me. "I added it last week, but someone here didn't believe me. As if I'd want to drink something watered down. I don't think so."

The competitiveness had amped up early this time. Better get to work. I cuddled both cats to my chest. Thankfully, they spent so much time together, they didn't mind being so close. Made me sad my two cats didn't even like being in the same room. "Let's get these pretty girls even prettier."

Both ladies beamed, temporarily over their tiff. After I placed first one cat, then the other, in the back of the van, I climbed the small steps that had automatically lowered as the doors had opened. Florence set their chairs near the back fender, then Lottie handed her a drink, and they got comfortable.

Percival jumped down from the front seat and trotted over to the table. He leaped up and stared at the ladies for a bit before seeming to decide they weren't doing anything exciting enough to hold his interest. He flicked his tail, then landed on the floor. The other cats, having been around him so often, didn't seem to mind his presence, though it was obvious they'd have preferred to have been alone.

My cat did the ceremonial procedure, edging close, sniffing them, and giving them each a quick lick on the head. The sphynx cats both closed, then opened their eyes toward Percival, a sure sign they approved of his existence. When Percival got bored with the exchange, he headed back to the front seat. I'd never had a problem with him jumping out the back and running off before, but always tried to keep an eye on him just the same. When he was with me on mobile visits, I put his special collar on him that had a bell. It made it easier to know his whereabouts when I was in the middle of something else.

When I'd first started the weekly grooming for their cats, the ladies tried to get me to join them in drinks. I finally convinced them they and their cats might not like the outcome if I was using grooming tools while under the influence.

Once the humans were ready, I reached for Helga. With the cats, I also had to change every week who got groomed first. Believe me, the ladies paid attention to what I did. I'm not sure the cats cared, because as soon as I'd set them in the van, they curled up together for a nap as if that had been their plan all along.

Helga grumbled and huffed when I picked her up, having settled into a comfortable position on a soft blanket. Eleanor closed her eyes and went to sleep. She'd have her chance to be groomed soon enough.

While in the past, I'd always ask the ladies about anything newsworthy they'd heard to keep them occupied as I worked, this time, I was hoping for useful bits which could aid in my search for the killer.

I placed Helga on my table and removed her pink sweater. Sphynx cats didn't like this part as they were always cold, but the nice warm bath I had prepared made up for it. They didn't fight me or try to get out but seemed to enjoy the warmth soaking into their sparse fur. Helga sighed as I placed her in the sink and poured water in small increments over her back and shoulders.

I kept working and didn't bother looking down at the ladies before I spoke because they were always watching my every move. "So, anything exciting happen you two have heard about?"

A thunk of glass on concrete sounded as one of them set her glass down on the driveway.

"Well," said Lottie, "you 'll never guess what we heard today."

"Oh, what's that?" I lathered some special sensitive skin cat shampoo on Helga's skin, working it down her back, around her tummy, and down her legs.

"Why don't you let me tell it?" Florence's voice was petulant.

"Because I started telling it. You had your chance."

"Not really. You bulldogged your way in there."

I glanced over to see Lottie raising her hand in a surrender gesture. "Now, now. Let's not argue. We can both tell it."

"You're right. We both can."

Silence.

I watched them and waited. When nothing more happened, I smiled. "Is someone going to tell me?"

They eyed each other, gave their silent signals, and Lottie nodded. "I'll start. When we were at Paula's Pastries this morning, we overheard something interesting."

I took my time as I poured a pitcher of fresh, clean water over Helga's back. The water drained slowly from the tub, but I kept rinsing her until the sink was empty of soap. After the warmth of her bath, I worked fast to get her to a thick warm towel so she wouldn't get a chill. "Really?"

"Yes, Ken Evers was talking to Frank Veerk about something which seemed to upset him."

Oh wow, this could be good. "Could you hear what they were saying?"

"Oh, my goodness, yes. Ken was talking loud, wasn't he, Lottie?"

"Yes, indeed he was."

Florence took a swig of her drink, which the ladies always assured me was for medicinal purposes, though I had serious doubts their doctor knew anything about their medicine. "He said Frank would get what he deserved."

My hand stopped mid-motion of drying off Helga, earning me a glare from the cat. "He said that?"

"Indeed, he did," said Lottie.

I dabbed gently with the towel around the cat's face, especially her eyes and ears. "Was there anything else?"

"Oh, my yes," said Florence.

I kept working but waited for more. When nothing came, I watched the ladies. They were once again signaling each other, this time with more exaggerated winks and hand circles. The medicinal alcohol must have kicked in. Unable to stand the suspense, I cleared my throat. "Did they say any more?"

Florence nodded and drained her glass—good grief, she was fast—and eyed Lottie, who jumped up and retrieved a pitcher from a table right inside her garage. Florence held out her glass for a refill. "Why didn't you bring the pitcher with you to start with?"

"Well, I had two glasses to carry, didn't I? Was I supposed to place the pitcher on my head and glide straight and slow like our school deportment lessons so I wouldn't spill it?"

Finally settled, each with a refilled glass, Florence looked up at me. "While we were there, we got an exciting show, didn't we, Lottie?"

"Indeed, we did." She took a giant slurp from her fancy straw, burped, excused herself, and took another drink.

Florence leaned forward in her chair. "There was shoving and growling."

"Oh, it was exciting." Her friend nodded her head vigorously.

"When Ken balled up his hand, I thought sure they're resort to fisticuffs."

Lottie fanned herself with the hand not holding her drink. "Me too. It would have been so exciting." She turned to Florence. "Can you imagine if the two men were having their quarrel over a woman?"

She sighed. "It would be exactly like the book." Eyeing me, she said, "Have you read the book yet?"

I rubbed some lotion on Helga's skin. "Uh, no, haven't had the chance."

"Well, you simply must read it. I think it would give you valuable information on your quest."

"Quest?"

"You know. For a man."

"Not any man," added Lottie. "The cute animal doctor. The book would give you tips on the birds and the bees."

Florence waggled her eyebrows. "Oh boy, would it." The ladies fell into a fit of giggles, Lottie splashing part of her pink drink onto her lap, but she didn't appear to notice.

I rolled my eyes. *Here we go.* "I'm not after Hank Chenoweth."

Lottie stared at me. "Of course you are, dear. Everyone knows it."

"What do you mean, everyone? Not that it's true, but even if it was, how would they know?"

Florence giggled. "Well, we've told them, of course."

My face heated. Perfect. Did the whole town think I was some sort of hussy trying to snag the kind, sweet, gorgeous, hunky— For Pete's sake. Now I was doing it too. "Listen, I'm not after the vet."

"I think you're wrong, Molly." Lottie stirred her drink with her straw.

"I'm...wait a second. Wouldn't I know if I was after some man?"

Florence shook her head. "Sometimes the people involved are the last to know."

I sighed. This wasn't getting me anywhere except more embarrassed. "Uh, back to what you heard at Paula's Pastries. What else happened?"

"Well, they started talking about the library." Lottie gave a finger wave to her cat, who was now facing her from my table.

Ah, now we were getting somewhere. When I'd overheard the men in the nonfiction animal section, their argument had gotten pretty intense. I redressed Helga, then gave a quick trim to her toenails. Having already checked her eyes and ears while bathing her, she was good to go.

I set her back on the pillow. "What did they say about the library?"

"Frank said something about cheating."

I gave the tub a good scrubbing with cleanser, rinsed it well, and then turned on the warm water spigot for Eleanor. As the tub refilled, I faced the ladies. "Did they say anything specific?"

"Frank said Ken must have finagled things so he'd get the contract instead of Durbin's firm."

Lottie nodded. "Yes, that's right."

"And then Ken said, 'I don't care what you think. I'm getting what should have come to me all along,' didn't he, Lottie?"

She winked. "Exactly those words."

While I couldn't be sure their memories while inebriated would call up the exact wording of another person's conversation, they were usually pretty accurate when it came to overhearing someone else's business, especially if they found it exciting.

I picked up Eleanor and removed her sweater. It was identical to Helga's pink one because the ladies called each other every morning to decide what their girls would wear. Then I lowered her into the water. Eleanor was more congenial than Helga and didn't even give me the stink-eye when she was sitting there naked. She even purred when I set her in the sink and closed her eyes in apparent ecstasy as the warm water covered her back.

"What happened next?" I repeated the bathing procedure as I'd done with Helga.

"Well, it's quite interesting." Florence tapped her drink with her fingernail. The sound made me cringe at what had happened to mine in the salon. Once I saw what Trixie had done to them, I'd balked at the thought of wearing the awful color and design around for however long the treatment lasted. But the first time I tried to groom a cat afterward, the nails had to go.

Veronica had watched, horror-stricken, as I'd taken the grooming clippers to them and had removed the majority of the fake nails because of the cost involved in having gotten them. It was either get rid of the ghastly, expensive nails, or accidentally poke, scratch, or terrify my clients. Wasn't gonna happen.

After a few seconds, when the ladies hadn't elaborated on what was so interesting, I gave them an indulgent smile. "You were saying something had been interesting."

Lottie's eyes were half closed. Had she been about to take a nap? Her eyelids flew open, and she blinked, as if my image was blurry. Was she seeing two of me? She finally shook her head and gave me a lopsided grin. "Oh, right. Let me think."

Florence poked her on the arm. "Don't you remember? The men got so loud and rambunctious, Paula finally asked them to leave."

"That's right! Thank you for reminding me."

"Any time." Florence's speech wasn't as sluggish as her neighbor's, but from the way she kept spilling drops of her drink on the driveway, she wasn't far behind.

I finished up Eleanor's bath, dried her, and applied lotion. As I was redressing her, Percival jumped up and gave her the sniff test. She mainly ignored him but did give a brief glare when he tried to sniff her nether regions.

"Honestly, Percival. How rude." I glanced at the ladies to make sure they weren't upset by the interlude, but they were both mostly asleep. After shooing Percival from the table, I placed Eleanor with her sister on the blanket. They immediately began giving each other simultaneous tongue baths, trying to undo what I'd done to them. Leave it to cats to try to bathe away cleanliness.

When they'd calmed some from their frenetic bathing, I tied a pink ribbon around each of their necks to match their sweaters. "Okay, girls, you're good to go." I climbed down the steps, reached into the van, and retrieved first Eleanor, then Helga, who growled a little at being moved around so much.

I stepped slowly toward the ladies, not wanting to frighten them in their sleepy, tipsy state. Keeping my voice low, I said, "All right, your girls are clean and dressed. They're ready to see their Mamas now." Waiting for the women to acknowledge my presence, I stood and held the two cats.

First Florence, then Lottie stirred, both blinking repeatedly and frowning. Trying to figure out what year it was, maybe? When they'd regained their senses, they both stood, albeit slowly and a little wobbly, to take their respective cats.

Thank goodness they opted for my mobile visits. No way could they have driven home after so many medicinal drinks. I had a rather good idea the women and their cats took a long nap each week following their appointment.

Chapter Twenty-Two

Veronica hurried from the back room. "I can't believe I forgot to send it."

I glanced up from stocking some shelves with new cat collars we'd gotten in. "Send what?"

She held out a package. "I got a sweater a few weeks ago. Pretty pricey, but I'd loved the color. Anyway, when I got it, the sweater was the wrong size. I'd intended to return it, then misplaced it, and then forgot about it and accidentally came across it again last night. When I read the paperwork just now that came with it, today is the last day I can return it to get my money refunded. Wouldn't you know I have back-to-back appointments. By the time I get finished, the post office will be closed."

"Can't we give it to Ricky when he drops off our mail?"

Veronica rolled her eyes. "You know Ricky. With the way he gets to talking sometimes, he might or might not remember to send it out today. I like him, but he's not always the most reliable. Plus, my next appointment is with Mrs. Collings. You know how upset she gets when she and Skippy have to wait."

"You're right about Ricky and about Mrs. Collings." I looked at my watch. "Listen, I have time before Mr. Ware brings in Andy for me to groom. I'll take the package."

Her eyes lit up. "You will? Thank you. I owe you."

"You can make it up to me with anything from Paula Pastries." I laughed.

"Done."

"I was joking. "No need to—"

She held up her hand. "I want to. Thank you."

155

I smiled and took the package from her. "My pleasure. Don't know what I'd do without you around here, so this is something small I can do for you." I glanced over to see what the cats were up to. Percival was zonked out on a pillow on a half-empty shelf. Only half empty because he'd shoved off some packages of cat vitamins I'd put there yesterday when he wanted room for a nap.

Jasper, however, was wide-eyed, his tail swishing as he stared at me. He needed more attention than I'd been able to give him lately. Maybe he'd like to come along. Making the decision, I reached for his leash and harness beneath the back counter. "Come on, mister. Let's take a walk." I grabbed my purse from below the counter and slung the long strap over my shoulder.

Once we were ready to roll, we headed out of the shop and into the cloudy but humid day. Even though the sun wasn't visible, Jasper lifted his face to the sky. Maybe he knew the sun was there somewhere, and he'd be ready to soak it in when it reappeared.

We strolled several blocks to the post office, me making sure not to move too fast so Jasper could keep up and Jasper stopping every few feet to sniff blades of grass or pebbles.

I opened the door and allowed Jasper to enter first. Once I'd laid the package on the front counter, I picked up the cat. Although they didn't mind people coming in for brief stays with their pets when they picked up mail, they might frown on animals wandering around sniffing everything, especially if there was a customer already in there who didn't like pets.

The place was empty today except for Edna Garing, the postal assistant. She mainly stayed in the office, sorting mail, and seeing to customers who stopped in. Ricky did the actual walking route, and Edna only did it if Ricky had to be out. She didn't seem to mind the office, though. As chatty as she was, I bet she liked having lots of conversations with everyone.

But then, so did Ricky. It was the reason our mail was sometimes late. And the reason Veronica couldn't trust him to get her package back out today. I didn't blame her. I loved Ricky, but reliable, he was not.

Edna grinned up at me when I approached the counter. She was even shorter than I was. Poor woman. "Hi, there. How are you?"

"I'm good."

"And who's this little cutie?" She reached across the counter and scratched beneath Jasper's chin with her skinny fingers. His purr boomed out, making her laugh.

"This is Jasper. He was… Durbin's."

Her smile fell. "Oh, poor little kitty. Are you keeping him now?"

"Yeah. I'd had him with me following a grooming when I found—"

She gasped. "That's right. You found poor Durbin. I guess I haven't seen you since it all happened."

"No, guess not."

She petted Jasper again. "Well, what can I do for you two today?"

As I shifted Jasper to my left hip —he snuggled up like a toddler— I tapped the package with my other hand. "This needs to go out today. Sorry for the short notice."

"Not a problem." She set it in a box to her left on the counter. "This is our outgoing for this afternoon."

I sighed. "Glad I didn't miss it."

"You're good. Was there anything else? Or did you just want to chat?" She laughed. "I always like seeing you, you know. Especially when you bring in a friend." She winked at Jasper, who winked back. She eyed me, then her face fell. "Wait. You still have Percival, though, right?"

"Oh, yes." I nodded. "He's fine."

"That's good to hear. I like it when you bring him in to see me. How's it going having two cats at once?"

"Not so good. They're having trouble adjusting to each other. Mostly Percival."

Her eyebrows went up and down. "Why don't you get the cute vet to help out? Bet he has some good ideas."

I wanted to roll my eyes so bad. "Um, he's given me some advice already."

She leaned closer and looked both ways even though we were alone. "Only advice? I thought maybe…."

Good grief. Was the whole town in on hooking us up? "Nope, advice. We're just friends."

"Not from what I've heard." She crossed her arms.

I opened my mouth to ask what she'd heard, then decided I didn't want to know. It might be some wild, embarrassing tale I didn't want to hear. I snapped my lips shut and shrugged.

The door creaked open, and a man came in. He stepped over to the post office boxes, opened his with a key to get his mail, then left, all without saying a word.

It took me a second to remember where I'd seen him before. Then it hit me. He was the one from the library who'd argued with Ken. Durbin's partner. Who, according to Candi, had argued often and loudly with Durbin before he died. Frank Veerk.

Edna thumbed toward the door. "Strange duck, that one."

"How so?

"Rarely says anything, but when he does, he's grumpy and has a mean look about him."

"Oh, gee. Sounds lovely."

She snorted. "Yeah, sure."

"I've never met him."

"You're not missing much," she said.

"Does he live close by?"

"Yep, three blocks over on Terrence Ave. You know the old house that sat empty for so long?"

I nodded. When we'd been kids, it had been scary looking and sad.

"He bought it and fixed it up. Looks real nice now. At least from what I've seen when driving by."

I could well imagine she happened to drive by lots of places out of curiosity. Maybe she would have preferred the walking route Ricky had, if it meant she could check out what people were doing around town.

Edna said Frank never talked much, but it didn't mean she hadn't heard things about him. "Someone, I can't remember who"—I wasn't about to start tossing other people's names into the mix for Edna to pass along— "said that he'd been Durbin's partner."

"Yep, that's right. From what I hear, the two didn't see eye to eye."

I nodded, having discovered if I didn't add anything, they often filled in the silence with something useful.

She pointed to Jasper, who was now dozing with his head lolled against my shoulder. And he was drooling. "Even though Frank seems to be a meanie, he might actually be a cat person."

"You think so?"

"Yeah. When Ricky delivers mail there, he said lots of times there's a scraggly looking white cat sitting on the porch."

"Maybe it's a stray," I said.

"Ricky doesn't think so. Said there's a small cat house on the front porch with a dish for food and water. Like it lives there."

"Hmmm. Very interesting."

"It is?"

Hmmm. I needed information without spreading more gossip than was already floating around town. "Just that he has a cat. You know how much I love those." I patted Jasper, who sighed.

She smiled. "Sure. Everybody knows that."

Good. If she told everyone who came in later today Molly Stewart loved cats, it wouldn't be a revelation or anything titillating to tell others. Not like whatever people were saying about me and Hank. My darned face heated. Why did it keep doing that?

"Molly? Are you all right? Your face is flushed."

I waved my hand. "Nope. Fine. A little warm today."

"Isn't it the truth? Everyone who comes in here complains about the humidity, but no one does anything about it." Her loud laugh startled the cat. His eyes popped open, and he looked directly at Edna.

She grimaced. "Sorry, Jasper. Didn't mean to interrupt your nap."

I patted him until he relaxed. "He's fine. No worries." After hearing Frank had a cat, it gave me an idea. "Say, Edna, could I buy an envelope and a piece of paper from you?"

"You don't need to buy them. We have a million. Here ya go." She handed me a business-size one from an overflowing box behind her on a counter, then grabbed a sheet of paper from the tray below her copier.

"Thanks so much."

"Need to mail a letter? Need a stamp?"

I shook my head. "Just this." I held them up. "Thanks again."

"No problem." The door opened again, and a woman entered. Edna looked behind me and then back. "Anything else I can do for you?"

"Nope. That's it. You've been a big help."

"For an envelope and paper?" She waved her hand. "It was nothing."

I smiled and waved Jasper's paw at her, causing her to laugh.

No, what she'd given me might be a huge help in getting me more clues.

As soon as Jasper and I were back outside, I set him on the sidewalk. He stretched his front legs, then his back. When he'd straightened again, I coaxed him a few yards away to a bench situated against the side of Lavender Lingerie. He hopped up and sat, immediately washing his front paws.

I sat beside him, put the paper and envelope on the bench between us, and fished a pen from my purse. If someone had a cat, especially if Ricky was correct in his description of it being scruffy, maybe the person would appreciate a complimentary cat grooming.

I scribbled the invitation on the paper and included my name, phone number, and the shop's address. I tried to print legibly even though I'd been told my writing wasn't always the best. Typing the note would have been more professional looking, but I was in a hurry. Frank didn't live far away, so Jasper and I could get there quickly. I hoped Frank hadn't gone home after visiting the post office. Wouldn't want a repeat of showing up at someone's porch only to find them standing there, like I had with Wilma.

I folded the note, stuck it into the envelope, and jotted Frank's name on the front. Jasper and I took off at a fast clip down the street. He didn't seem to mind the pace this time. Instead, he trotted along happily beside me. Durbin had taken his cat for frequent walks, and I hadn't been doing that. Maybe the cat had missed getting out for some exercise. I had to remedy that.

We reached the house in no time. Edna had been right. The old place didn't resemble the ramshackle heap anymore. It had new siding, new shutters, and the roof was no longer sagging. Flowers were planted in a brick box in the front yard, and the grass was trimmed, full, and lush.

I stopped and admired it from the sidewalk. Wow, what a difference. Eyeing the driveway, I smiled. There wasn't a vehicle parked there. Maybe he was at work.

Giving the leash a light tug, I led Jasper up the drive and to the porch. Just as Edna had said, there was a kitty house and food dishes present, but no cat. Would Frank have left the cat inside his house when he wasn't home? Though it wasn't my plan to speak to him, only leave the note, I nevertheless knocked on the door.

No one answered. Good. He must not be home. I tried the screen door, which was unlocked and opened it a fraction, then closed the door so he'd see the envelope sticking out from the outside.

Jasper pawed at something to my right. A loud meow followed but didn't sound like his.

A long-haired white cat, indeed, scruffy-looking, poked its head out from the opening of the cat house. Its sleepy blue eyes met mine, and it blinked.

I crouched down. "Hey there, little one. How are you?"

When the cat got closer and turned, I saw it was a female. She didn't seem too alarmed to see me, or even Jasper. Maybe he'd startled her from a nap when he'd pawed at her house, and she was still sleepy.

The cat came closer and rubbed her head against my hand, then did the same to Jasper's head. I frowned. Why couldn't Percival do the same with Jasper? He had no trouble with other cats. I thought about Veronica's words about needing Hanks' advice. My face heated again. Would it do it every time I thought about the guy? Sure, I was growing to like him more and more, but until I knew it was reciprocated, I refused to get my hopes up.

Jasper bumped his head against my hand, making me glance at my watch. Good grief. We needed to head back to the shop, so I wasn't late for my appointment. I petted the white cat one last time and picked up Jasper.

"See ya later, kitty. Hopefully soon."

The cat blinked, then began grooming her paws. She wasn't dirty so much as her long fur needed some thorough brushing and a light trim. From experience, I knew how hard it was to keep long fur tangle free and brushed. Her fur would stay tangled, if she stayed outside a lot and Frank didn't have the time or tools to help her..

Tools. Durbin and the left-handed garden implement.

I crossed my fingers Frank would take the bait and contact me for a free grooming for his cat. It seemed the best, and maybe only way I might get to speak to him and find out more details about his relationship with Durbin.

After work was finished for the day, I called Russ and filled him in on what I'd seen and heard since we last talked. Poor man sounded exhausted. I was more determined than ever to figure out who killed Durbin, so my uncle could get out from under the sheriff's thumb.

Chapter Twenty-Three

When Veronica approached me the next day, eyes wide with excitement, she had my attention. I pointed to her smile. "What's up?"

"Guess who called to make an appointment?"

I shrugged. "Santa and Rudolph?"

"Nope. Guess again."

"Do I have to? I'm terrible at this game. You always end up laughing at my guesses."

She rolled her eyes. "You're no fun. Fine. It was Frank Veerk."

"Wow. That was fast." I hadn't been sure he'd even take the bait at all.

"Now's your chance to find out more about him. He wanted to drop off his cat—"

"Oh, but—"

She held up her hand. "I told him a mobile visit was better."

"Good thinking. Thank you."

Veronica held up one finger. "And, for the initial grooming appointment, that you liked the pet parent to be present to make sure things go smoothly. Plus, you might want to ask questions while doing the grooming. I didn't say what kind of questions he might be asked."

I crossed my arms. "Ooooh, aren't you the clever one?"

She glanced down, acting like she was examining her fingernails. "Well, yes."

I laughed. "Okay, so when do I see them?"

"You had a cancellation for this morning, so I put him in." She pointed to the computer screen to my left.

My eyes widened. "So soon? I haven't had time to formulate questions about his partnership with Durbin or think about what my responses to his possible questions might be or—"

"Don't get yourself into a tizzy." She patted my arm. "You'll do fine. You always seem to come up with the right thing to say to people." She made a face. "As long as you're face to face and not on the phone. What is it with you and being nervous on the phone, anyway?"

"I think it goes back to when I was a teenager. My mom had a habit of standing right around the corner, listening to my conversations."

"Oh, wow. Especially for a teenager, having a parent listening in would be...."

"Mortifying, yeah. I guess the discomfort of speaking into a communication device stuck. Texting doesn't seem to bother me, but actually talking? Blech." I patted her arm. "I'm doubly glad you are so good at phone etiquette."

She batted her eyelashes as if having been told she'd won a beauty contest. "Thank you."

I grinned. "So, I need to do Miss Kitty's grooming, a couple more appointments, then head over to Frank Veerk's."

"Yep." She eyed me. "Hey, you'll do great. I have no doubt you'll know what to ask when the time comes. You're getting rather good at this sleuthing thing."

"Guess I have to, since the sheriff won't look farther than my uncle."

Veronica's eyes narrowed. "You're doing the job he's paid to do." Her indignant expression made me laugh.

"It's okay. I want to give Durbin some justice. I wouldn't feel right after seeing him the way he was, and letting the real killer go free."

"You're a good egg, Molly."

"I do try."

Veronica winked, then headed to the back of the shop.

The door opened, and Maribelle Lane brought in Miss Kitty on a leash and harness. Usually, parents brought their cats in their carriers, but occasionally they were leashed. Then there was Rose Renfield, who had the habit of carrying her cat, Queenie, on a large red pillow. She insisted her cat wasn't spoiled. No, not at all.

Instead of tying a ribbon on Queenie's neck when I'd finished with her grooming, Rose always brought along a tiara. An actual cat-sized tiara for me to place on Queenie's head.

It took all kinds.

Maribelle stepped closer, speaking reassuring words as she coaxed Miss Kitty along with her. Finally, she bent down and got her cat, then placed her on the counter. "Sorry if we're a little late. Miss Kitty was a being pokey today." She placed a kiss on her cat's head. I'd guess nothing her baby did would upset her. Even being pokey.

"No problem. We're fine on time."

My next couple of hours flew by with kitty baths, brushings, lotions, and pretty neck bows. Before long, I gathered up supplies for my mobile appointment.

Percival and I headed back to the house where I'd met Frank Veerk's white cat. I parked in his drive, surprised not to see a vehicle already there. Had we gotten the time wrong? Or maybe he was home but had parked inside his garage.

I got out of my van, leaving Percival in there, much to his dismay, and headed up the stairs. The white cat greeted me like an old friend. As I bent down to pet her, the front door opened.

Frank stood there frowning. "I assume you're Molly Stewart."

I stood and extended my hand. "Yes, nice to meet you, Mr. Veerk."

He looked at my hand for a few seconds before shaking it.

Alrighty, then. This guy might be a tough one to talk to, but I knew about it going in.

"Call me Frank."

That was better. "Thank you for calling about your free grooming session for your cat. I'm looking forward to it. What's her name?"

His eyebrows rose. "How do you know it's a she?"

Hmmm, yes, how indeed. He didn't know I'd already met her. "I…"

Frank crossed his arms, making his shoulders and arms seem even bigger than before. Up close, he was taller and more imposing than I'd remembered from the library. "I suppose you're going to tell me cat people like yourself automatically know these things."

What else could I say? The truth certainly wouldn't work. "Something like that."

He harrumphed. "Well, let's get this over with."

Gee, nice to meet you, too, Mr. Grumpy.

He tapped his foot in a rapid beat on the step. "What do we have to do?"

I pointed to my van. "Everything we need for the grooming is inside my mobile grooming station."

"You do your job from inside there?" He made it sound as if I'd be taking his cat into a storage facility for toxic waste. Hey, I kept my van clean. His implication made me defensive. *No, don't go there. Have to play nice to get the guy to talk to you.*

I nodded. "That's right." Before he could refuse, I picked up his cat. "Um, you never told me your cat's name."

"Oh, it's Daisy-belle." His face reddened, and he looked away.

I bit my lip, trying not to smile. A big gruff man might not like to admit his cat was named for some flower and resided in the deep south and drank mint juleps. Instead, I turned the cat so she faced me, "Nice to meet you, Daisy-belle."

The cat closed her eyes and placed her paw on my chin.

Frank's eyes widened. "I've never seen her do anything like it before. Why did she do it?"

"She's saying she's glad to meet me too."

He frowned. Was he jealous his own cat had never shown him that particular form of affection? Or did he think I was blowing smoke and making her reaction up?

I cuddled the cat to my chest. "Why don't we head down to the van and start the grooming. Is that okay?"

He grumbled from behind me, stomping down the stairs. Why did he even want the grooming if he was so irritated about it? Not that I was complaining, but it didn't make a lot of sense. If I got an ad or offer I didn't want, I tossed it in the trash. Maybe he just accepted because it was free? Some people, no matter how much money they had, couldn't stand to pass up a deal.

I handed the cat back to Frank temporarily. "Let me get the back doors open first. Be sure to stand back a few feet until I get them open, and then let the steps down."

As I rounded to the driver's side door to press the remote to get everything ready, Frank mumbled something like "wasted time."

Sounded like I was lucky to even get this one session with him and Daisy-belle. I'd have to make the most of whatever conversation I was able to get from him.

I returned to the back doors and climbed up the steps into the van. Leaning down, I held out my arms. "Go ahead and give me Daisy-belle."

Frank frowned but handed me the cat. He glanced toward the street. Was he afraid a neighbor might see him conversing with a lowly person who did business out of a van? "Er, um, the woman I spoke to on the phone about the appointment… She said I needed to stay here while you do the grooming."

"Yes, that's right."

He harrumphed. "May I ask why?"

I knew Veronica would have already covered this in her conversation with him when she booked the appointment, but I needed to get this guy talking, and if this was the way in, I'd take it. "Of course. It helps me, at least during the initial grooming, to get to know more about the cat by talking to their human."

"Their human?"

"Their owner."

He shook his head. Must have thought the way I talked about cats and their people was silly. But I didn't care. I was used to non-cat people, or those like him, who had one but didn't seem too invested in them, scoffing at my thoughts on cats and their care.

I petted the cat, hoping to calm her before I began the grooming. "I'll explain what I'm doing as we go along for Daisy-belle's grooming. How long have you had her?"

He shrugged. "She kind of was here when I was renovating the house. Just hung around and refused to leave. My construction guys started leaving food out for her. Also, somebody brought over the cat house she sleeps in. I guess she didn't have any owners."

"Until now."

"Right. Yeah. Until now."

I ran a brush through her fur, taking care to be gentle. She did have a lot of tangles. I explained to Frank how to do it. "Does she ever go inside your house?"

"When the weather is bad, I've let her in. Not often, though."

I nodded slowly.

His hands landed on his hips, in an almost aggressive stance. "Is it wrong? To leave her out?"

"Not wrong. I've just found cats enjoy being inside a home for the most part. It's warmer and safer. They feel cared for and more relaxed in general."

He pointed to his porch. "She seems to like being outside. At least if it's nice out."

"True. Some cats do." Percival picked that moment to hop up onto a nearby stool. "My cat here, Percival, likes me to take him for outings on a leash to get some fresh air. Otherwise, he's inside either my house, shop, or van."

Frank's eyebrows lowered. "You bring your cat to take care of other's people's cats?"

I smiled at Percival, who was now staring wide-eyed at Daisy-Belle. She was watching him too but didn't seem upset he was there. "Yep. He likes it."

"What if the cat's, uh, human doesn't approve?"

"I have only two clients who'd prefer I not have Percival when I do their cats. I abide by their wishes, of course. Why? Does it bother you? I can put him in his carrier if it does."

Frank watched Percival, who was now sitting quietly on his stool, washing his front paw, and seeming not to care what anyone else did, said, or thought. "No, I suppose it's all right."

I ran my hand over Daisy-Belle's long fur. "Great." I lowered the cat into the warm bath and explained everything as I did it.

Frank crossed his arms, still looking annoyed, but didn't make a move to leave. I considered it progress.

"How did you come up with your cat's name? It's pretty."

"Well, my girlfriend suggested it."

"Oh, how nice."

"It was until she decided I wasn't worth seeing anymore." His eyes widened. "I can't believe I said those words out loud."

"It's okay. People tell me all kinds of things." If I was lucky, he'd spill a whole lot more, and not just about an ex-girlfriend.

"It's just, as a rule, I don't talk about personal matters."

Acting as if I wasn't thrilled he was starting to open up, and not wanting to scare him away, I shrugged. "I don't mind. There's something relaxing about watching a cat being bathed and brushed that often makes people relax. Almost like they themselves were being treated to a massage."

He rubbed the back of his neck, as if it was sore. "Massage. I used to get those. A long time ago."

"Not now?"

"Being sort of new in town, I don't know who would be a good one to go to. Or if there's even a place here. It is a small town, after all."

"It's small, that's true. However, we do have a place. When we're through here, I can write down the information if you'd like" I said.

His mouth opened, then closed. He studied me for a few seconds. "Why, yes. That would be great."

Wow, he nearly smiled. Progress, indeed. I finished Daisy-belle's bath and dried her with a thick towel. "When we were talking about cats being inside versus out, there's something you might want to consider."

"What?"

"Lots of bad things can happen to a pet if they're left outside all the time."

"Bad?" His hands balled into fists at his sides.

"Yeah, there are predators around."

His eyebrows lowered. "They might get a cat?"

"Yes. Unfortunately. Coyotes. Owls. There are others."

He shook his head. "Guess I never thought about it."

"Also," I tilted my head toward the street. "Lots of traffic. Sometimes they get…," I lowered my voice, "hit."

"Oh." He looked at his cat. "I don't think she'd do that. Go out into the street, I mean."

"Do you know for sure? I'm guessing with whatever your job is, you might not be home all the time?" Maybe my question would get him to talk about work somewhat. Then, in turn, it could lead to talking about Durbin.

He eyed his house. "Well, true. I'm not here all that much some days."

I kept my attention focused on the cat, as if I wasn't all that interested in the conversation. "Where do you work, if you don't mind my asking?"

"At Durbin Construction."

"Oh. Really?"

"Do you know of it?"

"I know some people who've worked there." I trimmed the cat's nails, then checked her eyes, ears, and teeth.

"Like who?"

"Well, Candi Jones. She's a client of mine." While I wouldn't usually divulge who my clients were, in this case, I needed an opening for him to talk more.

"Ah, yes, Candi. Seems okay at her job. Maybe a little flighty."

I bit my lip. A little? Try dramatic and hyper. Instead, I smiled. "Oh, and… well, there's, there was, Durbin Haines."

His face darkened. "You knew Durbin?"

"I did, yes."

"Another client of yours?"

"Yes. I'd known him for most of my life, actually." Should I tell him I was the one who'd found Durbin? He didn't seem to know. Maybe I'd wait a bit and see what panned out. "Such a shame what happened to him."

Frank didn't answer at first, seeming distracted. "What? Oh, yes. A shame."

Did he really think it was a bad thing Durbin was gone? Or was he truly sorry his co-worker had died? I finished drying Daisy-belle's fur, then re-brushed her. The difference in her fur texture and color was amazing. "Had you worked with Durbin long?"

"No. Not very long. Long enough to…."

"To…"

170

"Nothing."

As I finished with Daisey-belle and tied a pink ribbon around her neck, I realized I wouldn't get any more information from Frank. He did, however, seem interested in further groomings for his cat. That, at least, was something.

Chapter Twenty-Four

I took my bank deposit to the local bank. Veronica offered, but she did so much at Fabulous Felines already, I hated to ask. As I came around the corner from their parking lot, I nearly ran into Andrea. Maybe she was there doing the same thing for Hank.

"Hey, Andrea."

She gave me a half-hearted wave but said nothing. She disappeared around the corner. How odd. She was one of the friendliest people I knew, to the point of seeking people out to hear the latest news about anything and everything.

Shrugging, I headed inside and waited through two other customers before making my deposit. If I hurried, I'd be back at the salon before Rose Renfield came in with Queenie.

When I returned to my van, I opened the door, then stopped. Why was Andrea's car still here? I knew it on sight from the many times I went to their office, and it was usually parked out front. Was she having car trouble? I shook my head, thinking about my van breaking down in front of the jeweler. Maybe the vehicle illness was catching.

I shut the van door again and headed across the small lot. Andrea wasn't on her phone as I'd expected, maybe trying to call the garage or someone else. Instead, she was sitting in the front seat in tears as she stared out the windshield.

I knocked on her window, and she jumped. After blinking a few times, she lowered her window. She looked up at me, eyes red from crying.

"Andrea? What happened?" I knew better than to ask if she was okay.

Something was way off.

She grabbed a tissue from a small box in her center console. "It's so awful."

"Something happen with your family? Or at work?"

"The first one."

I nodded, even though I had no clue who in her family was the problem or why. She mopped away some wetness from her cheeks. I'd never seen her like this. Something awful must have happened. A glance at my watch told me I still had a little bit before I had to return to work. "Need someone to talk to?"

She turned and looked at her car passenger seat and removed a shopping bag, setting it in her back seat. "Yeah. I think I do. If you don't mind."

"I don't. Want me to get in?"

She nodded.

After skirting around the front of her car, I hopped into the empty seat. I set my purse on my lap. "You can tell me as much as you want. Or as little. Or...we can just sit here if that would help."

Andrea tossed her used tissues in a small waste bag behind her seat. After grabbing a few clean ones, she turned in her seat toward me. "I still can't believe what he said."

Since she'd said it was family, I knew it wasn't Hank. Though, I couldn't imagine him ever saying anything to make someone cry at any rate. "Do you want to talk about it?"

She lifted one shoulder in a shrug. "I think so."

"Okay." I folded my hands together over my purse and waited.

"See, my brother, Ken, has always been great to me. We've always been close. We're actually twins, did you know?"

"No, I didn't."

"All our lives, we've stuck together through everything. Especially when our parents divorced when we were sixteen. He and I got even closer."

A minute went by while I waited, but she said nothing more. I turned a little more toward her. "Did something happen to Ken? Is he okay?"

"He's not okay, but the problem isn't his health. At least not his physical health. Mentally?" She shook her head. "I'm not so sure."

Poor girl needed someone to talk to. Maybe if I prodded her a little, she might be able to get out what was bothering her so much. Deciding to jump into the conversation and ask questions, I touched her hand. "Why do you think there's a mental issue?"

"There has to be. I mean, the way he talked to me a little bit ago. It's never happened before. I don't even know what to think." She glanced out the window.

"What did he say?"

Her gaze met mine and at first, I didn't think she'd answer. What he said was, 'I don't want anything to do with you. Ever again.'"

I let out slight gasp. If a member of my family or anyone close to me had said that, I'd be in a puddle of tears too.

Andrea blinked several times. Was she going to cry again? "I don't understand where this is coming from. It's not like he's had some major life change, like a bad divorce or the death of someone he loved. I realize people take out their grief in strange ways. It might come out as anger, but since there doesn't seem to be a reasonable explanation for it, I don't know what to think."

"Did you ask Ken why he'd said it?"

She crossed her arms protectively across her chest, as if warding off any further verbal insults. "I asked."

"What did he say?"

"To leave him alone. Forever."

Another gasp from me. I could see why she'd been so upset. I would have been a mess.

Andrea shifted in her seat. "If I knew it hadn't only happened to me, if he'd been this way to someone else, I guess it might help somewhat. It wouldn't make it right, but then at least I'd know it was something going on with him and not me. Part of me thinks I've imagined it. Of course, I know that's not true. I can't wrap my mind around why he'd say those things to me."

I'd had zero intention of ever telling Andrea the things her brother had done and said in my presence at the garage. I hadn't wanted to hurt her. Now? It sounded as if she needed confirmation she wasn't crazy, that her brother had something going on and had spouted off at somebody besides her.

"Hey." Andrea bumped my arm with hers. "You okay? You zoned out for a second."

How should I say it? Although what Ken had said to me that day wasn't anything compared to what he'd said to his own sister, he'd been hateful, demeaning, and awful.

"Do you know something? Have something you need to tell me? If you do, I wish you would. It can't be worse than what I've already told you."

She was right.

I placed my purse on the floor, then looked right at Andrea. "Okay, I wasn't going to ever tell you this."

Her eyes widened. "Did something happen? With Ken?"

"I'm afraid so."

"Can you tell me? I mean, was it…."

I cringed, remembering his aggressive stance. His harsh words and threatening tone. "It wasn't good."

"I know you think it may sound strange I want to hear something bad about Ken, but I need to know what's going on with him. Going by what he said to me isn't telling me anything. I need more information if I'm going to figure it out."

Yep, I sure understood. Wasn't it the same thing I'd been doing? Trying to find out all the information about Durbin to figure out the mystery?

Sounded like I needed to just say it. Maybe, hopefully, it would help her in some way. "Okay, what happened was this. My van had broken down in front of the jewelry store, and I had to have it towed to Ollie's Garage."

Andrea nodded, her full attention on me.

"While I was waiting there, Ken came in and was arguing with Ollie and Ernie. It seemed intense. When he came out of the office where they'd been, he spotted me and stormed over. He thought I'd been listening in and would tell someone what I'd heard. I heard them yelling, yes, but had no intention of spreading anything around. I didn't even know what they were talking about. It seemed odd he'd do that. Come rushing over and even threaten me and Percival, who happened to be with me."

"My brother threatened you? And your sweet cat?"

I nodded, still hating having told her, but hoping it might help her in some way figure out what was happening with her brother.

She pressed her hand to her chest. "Gosh, I'm so sorry."

"It's not your fault."

"I know, but you know how when you're connected to someone, and they do something to hurt another person, you feel responsible?"

"Yeah, I do."

She looked at her watch and sighed. "Well, time got away from me. I need to get to work. Hank will be wondering where I am."

"Does he know about what's going on with Ken?"

Her shoulders slumped. "No. I haven't told him. It's uncomfortable talking to your boss about family stuff. Plus, the workplace doesn't seem like the right venue to spout off about non-work stuff."

"I'm sure he'd like to know if something is wrong. He cares about you."

Andrea nodded. "I know he does. He's a good guy." She opened her mouth as if to speak, then closed it. Tilting her head, she said, "If you... No, I shouldn't ask."

"If I what?"

"I know you and he are friends. Maybe if you...." She shrugged.

"Would you want me to tell him for you?"

Her eyes brightened, despite the redness from tears. "Would you?"

"Of course."

She leaned over and hugged me. "That's great. Thanks so much. Thank you for checking on me. And listening."

I smiled. "It's what friends do." Until now, she and I had been acquaintances, but I was pretty sure we'd be more than that from here on. "You go on to work and try to have a good day, okay? I'll give Hank a head's up for you."

"Thank you, again."

I got out of the car and closed the door, giving Andrea a wave as she started her car and left the lot.

Realizing the time, I hurried to my van and drove a little too fast back to work.

When I walked back into Fabulous Felines, Veronica was frowning. She pointed to the clock. "Are you all right? Rose and Queenie are here and waiting in the back. I got out your supplies and told you you'd be right with them."

"Thank you. Sorry about that. Let me do their grooming and then I'll fill you in on what's going on. Don't worry. I'm fine." I smiled and hurried to the back.

After the appointment was finished and Veronica had been filled in on things with Andrea, I texted Hank to see if he could talk soon. Within a few minutes, he texted back he had a break for the next couple of hours and would be at my salon.

When Hank entered, Veronica made herself scare, darting to a side room and closing the door. That was something considering her tendency to listen in on conversations. But since I'd already told her everything, her curiosity was taken care of, for now. At least, I hoped so.

"Hey, Hank. Thanks for dropping in."

His eyebrows were lowered, and he wore a frown. "You have me worried. Are you okay? Is it about Percival and Jasper?"

I motioned to some chairs in the corner, and we sat down. "I'm fine. The cats are the same. Still working on it. No, actually, it's about Andrea."

"My receptionist, Andrea?"

"Yes."

"I saw her right before I came here. What's going on?"

"I had to run to the bank a little while ago. When I came out, I found her crying in her car in the parking lot. She was pretty shaken up," I said.

"This is news to me. When she came in, her eyes were red, and I asked if she was okay, but she said maybe her allergies were acting up."

I placed my forearms on the table. "No, it wasn't her allergies. She wanted to tell you what happened but said sometimes it's uncomfortable telling a boss about your personal stuff when you're at work."

"I get it. Yeah, I understand." He studied me for a second. "So why are you telling me?"

I held up my hand. "I have her permission to tell you what's going on. She wants you to know. Just having trouble saying it to you."

Hank crossed his arms and sat back against his chair. "All right. What's happening?"

"It's about her brother." I hated to go into it, but it was Andrea's wish, and I'd agreed. Hopefully, Hank would be able to discuss things with her later, if she wanted.

His eyebrows lowered. "Ken? Is he okay?"

"Not really. I think he's fine physically, but something's going on with him."

"Do you know what's happening?"

I lifted my hands, palms up. "His personality seems to have changed and Andrea doesn't know why. Apparently, right before I saw her, she'd had an argument with Ken, something which never happens. She talked about how close they'd always been."

"Yeah, I did know that. I mean, they'd be together every single holiday and always did lots of things together. She'd also told me in the past, they'd gotten closer since their parents split up. What changed?"

"She doesn't know. Just that Ken all of a sudden is argumentative and mean. I won't repeat what he said to her, but it was painful. If a member of my family said it to me, I'd be in tears too."

"Oh, the poor girl. No wonder her eyes were so red. Why do you think she opened up to you? Are you guys close?"

"Not really. I think because I happened to be at the same place right when she was, it was her opportunity to tell someone. Also..."

Hank leaned forward. "What?"

"She was trying to figure out why Ken had been that way to her, but she hadn't heard of him doing it to anyone else. It didn't make sense to her. She asked if I heard of anything about him that might help her figure it out, like if he'd been rude to another person."

"And had you?"

"Unfortunately. It was to me, when I'd had my van towed."

Hank's eyes narrowed. "Wait, you had a problem with your van? Why didn't you call me?"

"Uh...." My face heated. For one thing, I always tried to take care of problems by myself, if possible. Also, it hadn't occurred to me Hank was someone I could call in an emergency. But, good to know. "I didn't want to bother you."

"Well, next time, call me. It's not a bother, believe me."

I smiled. Maybe Hank did see me as more than a casual friend. If not in a romantic way, it sounded like something a good friend might say. "Thank you."

He squeezed my hand. "What happened when you had to have it towed?"

"Ollie got me and Percival, who was with me, and took us to his garage. Wilma Haines had harassed us while we waited in front of the jewelry store where the van broke down, but it's a whole other story. It's fixed now, but while we were there, Ken barged into Ollie's office and started yelling at them."

"That's weird. What about?"

"I'm not sure. I could hear loud voices, but whatever they were talking about didn't make a lot of sense to me. But when he exited the office, he saw me and came over, yelling and making threats to me and to Percival."

Hank's mouth dropped open. "Threats? You're kidding."

"I wish I was. It was awful."

Hank shook his head. "Andrea's right. Something is way off with her brother. From what I know of him, he's never caused anybody trouble before. Thank you for telling me. I'm sorry she's feeling like this, but I'd rather know than not."

I let out a sigh. "I'm glad I was there to see her earlier and that she told me. She wanted you to know, just...."

"Yeah, it's okay. I get it. I don't usually tell everyone my business, either. Although now that she's given you permission to tell me, I have the opening to talk to her myself." He stood. "I'll let you get back to work, and I'll head to my office and see if she and I can talk a little before my next patient. Thank you again."

"Glad to help." I stood too and pushed in my chair. "Let me know if there's anything I can do for Andrea."

"I will." He headed toward the door with a wave and stepped outside.

Rapid footsteps came from the back. Veronica sidled up beside me. "Wow, what a nice guy Hank is, being concerned for Andrea and for you."

I rolled my eyes. "You were listening again? I'd already told you what was going on so you wouldn't feel the need to do it."

She shrugged. "Might have been something juicy that happened after he got here."

I shook my head in mock exasperation. Her being as curious as a cat could be annoying, but I loved her dearly and couldn't stay mad. "You're incorrigible."

"It's why you love me."

I laughed. "True."

Chapter Twenty-Five

When I entered the front area of the shop, Veronica was deep in conversation with Ricky. Veronica turned to me, eyes wide. She waved me over. "You've got to hear this."

What on earth was so fascinating? Were the Christmas catalogs coming way early? Veronica was a shopaholic, after all. "What's up?"

Ricky set his mailbag down on the floor, then leaned his elbows on the counter. "I was telling Veronica here that I witnessed the most incredible thing on my route this morning."

Sometimes Ricky got excited about subjects that might not interest everyone else. Parking lot gravel. Garden slugs. Earwax.

My grandma would have said the guy was nice but had a personality as dry as dust. However, the stunned expression on my assistant's face drew me in. It must be something huge. "What happened?"

Beside me, Veronica buzzed with excitement. "Go on. Tell her."

Ricky raised his eyebrow. "I was getting to that."

"Somebody tell me, okay?" I held in a sigh.

Ricky eyed me. "You won't believe it. You just won't."

This wasn't going well. I had a grooming appointment in ten minutes. As slow as Ricky told stories, it might actually be Christmas before I found out whatever this astounding news turned out to be.

Veronica wound her hand in a circle. "Ricky, if you don't tell her, I will."

He frowned. Did he not want to lose the chance to tell the juicy tale? I eyed the wall clock. Ricky was over an hour late in bringing the mail. If he was telling this story at every stop and took this long to get to the point, he'd still be handing out bills and fliers at midnight. He ran his hand down his chin. "I'm going to tell her."

I watched him, hoping it would be sometime today. If Veronica wasn't so insistent and excited about his story, I wouldn't spend time standing around waiting.

Finally, he grinned and faced me. "You're going to be totally amazed."

I nodded, even though his last totally amazing story was about the moldy piece of cucumber he found in his fridge.

"What I saw was this…. On my route today, I was taking mail to the west side."

"Uh-huh."

"And I had a few pieces of mail for Wilma Haines."

"Okay."

"It was odd because normally she doesn't get mail on a daily basis, must do her business online. You know, lots of people do it now. Some days, I don't have all that much to drop off in boxes. Makes a body wonder if there will even be a need for the postal service in the future."

Wanting to hurry him up, I patted his hand. "I'm sure your job is safe."

He bobbed his head. "You're probably right."

When he hadn't gone on yet, Veronica pointedly knocked on the counter with her knuckle.

Ricky blinked. "Anyway, at Wilma's house, she was doing something odd."

When more wasn't forthcoming, I looked behind him at the front door. Any time now Agnes Temple would bring in Lulu for her weekly brushing and ear check.

He glanced behind him too, as if someone was standing behind him, then back at me. "As I was saying, she was doing something out of the—"

Veronica huffed out a breath. "Honestly, you've got two seconds before I tell her."

"Fine." He held up his hand. "My goodness, you're impatient. So, when I got to her house, I started to put her mail in her box. You know, like I normally would."

I held in another sigh and nodded.

"I saw her standing by her garden."

The garden? That got my attention "What was she doing?"

"I decided since she was outside, I'd bypass the mailbox and trot on up their steps to personally hand her the envelopes. See, I think a personal touch makes folks feel valued. Like they matter. Not just a part of my job, you know?"

"Um, sure. So…"

"When Wilma saw me coming toward her, she kind of jumped, like I'd scared her. I didn't realize I was so scary to look at." His laugh came out loud and creaky, sounding like a rusty hinge.

I forced a smile. "Nope. Not scary. So, Wilma?"

"Yep, she was standing by the garden, like I said. Holding something."

"And it was…."

"A shovel."

Oh boy. That piqued my interest. "She was digging something up?"

He shrugged. "Or had buried something. Couldn't tell. There was a mound of dirt there. I guess she could have been planting some kind of vegetable, but it's not the right time of year, you know?"

No, definitely not vegetable season. I looked at Veronica, whose eyes were opened wide again. She gave me an elbow bump. Yep, way more interesting than a moldy cucumber.

Ricky tilted his head. "It's funny, though. Other people I told this to didn't seem all that interested. Not like you."

If the others had discovered a body there, they might have been more enthused about what he had to say.

The door opened, and in walked Agnes.

I smiled at Ricky. "Thanks so much for the information. It's interesting. And valuable."

He stood up straighter. "You are quite welcome. Glad to deliver some news you could use." After picking up his mailbag, he winked. "You ladies have a nice day now."

"You too, Ricky."

I so wanted to discuss the latest information with Veronica, but along with my client, came hers. It would have to wait. Our morning and early afternoon were packed. It was a flurry of meows, purrs, and fur. Every so often, I'd catch her eye from across the room. Her raised eyebrows indicated she wanted to discuss Ricky's revelation as much as I did.

I had a little free time afterward, but Veronica had rushed off to a dentist appointment. So much for comparing thoughts on Ricky's revelation. Heading outside for a bit, I took advantage of the bright sunshine to soak in some vitamin D. A voice carried from outside Carrie's Coffees right up the sidewalk. It was Wilma, talking on the phone.

She had her back to me, but her words were clear. "That's right. I'm not available this evening. Have a bridge date with the girls starting at five. What? No, not at my house. At the club." She turned toward me, and I peered across the street, acting like I hadn't been eavesdropping on her conversation.

She'd be gone this evening? I knew where I'd be—checking out her garden. Maybe she'd buried something to link her to her husband's murder.

Veronica had cleared some of her afternoon appointments, not knowing how long the dental appointment might take. I groomed two more cats, then closed up for the day. I stopped at home, hoping beyond hope the cats were snuggled up together in a chair, now friends forever. While I brought them into the salon now because of the threatening note about them, today wouldn't have worked well with Veronica gone part of the day. I needed her help to keep an eye on them.

Jasper met me at the door, meowing incessantly, as if telling me what terrible things he'd endured from Percival.

And Percival sat in the doorway to the living room, eyes wide and unblinking. The picture of innocence and sweetness. But I knew better. He'd most likely been harassing Jasper again. I'd given up trying to separate them since Percival kept escaping from whatever room I had him trapped in. Besides, the two had to start sharing breathing space sooner rather than later. I was determined they'd get along. I just didn't know how yet.

After feeding them, I left and headed to Durbin and Wilma's house. Although, it was only Wilma's now.

When I pulled up in front of the house, I groaned. Someone else was parked there too, and I had a good idea who. Had he also heard from Ricky that Wilma had been using a shovel in her garden? The whole town must have heard.

When I climbed the cement steps and headed around to the side of the house, my suspicions were confirmed. It was Buford. The other person with him was a surprise. It was Ken. Why would they both be here? Did it have something to do with them together in Evan's picture from the pastry sale?

They hadn't seen me yet, so I hugged the corner of the house, holding still, peeking around the side. They were both on their hands and knees, staring intently at the dirt. Either they were hunting for worms, which I highly doubted, or something was buried there they were keen on digging up.

Ken pointed toward the ground. "Well, it is there, or isn't it?"

Buford huffed out a breath. "It should be. I don't understand why it isn't."

"You promised me I could have it today."

"I know. I...I thought..."

"Listen, if you reneged on our deal—"

"No. I'm not reneging. Give me a little more time, okay?"

Ken shook his head. "I shouldn't. I've waited too long already."

"Please. It's not my fault it's not here," said Buford.

"You'd better get it for me. Quick. Or else..."

Buford leaned away. "No. You wouldn't."

"Don't tempt me. I mean it." Ken stood.

"I'll get it for you." Buford struggled to his feet. "I promise."

They'd both turned toward me. They were heading this way! It was too late to run. Besides, they'd see my van parked out front. Not too bright on my part. Although, I hadn't expected to find anyone else in the garden when I'd come over here.

I backed up a little, then came around the corner, forcing a smile. "Hey, there. What's up, guys?"

They both stopped in their tracks. Buford's eyes were wide. Ken wore a frown.

Buford's face darkened. "Why're you here?"

Good question. I couldn't tell them I'd hoped to discover a clue about the murderer since I still had no idea who it might be. "Um... Well after poor Durbin was... er, since he died, I've been caring for his cat. You know that, Buford, right? Since you saw him in my shop the other day?"

He shrugged. "Yeah, it's true."

Ken crossed his arms. "Then why are you here? Isn't the cat at your house?"

Why would he ask that? Was he the one who'd sent me the threatening note about my cat? "Well, Jasper's favorite collar is missing, and since he often played out here in the garden"—not true, since Durbin had been ultra-protective of his cat and never let him outside, but they might not know that— "I hoped maybe it was in the yard. Or maybe the garden."

Ken eyed the garden, then me. "Well, we didn't see anything like that, did we, Buford?"

"What?" He frowned. "Oh, right. Um, no. Nothing like that."

It was my turn to cross my arms. "Then what did you find?"

"Nothing. It's...." Buford blinked and glanced at Ken. "Just dirt. Nothing else."

"Yep. Dirt," said Ken.

I stepped closer. "Why are you guys here, anyway?"

Silence. The men looked at me, then each other for a few seconds. Finally, Ken elbowed Buford, raising his eyebrows. Did he hope Buford could get them out of this jam?

Buford's mouth opened, then closed. He took a deep breath, then let it out. Facing me, he frowned. "Why are you asking all these questions? I'm Durbin's nephew. He's my family. Don't I have a right to be at his house?"

If, according to Lottie and Florence, Buford hadn't liked his uncle, he wouldn't be here for sentimental reasons. There wasn't much I could say now, with Ken standing right beside him. It was obvious I wasn't going to get any information out of either one as to why they were skulking around the garden. I shrugged. "Sure. Of course, you've a right to be at a family member's house." Pointedly I eyed Buford, who quickly glanced away. "Never knew you and Ken were friends. You hang out together a lot?"

Ken flung his arm around Buford's shoulders, making the other man stiffen.

CHAPTER TWENTY-FIVE

"Oh. Sure. Best pals. Always have been."

Buford's face turned white, and his hands shook.

Right, pals. Shrugging, I knew when I'd been bested. I'd have to wait until they were gone, then come back and try to check the garden later. Though, finding another time when Wilma would definitely be away from home might be a challenge. Shaking my head, I turned and headed back to my van.

Chapter Twenty-Six

I had several morning appointments, but they were scattered on the schedule. Veronica was manning the store, so I decided to do some shopping while I had the chance. I'd been eyeing a few items in store windows down the street from my shop. Now seemed the perfect opportunity to do more than look. Besides, a small break doing something normal for a little bit might be just what I needed to recharge after the recent hours spent searching for something to help out Russ.

Upon entering Designs by Amelia, I was enveloped by the sweet scent of cherry blossom. Soft music caressed my ears, and I immediately relaxed. What a great way to put shoppers in the mood to buy something. My feet, as if having minds of their own, propelled me toward the corner where Amelia Lacey had placed the store's footwear on display. The cute ankle boots I'd been eyeing in the window looked even better up close. Plus, they had my size. As a large-footed girl, that in itself was a miracle.

Smiling as I exited with my purchase, I headed down the sidewalk toward Top of the Morning to check out some sweaters. Something gleamed in the window beside me. Stopping to look at the reflection, I frowned. Burford was across the street. Sunlight caught the metal on his—Durbin's—large fish tie tack. Why was Buford staring at me? I shook my head, hoping it might deter him from watching me. It worked. He startled, stumbled, then scurried toward a nearby shop door and hurried inside.

When I glanced at the name on the store window, I laughed. Did Buford realize he'd stepped into Lavender Lingerie? Poor guy would implode when he found out. I'd never known him to have a girlfriend. Nor had I seen him speaking to a member of the opposite sex in any way, which might have led me to believe he'd been interested in a romantic interlude.

Amused, I stood there and waited. Sure enough, he burst out of the doorway a few seconds later, tugging at his collar as if he couldn't breathe. Not wanting to waste any of my brief time off from work, I went another half block to the Lower Half Jeans store. The last time I'd bought any new jeans had been...oh, good grief. I couldn't remember. Well, I'd take care of that little problem right now.

A while later, I left the store, my wallet lighter, but my future closet space fuller after the purchase of three new pairs of jeans. Checking my watch, I sighed. It was close to time for my next grooming appointment. Maybe I had time for one more stop at—

Once again, Buford was directly across the street, but I'd moved on down the block. Was he following me? Why? Maybe I'd spooked him when I'd caught him in the garden with Ken. A chill ran across my shoulders. If he'd been doing something illegal, was it possible he'd been angry when I'd found him in his uncle's yard?

I'd never witnessed Buford act like anything fiercer than a timid mouse. Maybe it was all an act. Could the mild-mannered man have a mean side? Was he following me to catch me alone to hurt me or—

Get a hold of yourself. He's so skinny you could snap him like a twig. Straightening, I marched across the street. With every step I took, Buford retreated a few more inches. By the time I reached him, his back was scrunched against the shop window, the fabric of his suit squeaking against the sparkling clean window.

"Buford, why are you following me?"

His face reddened. "I'm not."

Pointing up the street, I said, "Do you frequent Lavender Lingerie on a regular basis?"

Now his skin was beet purple. "No."

"Then why did you go in there?"

He rubbed his chin. "I thought it was...the men's shop."

"It's on the other side of town, and you know it. Fess up. Why do you seem to be stalking me every time I go into a store?"

He shrugged.

"That's not an answer. You're up to something. I just can't figure out what."

He turned halfway to the side, took a step away, then full-on ran back up the sidewalk, his dress shoes scuffling against the cement.

What an odd duck. I repositioned my shopping bags in my arms and headed back to Fabulous Felines. So much for checking out another shop on my break.

When I reached the grooming shop, Veronica met me at the door. "I'm glad you're here."

"What's up?"

"James Larabee thought Minnie's appointment was now instead of this afternoon. Do you have time to see them?"

I peered around her to spot James standing at the counter. "Sure. No problem." I waved to my pet parent, then edged behind the counter and stashed my purchases.

James ran his hand along his cat's fur. "I know I normally stay and hold Minnie's paw when she's groomed, but I need to run to the pharmacy across town." He ran his finger down the cat's spine. "Do you think you'll be okay while I'm gone?"

I waved my hand. "Sure. I'll be fine." Things progressed better when pet parents weren't hovering. Hovering. That made me think of Durbin, who'd always been right at my elbow, except the last time when he'd gotten an urgent text.

"I was talking to Minnie."

Startled from my thoughts, I focused on James. "Oh. Sorry."

After giving Minnie three kisses on top of her head, James hurried across the shop floor and outside.

Veronica stepped closer. "I would have gladly taken Minnie since you were out but, James insists it has to be you."

"It's okay. I know you would have." I smiled. Glancing out the door where James had just left, I shook my head. "Must be my day to encounter strange ducks."

"Ducks? Are we going to start grooming things with feathers now?" She smirked.

"Not exactly. James has always been eccentric."

"That's the truth. But was there someone else too?"

"Yeah. Buford," I said.

"What now?"

"He was following me. Every time I came out of a store, he was across the street, watching me."

"Creepy little dude."

"Agreed."

"Why do you think he was doing that?"

I shrugged. "The one thing I can come up with is he's getting back at me from finding him and Ken at Durbin's garden."

She grabbed my hand. "Should we be worried? Could he possibly be the killer?"

I gave her hand a squeeze. "That's what I'd like to know too. Hey, are you free tonight?"

The shop door opened and closed behind me. Was it time for my next appointment already?

Veronica looked over my shoulder, then back to me. "Why do you ask?"

"I'm thinking of doing a stakeout. Could you go with me?"

Again, she glanced toward the door. What was going on? I pivoted around. Hank stood there, arms crossed. Great. Had he heard us talking about a stakeout?

Veronica yanked my hand, so I gave her my attention. "I can't tonight. But…." She angled her head toward Hank.

What? No. I shook my head. Wouldn't work. Me, alone in a vehicle for who knew how long with the gorgeous veterinarian?

Steps came up from behind me. "Hey, Molly. Stakeout huh? Well, I'm free tonight."

Veronica snorted, then after wiggling her eyebrows up and down, darted off to the back room. The traitor.

I faced Hank. "I'm sure it's something I can handle all by myself. Thanks, anyway."

"Do you really want to sit in a car and watch someone at night all by yourself?"

All right, he had me there. I'd never been a fan of being out alone at night. Why couldn't Veronica just go with me? "Well..."

"Great. I'll be going too. By the way, who are we watching?"

I sighed. "Buford."

"I assume you think he's the killer?"

"Don't know. That's the purpose of a stakeout, to see what he's up to."

"Will you be bringing snacks?" he asked.

"What?" I frowned.

"On the stakeout."

"You want me to bring food?"

"Well, yeah. Or I can if you'd rather. Sometimes stakeouts can last hours. We might get hungry," said Hank.

"How would you know? Have you ever been on one?"

"No. Have you?" Hank crossed his arms.

"Well, no."

"Better safe than sorry. Tell you what, I'll bring food if you bring drinks. Sound good?"

Good grief. How had me having an idea for a stakeout and talking to Veronica morphed into Hank and I sitting close together, alone in a vehicle at night? My face grew hot.

"Hey, are you okay? You look—"

"Fine." I rubbed my cheek. "It's stuffy in here."

"Not so much. I was going to say it was chilly."

"So anyway, uh, tonight around seven?"

"Sounds good. I'll pick you up."

I placed my hands on my hips. "No, I'll pick you up."

Veronica stuck her head out of the doorway. "Will someone decide who is picking who up, already?"

She'd been listening again. I waved my hand to her in surrender and eyed Hank. "Fine. You pick me up. Bring food. Don't forget chocolate. I'll bring drinks."

He wrapped his knuckles on the counter. "All right, see you then." He gave a big cheesy grin. He was enjoying this. Must I be the object of ridicule for everyone?

Glancing to my left, where Veronica had sidled up beside me, I took in her big smile and exaggerated eye winks. Apparently, yes, everyone was taking great delight in my discomfort.

Chapter Twenty-Seven

When a vehicle pulled up in my driveway, I frowned. It wasn't Hank's huge pickup truck. It was a tiny blue compact car, which looked familiar. Sure enough, Hank was sitting in the front seat, waving at me. I opened the screen door, then turned to Percival. "Okay, I'm going out for a while." I pointed right at his innocent expression, which I knew to be false. "And you, be nice to your new brother."

Percival blinked, then flipped his tail. Great. What would I find when I got home later? I glanced up to see Jasper sitting at the top of the stairs. His tail was lashing too. They were going to have a long night. I just hoped they'd be safe here alone. But my only recourse would have been to take them with us on the stakeout. Probably not a great plan.

Hank honked his horn. I turned and glanced out the doorway again. He pointed at his watch. Looked like I might have a long night too. Dragging my small cooler filled with drinks, I closed the door and headed down my driveway.

When I reached the car, Hank jumped out, ran around the front, and opened my car door. He was acting like this was a date. Did he think it was? Did I?

Stop. This is no date.

I lifted the cooler. "Brought drinks, as promised."

Hank took it from me and placed it in the backseat next to a large grocery sack. "Hi. What were you doing up there in the doorway?"

I got into the car and waited while he shut the door behind me. He jogged around to his door and got in. I fastened my seat belt. "Do you always shut

194

a door and leave right after asking someone a question?"

His eyebrows lowered, but he must have noticed my smirk because he grinned. "Nope, want to get this show on the road. What were you doing up there?"

"Giving the boys instructions for when I'm gone tonight."

"Instructions?"

"Basically, not to harm, maim or maul each other."

"I won't ask how they're doing, then."

"Yep, no point in that."

He backed the car out of the drive and headed down the street. "I haven't given up getting those two to get along. Just haven't figured it out yet."

I shrugged. "I hope you figure it out soon, Doc. Because I've tried everything I can think of. I don't want to come home to two piles of angry fur."

"I'll get those guys to be friends. Don't worry." He pointed his thumb over his shoulder. "What kinds of drinks did you bring?"

"Grape and orange sodas. That work?"

"Yep."

"I assume you brought chocolate. Mass quantities?"

"How much is mass?"

Glancing to the back seat, I eyed the bag. "If the whole sack is filled with the heavenly goodness and sugary delight, then we're okay."

He rolled his eyes. "We may have to make a store run partway through the evening."

I smiled. "I knew I liked you."

His face turned pink. "Uh, thanks. I like you too."

Why did he look embarrassed? I'd been kidding around. Did he think I…. Turning, I made a show of being interested in Mrs. Jackson's azaleas as we passed her yard. I did like him. A lot. But I didn't want him to know it. At least until he felt the same. He'd said he liked me, but was that simply him being polite?

When I turned back, his eyes were trained on the road ahead, but his face had faded from red to a faint pinkish hue. Time to talk about something

195

else. "Say," I patted the edge of my seat. "I was expecting you to pick me up in your truck."

His shoulders relaxed. Was he glad I'd changed the subject? "Andrea said it was okay for me to borrow her neighbor's car. Andrea is watering their plants while they're gone, and they left their car keys in case she needs it."

"Is something wrong with your truck?"

"No, it's fine. Thought this might be less conspicuous than my huge truck." He glanced at me, with one eyebrow raised. "And much less conspicuous than your mobile cat van."

He had a point there. I was so used to driving my van everywhere, I hadn't considered sitting in front of Buford's house in it would be so obvious. "That was nice of Andrea."

"She's a good egg." He glanced out the window and back. "You know, even though we're watching Buford tonight, all the things he's been doing might be circumstantial. It might have been someone else who did that to Durbin."

"Circumstantial. Listen to you. Talking all law enforcement-like."

He smiled. "It's what tonight it all about, right? The business of catching the person who killed Durbin."

"Yep." I crossed my arms. Part of me wished we were on a date instead of a stakeout. Why did I now view Hank as more than a friend? I'd given it some thought over the years, but after so many bad dates with others, hadn't been inclined to take it further. Maybe when—

".... house?"

I jerked. "What?"

"I said, did you want across the street from Buford's or a little down the side street from his house?"

How had we gotten to Buford's house already, and I hadn't even noticed? I sunk down a little in my seat. I needed to keep focused on tonight's mission, not the fact that a hunky guy sat extremely close to me in the confined space of a teeny tiny car. "How about on the side street? We could watch him from a short distance away if we park under one of those trees."

Park? Oh, the visions I got from the image made my temperature rise. I lowered my window, hoping to cool things down.

"Okay, sounds good." Hank went left down the side street, did a U-turn, and edged the car next to the curb beneath a maple tree. It was still light out enough to see, but with the lengthening shadows, soon the streetlights would come on. We'd still be hidden where we were stationed.

Buford's house was small, nestled close together with his neighbors on each side. The little house needed some work—paint, bushes trimmed, lawn mowed. It was hard to imagine Buford, in his spiffy clothes and dress shoes, pushing a lawn mower around his yard. Maybe he didn't like to get dirty and didn't bother doing the work. He could hire someone else to do it, but maybe he didn't have the funds. Then I remembered him in Durbin's garden with Ken. There must have been something super interesting to get him that close to dirt.

Hank and I sat for a few minutes, staring at the house. He gave my elbow a nudge. "Should we be doing something else instead of just sitting?"

I could think of a few things. "Like what?"

He shrugged. "Don't know."

I mirrored his shrug. I couldn't very well voice my opinion of what might be fun. "I've never done a stakeout either. I should have gotten the book, Stakeout for Dummies, I guess."

Hank grinned. "Why didn't I think of that? Well, until he decides to come out of his house, I guess we could talk."

"Uh, sure." I'd planned to do this with Veronica. Finding something to talk about with her was never a chore. She talked so much, she could have a conversation all by herself. I had a sneaking suspicion she'd actually been free tonight and had maneuvered me and Hank together when he'd walked into Fabulous Felines at the right moment.

Now, I'd have to try to find things to discuss with Hank that wouldn't make me conjure up images of him and me alone in this car, which would get me into trouble. There was at least one safe subject we had in common. I turned a little in my seat. "Hey, how is Beatrice doing?"

His face lit up. "My little cat is amazing."

"How so?" After all my work with cats and their pet parents, I knew getting people to tell me their cat was the most wonderful feline in the world wasn't

197

a problem.

"She's the smartest, cutest…." His gaze met mine, and glanced down. "That sounded lame, huh?"

I touched his hand. "No, it didn't. You obviously love her."

"I do. It's crazy how much. I mean, I adore all of my patients, of course, but having her live with me is way different."

"I know. It's the same way with Percival. He's my family. Now so is Jasper. Wish they'd stop fighting."

He smiled. "We'll get them there. I'm not giving up. There has to be a reasonable explanation considering all the time Percival spends with other cats and never has an issue with them. Jasper is a friendly cat too. Don't worry, we'll figure it out." He reached into the sack in the back seat and grabbed a chocolate bar the size of my hand. "Here. This will help."

I eyed the goodness in its brown wrapper. "You think a candy bar will make everything better?"

"Doesn't it?"

I removed the wrapper and got a whiff of the chocolate. My darned saliva glands went into overdrive. "Well, yeah. It does."

Hank chuckled. "Good."

"Hey, is the bag full of only chocolate?"

"Well, there are a few other things. Chips. Peanuts. Jerky."

"Jerky?" I made a face like he'd offered me raw turnips.

"You don't like it?"

"Blech. Keep the chocolate coming, and no one gets hurt."

"Good to know. I'll save it for when I get home."

A door slammed from the direction of the row of houses. I turned, mouth full of chocolate, to see Buford trotting down his front steps. I couldn't form words. Why did I have to pick now to take the single largest bite of chocolate known to man? I smacked Hank on the arm to get his attention.

He frowned. "What? Are you okay?"

Waving my arm, I pointed to Buford, who was heading right down the street toward us.

Hank's eyes widened. "Should we leave? He wouldn't know this car. We could just—"

Buford, walking at a fast clip, was getting closer. If we left now, he'd notice. I swallowed the baseball size piece of chocolate and gasped. "No...stay... here." My voice was a wheeze, like a clogged vacuum cleaner that had picked up too many hairballs.

"We could—"

"Stay. Here." I slid down in my seat as far as I could. My lower body was crumpled onto the floor, and from the shoulders up, I was in an uncomfortable pretzel shape on the seat, trying to keep below the window. I tugged at Hank's sleeve, then pointed toward the floor.

"You've got to be kidding. I can't fit down there."

I narrowed my eyes.

"Fine." With a lot of effort and I was fairly sure some muttered curses, Hank got most of his body on the floor, squeezing past the steering wheel. He gave a yelp when his chin connected with it.

We sat there, unmoving, the only sound our rapid breathing and Buford's footsteps as he got ever closer. If we could just stay down, maybe he wouldn't notice us. He'd appeared to be in a hurry to get somewhere, so he might be too preoccupied to care about a parked car. Also, it was getting darker. He might pass on by. If we could hold out a little bit longer, we could escape our burrows and climb back up to the seats. My muscles would regret this awkward position later tonight.

Something tickled my nose. I had to sneeze. No, not now! I pressed my hand over my face, needing to keep from sneezing for another minute until he had passed us.

Hang on, whatever you do, please do not sn—

I had to admit, as far as sneezes went, it rivaled my grandmother's. She was a little woman, but when she let one loose, neighbors two blocks away in any direction knew her hay fever was acting up. Was there a chance Buford hadn't heard me?

I glanced up. The window! Like a dunce, I'd left it open after I'd cooled off from those warm thoughts of Hank and me alone in the car. There was still a chance Buford hadn't—

Rapid steps came from the sidewalk, growing softer as Buford crossed through the small strip of grass before reaching the car. He leaned down. "Uh, Molly? What are you doing?"

I flapped my hand in his direction. "Well, see...."

Buford took a step closer to the window. "And who are you with? Hank Chenoweth? What are you two up to?"

With much effort and not a little groaning, I scooted back up on the seat until I was somewhat upright. It took Hank a little longer, as he had the steering column and longer legs to contend with.

I eyed Hank. He shrugged and angled his head closer to me. "Jig is up. Might as well get out of the car while we can still have use of our extremities."

He was right. What good would it do now to stay in the car? I waved Buford back as I climbed out, then flexed my toes, fingers, arms, legs, and neck for several seconds. Hank, on the other side of the car, did the same, then joined us.

Bufford's bag rattled as he changed it from the crook of one arm to the other. He frowned as he took in my appearance. What was the matter with it? Glancing down, I saw it too. My shirt was askew, my jeans were wrinkled and...I glanced into the car's side mirror, my hair looked like Pericaval had used it for biscuit-making practice.

Hank's wasn't much better. The fact he was now re-tucking his shirt was even more noticeable. Did Buford think we were...as if we'd been...

My whole body sweated. I was glad the sun was partway down. Maybe Buford wouldn't notice if my face was red. Sure, I'd pictured all of those scenarios myself while sitting so close to Hank just now. But to have someone else think that?

Buford shuffled his shoe in the grass. "So? What were you two up to out here?"

Instead of coming up with some lame excuse, I turned the tables on him. "Now, hold on. I have some questions of my own for you."

"What?"

I placed my hand on my hip, hoping to look somewhat intimidating. "Though you denied it, it was obvious you'd stolen the tie tack from your uncle at his funeral."

He frowned. "All right. I guess since you practically saw me…." He eyed me. Was he hoping I'd let him off the hook? No way. "Since my uncle reneged on giving me a job he'd promised, I wanted to get back at him. Taking his favorite tie tack gave me a smidgeon of satisfaction, like maybe I'd gotten something from him after all."

That was it? If he was telling the truth, I was somewhat deflated, with all of my conspiracy theories about Buford doing his uncle in. "Well, what about you and Ken at the garden? What were you two doing there?"

He sighed, like he knew there was no way he'd get out of telling me. Maybe my expression was as intimidating as I'd hoped. "See, we'd heard there might be jewels or something buried in the garden. Had overheard my aunt talking about it one day in the coffee shop. She didn't know I was there with Ken, sitting in a back booth."

"And about that. You hanging out with Ken. I never knew you guys were friends."

"We're not. Not really. See, Ken is a collector."

I narrowed my eyes. "Of what?"

"Anything he thinks he can sell."

Now it was making some sense. Why else would Ken and Buford, who'd never been around each other before and who were such different personalities, spend so much time together? "And you thought you'd dig up the jewels and sell them?"

"That was our plan. We never found anything, though. Wilma must have buried them someplace else, or deeper in the garden than we'd dug. You did interrupt us, after all."

I thought about Evan's photos. "Okay, but what about you two arguing at the pastry sale? And it looked like one of you was giving the other a package."

His mouth gaped open. Didn't he think in a large crowd of people at the sale, someone might have seen what they were doing? Buford avoided looking directly at me, instead stared at his shoes.

"Well? Out with it," I said.

"See, the tie tack I took from my uncle wasn't the only thing I, uh, helped myself to."

I gasped. "You've been stealing from your Durbin all along?"

"Not until after he died." He slapped his hand over his mouth, like he hadn't meant to say those words. "It irked me so bad when he'd gone back on his word for the job. I started, um, acquiring some of his things and selling them. It's not like he was going to use them anymore."

"Is that why you and Ken were together? Were you selling him something of your uncle's?"

He nodded, but still wouldn't meet my eye. "You won't tell the sheriff what I've been up to, will you? It's not like I killed him or anything. Honest, it was after he was gone that I took those things."

I glanced at Hank, who shrugged. "Okay, Buford, here's the deal. You stop stealing stuff, and I won't tell him. But you have to stop. Understand?"

Buford nodded. I half expected him to utter 'Yes, ma'am,' but he said nothing.

All of it explained a whole lot. Yet, there was still one more thing. "Why were you following me the other day?"

"What do you mean?"

"When I was shopping on Main Street. Every time I came out of a store, there you were."

"How do you know I wasn't shopping too?"

I narrowed my eyes. "Come on. In a lingerie shop?"

Hank snickered.

Buford glared at Hank, then at me. "I…I entered the wrong door. I'd meant to go into another shop."

"Which one? The jewelry store? The clothing boutique with the cute boots?"—I turned to Hank— "which I bought, by the way." I pointed at my feet to the brown leather of the boots.

Hank winked. "Good choice."

"Thank you, I—"

Buford lightly smacked my shoulder. "Hello? Stop talking about your boots."

"Don't change the subject. Why were you out there on the sidewalk watching me every time I came out of a store?" I pointed at him, my finger an inch from his face. "You were up to something, and I want to know what."

Buford's sigh seemed to deflate his entire body. "Fine. If you must know, I was following you."

"I knew it. Why?"

"Because...I..." His shoes must have been remarkably interesting, as he stared at them and not me.

"Well, why? Just say it."

Buford shrugged. "I like you."

I blinked. "Um, what?"

"You're pretty and smart and...."

Oh boy. Had not seen that coming. Was it the reason he came into Fabulous Felines all the time, even though he didn't like cats? He had a crush on me?

From beside me, Hank cleared his throat. His muscular arms crossed over his chest.

Buford thrust out the sack he'd been holding, placing it awkwardly in my arms.

I almost dropped it, then fumbled and caught it before it could hit the ground. "What's this?"

"Look inside. It's for you. I was heading out just now to see you. At your house."

I peered inside the bag and held in a groan. A beautiful bouquet of yellow daisies sat inside the paper sack, its color so cheery I half expected it to wave. "Oh, Buford."

He edged a little closer. Was he going to try to kiss me?

Panic swept over me. What should I do? Step away? Smack his arm? Accept a kiss? Definitely no to choice number three.

Hank moved closer to me too. What was going on? Why were all the males in the conversation pressing in on me from every side?

Buford ducked his head, his words coming out in a mumble. "Molly Stewart, would you go out with—"

Hank's arm landed around my shoulders. "No. She will not."

Huh? I blinked at Hank. What was he doing? Even though I was grateful for his help, I still couldn't imagine what he had in mind.

Tugging me against his chest, Hank glowered at Buford. "She won't go out with you. Because… she's dating me."

Thank goodness Hank was holding on to me, or I would have ended up in a pile of wrinkled clothes, daisy pedals, and new boots.

Chapter Twenty-Eight

While chatting with Paula in her shop, I'd also been talking to Hank. It came as no great surprise he'd been playing a part when he said we were dating. A part of me wished it was true, but deep down, I knew it was for my benefit to get rid of Buford.

After Hank left, I stepped out onto the sidewalk and nearly smacked right into the sheriff. Great. I'd tried to stay out of his path since he'd scolded me before, but in a small town, avoiding someone for long didn't always work.

He glanced down at me with a frown. "And what might you be up to today?"

"Me? Nothing. I was just...." I pointed to Paula's Pastries.

"Don't see any crumbs or powdered sugar on your face or any other evidence of you being in there."

I reached up and touched my lips. Darn. On a normal day, I had it all over the place, and Veronica would get a chuckle out of my appearance. "Maybe I'm extra neat. I do like to use copious amounts of napkins. Ask anyone." No, maybe that wasn't a good idea. Anyone who'd ever shared a meal with me knew I covered myself in napkins from my chin to my lap, but only because I tended to be sort of careless and ended up wearing small dabs of whatever I'd had.

His eyebrows lowered. "You need to be careful. Been hearing talk of you wandering around town, going in and out of shops."

"It's called shopping. Need to see my receipts?" Thankfully, it was a challenge I could uphold. Good thing I'd made some purchases.

He scowled. "No need to get huffy."

He thought my behavior was huffy? This was nothing. I'd spent my whole life around cats and, if need be, could do a great imitation of hissing, growling, and flexing of claws all rolled into one.

The sheriff crossed his arms. "I thought we'd agreed that Russ Stewart was the one most likely to have killed Durbin."

Although I hadn't wanted to have this conversation with the man, it seemed he wouldn't let it go. "You're the one who thinks, wrongly, I might add, that my uncle killed someone. There's no way he'd ever do that. If you did your job properly, you'd be out hunting down whoever really committed the crime."

He held up his hand. "You're embarrassing yourself with all this nonsense. You don't want people to think you've gone 'round the bend, do you? Wouldn't do much for your reputation with all those cat people who pay you good money to fluff up their cats' fur."

Fluff up? I narrowed my eyes. The man was so rude. How dare he say—

Footsteps pounded against the sidewalk from behind me. I turned right in time for Candi to fling herself into my arms. What in the world?

Sheriff King took a step back. "Say, what's all this?"

I awkwardly patted Candi's back until she pulled away.

Studying her face, I gasped. She had angry red scratches running down both cheeks. "What happened?"

Candi pressed her hands to her face. "I was a-attacked!"

Sheriff King stiffened. "What?"

Candi blinked at him a few times, as if just noticing he was there. "That's right." She sniffled. When she faced me again, her eyes watered, then sudden streams of tears traveled down her face, plopping on her pink blouse.

The sheriff lowered his eyebrows. "Who did this to you? Can you identify them?" He mumbled aside to me, "Sure hope there's not some crazy stranger running around town accosting folks."

Candi wiped the tears from her face, then ran her palms over her pant legs to dry them off. "Oh, I knew who it was, all right."

He pulled out his notepad and pen, then eyed her. "Well?"

A few people had gathered on the sidewalk, obviously wanting to know the latest scuttlebutt happening in town. I leaned closer to Candi and waited. She looked behind me, and her eyes grew wide. Had she also noticed others staring at her? When her face paled, I turned to see what had her so upset.

It was Wilma.

Candi gasped again, pulling my attention back to her. Her hand shook as she pointed at the other woman.

I touched her arm. "Are you saying Wilma—"

"Yes. She's the one who scratched me with her pointy fingernails. Did more damage than an angry cat with claws could ever do."

I didn't have to check out Wilma's nails to know what Candi said about them was true. For some reason, Wilma liked her fingernails to be pointy. Even if I wanted to, I could never do that. Never mind my kitty clients wouldn't appreciate being poked when I groomed them, I'd be lucky not to stab myself in the eye while putting in my contact lenses. I'd always assumed Wilma had them that way because she liked them in a particular shape.

Maybe, it was more. Seeing the red slashed down Candi's face convinced me those nails also came in handy as lethal weapons.

Wilma, staring at us, wore an expression of shock. Sheriff King motioned her over. Did he not want to have to go through the growing, nosy crowd?

At first, Wilma shook her head. But when a few from the throng began whispering and pointing at her, she trudged toward us. Maybe she decided getting Candi's accusation over with might be easier than hearing everything the townspeople said, and what they would continue to say if they got wind of a conversation between her and the law.

She got closer, feet plodding along the sidewalk, head down, until she reached our group. Candi gave a sound like a hiss and hid behind me, grabbing onto my upper arms from behind. Did she think I'd protect her if Wilma lunged at her? I didn't want to be in the line of fire if it happened. However, Candi's grip on me was tight.

I tried to relax. But I'd sure keep a close eye on Wilma's movements. I'd seen firsthand how angry she could get when I'd spoken to her on her porch. Not that she didn't have reason to the day after hearing Durbin had cut her out of his will.

The sheriff held his pen poised over his notebook. "All right, Wilma. We've had a complaint."

Candi moaned.

"Uh, we've had an accusation."

Wilma clutched her hands together in front of her waist. Her face looked hard, like the cement we stood on, but her hands twitched. Was she trembling? Scared? I hadn't had much time to process what Candi had told me about Wilma, but it did sound plausible, given the relationship between her, Candi, and Durbin.

Looking behind her, then back at us, Wilma let out a long breath. "And what might this supposed accusation be?"

"It's not supposed. I heard it for myself. So did Molly, here."

Oh great. Drag me into it. Yet, when the sheriff watched me with raised eyebrows, I gave a single nod. I was already on his bad list. No need to make things worse.

Candi squeezed my arms harder—would I lose circulation?—and pressed her head between my shoulder blades. She must have had a lot of confidence in me coming to her rescue with Wilma. Truth be told, the older woman kind of scared me too.

The sheriff and Wilma glared at each other. Were they hoping the other would crack first? Hot breath seeped through the back of my shirt. What was Candi doing now? I tried to see her over my shoulder, but she was crouched down just enough and had a stranglehold on my arms, I couldn't even see the top of her head.

"…. kill me." Candi's voice, muffled by the back of my shirt, barely reached my ears. Had she said the word kill?

I leaned forward with force, then pivoted in a rush until Candi's fingers released their grip. I faced her. "What did you say?"

"I…." Her face reddened, the color of her skin now matching her tear-filled eyes.

Someone cleared their throat. I turned to see both the sheriff and Wilma staring at us. Sheriff King narrowed his eyes. "Yes, I'd like to know that too. What did you tell Molly?"

Wilma crossed her arms, her pointy nails biting into the skin of her lower arms. Had the attack on Candi just now happened? I craned my neck to see if there was any blood or bits of Candi's skin on them, but when she saw me looking, she jammed her hands in her pants pockets.

Darn. Was hoping I could help move things along with evidence of what she'd done to Candi. Then, maybe we could move on to the bigger subject of Durbin's murder. Wilma, now glaring at me, shot daggers so sharp, I could nearly feel them.

The sheriff stepped closer to Candi. I moved aside so I wasn't standing in between them. Candi gave me a withering glare, like I'd somehow betrayed her. Tapping his pen on the pad, the sheriff watched Candi. "All right, I'll ask again. What did you say to Molly just now?"

I bit my lip, silently pleading with Candi to say it so I wouldn't have to, because that would be the sheriff's next move if she stayed quiet.

Candi sighed and wrapped her arms around her middle. Her gaze landed on the sheriff but seemed to be more on his shoulder than his face. "I said she tried to kill me."

"Now, wait a second." Wilma stood up as tall as possible, which was already several inches taller than me. She scuffed her shoe against the concrete. "No one gets to say things like that about me. Tell lies. Especially her." She pointed at Candi, saw me looking again at her nails, then stuck her hands once more in her pockets.

The sheriff turned to Candi, whose tears were now dry, but still had blotched, red skin. "Candi, why would you say Wilma tried to kill you?"

Her eyes widened, and she pointed her index finger to one of her scratched cheeks. Her fingernails were rounded off like most women's. How odd for Wilma's to resemble tiny knives. Candi pressed one finger against her skin. "This is why I said it. Because it's true. The demented woman raked those sharp pointy fingernails down my face. I think she was trying to poke my eyes out. Or worse yet, maybe try to put her hands around my neck to choke me!"

Wilma huffed out a breath. "Pure fiction. So ridiculous. Why would I do that to you?"

Candi frowned. "Well, duh, because I had an affair with Durbin."

The crowd on the sidewalk had edged closer without me noticing. Now they stood quite close, near enough to have heard Candi's announcement. A general gasp floated over from the group. Now everyone would know. While Candi had told me after Durbin died that she supposed it didn't matter if the secret got out now, perhaps Wilma hadn't felt the same way. Had she wanted to keep it quiet? Is it why she'd attacked Candi?

The sheriff's eyebrows went halfway to his hairline. "Is that so?" He turned to Wilma. "Is what she says true?"

"Partly."

"Which part?"

"The last one. The part about...." She eyed the onlookers as her face reddened. "The hussy"—another gasp from the group— "had her way with my Durbin!"

The sheriff rubbed his hand along his jaw. "Seems to me it would be a good motive—"

My head jerked up. Motive? Did he finally believe me about Russ being innocent?

"—for you scratching Candi."

"No!" yelled Candi. "She tried to kill me. It's true."

Wilma's hands landed on her hips. "Not true."

"True."

I rolled my eyes. Somehow, in trying to discover who killed Durbin, I'd gotten dragged into a good old-fashioned catfight.

Sheriff King shook his head. "Listen. I think we should take this to the station. We're getting too much attention out here."

The sidewalk group groaned. If the conversation moved to a more private venue, they wouldn't be able to get all the facts.

Candi sighed. "Well, instead of doing anything formal, I guess I could let it drop."

I jerked. "You will? After all she did?"

She shrugged. "Life goes on. None of this will bring Durbin back."

The sheriff nodded. "If that's the way you want it. Here, give me your phone number in case I have more questions later."

She took the pen and pad he offered and wrote her number—with her right hand. Not that I thought she'd had anything to do with killing Durbin, but it did reassure me she wasn't left-handed.

Sheriff King asked for Wilma's number, which she gave verbally. Did she not want to touch the same pen Candi had used? He stuck his pen and pad in his pocket.

Candi wiped her cheeks. "I do have one condition, though."

Wilma, the sheriff, the group of busybodies, and I waited for her to continue.

Seeming pleased to be the center of attention, she gave a small smile. "The condition is Wilma would have to apologize for messing up my face."

Wilma stomped the sidewalk. "I will not! Why should I apologize for something I didn't do?"

Sheriff King sighed. "This is getting us nowhere. Come on, you two. We'll finish this conversation at the station. Looks like it might take a while."

When the three walked off, I hurried in the opposite direction. Better than being hounded by anyone else still standing there. Wait until I told Veronica about this.

Chapter Twenty-Nine

I'd just finished a grooming for Mrs. Kelper's cat, Cleo, and was tidying things up in the back of the van. She had taken the cat and had gone back into their house. Cleo, who spent much of her time in the Kelper's maple tree, had eventually come down on her own for her appointment when I'd shaken a plastic container of kitty treats near the base of the tree.

I stepped farther into the van and crouched down to pick up a stray tuft of Cleo's cream-colored fur from her brushing. As I turned, a long black tail disappeared from the back of the van.

"Percival!"

I made my way to the open doorway and hopped down. The crazy cat had crossed the street and was already halfway through the neighbor's yard.

I took off, legs pumping, wishing I could run as fast as my short-legged furry child. "Percival, come back here!"

He reached a small woods behind the house and stopped. Thank goodness. Maybe he wanted to play *chase me* for a bit. But the closer I got, he turned and stared at me. When I was a few feet away, he took off running again.

What was he doing? He'd never run from me before.

"Percival, get back here."

He edged around tree trunks and over fallen branches. I did the same but got smacked in the face more than once by branches that he'd been short enough to duck under. At this rate, my face would be scratched up like Candi's.

As I kept going, more light entered through the trees. Was I near the end of the forest? A few more yards and I came out in someone else's backyard. If I didn't catch my cat soon and had to keep trespassing on people's properties, Sheriff King would have something else to scold me about.

I stopped to catch my breath. Where had my spastic cat gone? As I checked around the yard for him, I heard voices from around the side of the house. Wait, I knew those voices. The more I studied the area, I realized where I was. Though I'd never entered from this direction before, I was standing in the Haines' back yard. One of the voices was Wilma. As I held still, the other became clear. Wilma was arguing with Candi.

Time to get my cat and get a move on. We'd have to retreat back the way we'd come, but no way I wanted to parade out in front of the two women and have to explain what the heck I was doing prowling around.

Prowling? By the way, where had Percival gone?

As I made my way across the yard, a tell-tale wagging tail stuck out from beneath a bush. Was he trying to spy on the women? Too bad he couldn't speak anything other than the language of meow to relay what they'd said. Might be something useful in discovering the identity of Durbin's killer, because Wilma was still on my list.

I crept up behind him, hoping to grab him before he took off again. As I leaned down and wrapped my hands around his middle, he let out a hiss, but when I pressed him to my chest, he calmed down, then reached up, pressing his paw to my chin.

I snuggled him for a few seconds and kept my voice to a whisper. "You scared Mama running away like that. Don't ever do it again. We need to get out of here before they know we're here and—"

The voices grew louder. Those two must really be having it out. I glanced down at my cat, who was squirming as if he wanted to get closer to the women. What was Percival up to? It was like he wanted me to be here. Had he led me here on purpose? Maybe his kitty-sense was in high gear, and he knew something I didn't. Most people would call the possibility absurd, but I knew cats. They were cleverer than people often gave them credit for.

As I petted him, he didn't thrash about anymore, but his muscles were bunched, ready to pounce on any unsuspecting person we happened upon. Glad he was on my side.

Wilma's voice sounded like a screech when she yelled, "How dare you show your face on my property?"

Wow. I bet at least one of the neighbors was already calling the sheriff to complain about the noise. This was much worse than when Wilma had spouted off to me on her front porch the day Durbin died, and the sheriff had heard about it later. Glad I wouldn't be on the bad end of his temper this time.

Candi's voice was equally as loud, but more petulant. "It wouldn't be your property if Durbin was still alive. It would be his."

"You have the nerve to mention his name? After what you did?"

"All I did was fall in love." Candi's words ended with a sniffle.

"Love? There's only one reason a man would want you, and it's nothing to do with love."

"You're no saint. Sleeping with the lawyer."

Wilma shouted, "That's none of your affair!"

"But it's obviously yours."

I tiptoed forward, staying close to the row of bushes, but wanting to make sure I didn't miss a word of what they said.

Someone made a sound like Percival's hiss. My cat's ears flattened, and he stiffened in my arms. I leaned down and whispered, "That wasn't meant for you."

Wilma shouted, "How dare you accuse me of scratching your face? And right in front of the sheriff. Do you know how embarrassing it was for me? How people now avoid me when they see me on the street. I can't believe I even had to apologize to you for it."

"It's the least you should have done."

"Why? I was innocent."

"You can keep saying those words to the sheriff. The proof is right here."

I imagined Candi pointing to her own face. This would be so much easier if I could see them. I'd have to be careful to keep quiet and make sure Percival did the same.

Candi gave a loud sob. "You're a horrible person. Treating your husband like a piece of garbage."

"I don't know what you're talking about."

"Messing up his cat's fur? So it would upset Durbin?"

Wilma laughed. "Oh, yes, it was classic. You should have seen his expression. Priceless."

"Believe me, I saw his expression quite often. He wasn't upset when he was with me. Not at all."

"Why, you little hussy. I ought to do you in, right here and now."

"You wouldn't dare."

"Wouldn't I? You have no idea what I'm capable of," yelled Wilma."

Silence. What were they doing now? I petted Percival again to calm him, then tucked him beneath my arm. With the other hand, I balanced as best I could and did a modified crabwalk to the corner of the house. Once there, I slid the cat to my lap but kept my hand firmly around his middle. I had no desire to chase him again today if he got another notion to run off.

Slowly, I checked around the edge of the brick. The two women were in profile, neither one facing me. Good. Maybe I'd be safe here until they were done talking. Or yelling, or whatever else was going to happen.

Wilma seemed pretty intent on doing some damage to Candi. Would it be worse than scratching up her face? I shivered, thinking about Wilma's pointy nails. Focusing on her hands, I noticed her nail color for today.

It was pink.

Wilma put her hands on her hips. "You're a worthless piece of trash. Appropriate name you have. All eye candy. No brains."

"You can't talk to me that way." Candi's voice dropped a level as she moved closer to Wilma. Was she getting ready to do something? Slap Wilma? "I'd so love to hurt you right now. But I won't. I'll be the bigger person. I'm leaving before—"

"Before what? I kill you? Believe me, I'd love nothing better than to squeeze your scrawny neck between my hands. Strangle the life out of you." Wilma's fingers opened and closed into fists at her sides.

I slid back behind the corner as Wilma turned her head toward me. Had she seen me? I held my breath, waiting. No footsteps sounded in my direction. Maybe I was safe.

Candi gave a frightened yelp. Rapid footsteps sounded. Then a car door slammed.

Holy cow! Wilma threatened to kill Candi! Wouldn't someone who'd killed before have little problem doing it again? Maybe committing a crime got easier over time. Or maybe she was getting desperate now, trying to tie up loose ends.

I took a chance and looked around the corner of the house again. Candi was indeed leaving. Wilma stood alone by the garden, her back to me, staring after Candi's car as its tires screeched down the street.

Percival kicked me in the side, wanting down. No way it was going to happen. I tightened my grip on his tummy, causing him to growl.

"Shhhh." Petting him with my other hand seemed to calm him a little. Yet, he still wanted to run toward Wilma. What did he think he'd do? Climb up her side and become a cat hat again?

More than that, there was no way I'd let her near my cat or any other. Not after the way she'd talked about poor little Jasper the day on her porch. Nope, Percival was stuck sitting with me.

Wilma turned and headed a few feet away to a small garden shed. What was she doing? After having a public altercation with someone in her yard, she had the yen to weed? She stepped out again, carrying an object. It wasn't a small hoe like had been found in Durbin's' chest. This was a shovel.

She made quite the sight in her dressy outfit and expensively styled hair, using a dirty old shovel with her pink manicured nails. Since the Haines had the left-handed tool in the first place, she must at least do some gardening. Still, she didn't exactly seem dressed for it today.

Time and time again, Wilma plunged the shovel into the brown Indiana soil, throwing aside scoops of dirt and tossing them in a pile. She wasn't gardening. No, more like hunting for buried treasure. She dug and dug. Whatever she hoped to find, she must have thought it important enough to search for it right away.

Buford had said they'd heard she'd buried jewels there and, even though they searched, hadn't found them.

The shovel hit something hard. Wilma gasped and took two more scoops of dirt. She tossed the shovel into the grass behind her and fell to her knees, digging in the soil with her fingers. Those claw-like nails would get her there fast.

A few seconds later, she gave a tug and pulled out some sort of cloth bag. She shook the bag, and something fell to the ground. Something red. It reflected a glint of light from the sun. A jewel?

Maybe she'd hidden them there so Candi wouldn't get a hold of them. Had Candi known they were there and had come to dig them up for herself? No wonder Wilma was in such a hurry to retrieve them.

There didn't seem to be any reason to hang around now since Candi was gone, and Wilma had found what she'd sought in the dirt. I backed up, made sure I had a good grip on the cat and hurried back to the woods. No way I wanted Wilma to have any idea I'd been hanging around. Even though heading back through the branches and brambles wasn't a nice thought, I had no choice.

It seemed to take longer to get back through the dense trees for the second time, but we finally made it. As Percival and I rounded the Kelper's house, I stopped short.

Oh no.

Mrs. Kelper stood there, a worried expression on her face, and who else but Sheriff King was with her. His arms were crossed, his brows lowered.

Since they'd seen me, I had little choice but to walk toward them. I put Percival in the back of the van, grabbed my purse, which I'd left sitting right out where anyone could have taken it, and closed the back doors.

Sighing, I turned to face them.

Mrs. Kelper rushed to me, taking my hand. "Oh, I'm so relieved you're all right. When I saw your van open and you were nowhere to be found, I got worried someone had snatched you."

My heart lurched, and I squeezed her hand. "I'm so sorry you were worried. I was ready to leave after seeing Cleo when Percival decided to go out on his own. I had to chase him down."

She smiled, her shoulders slumping. I hated that she'd been upset on my account. But at the time, my one thought had been my cat's safety. She released my hand. "Silly cat. I know how rambunctious they can be at times. Well, now I know you're safe, I'll go back to the house. Take care, now." She waved and headed to her front door.

If I was lucky, Sheriff King would forget the whole thing happened, go back to his office and—

He crossed his arms and leaned against my van.

Oh, well great. The only way I'd get out of here now was to possibly squash him beneath my tires. Although....

His frown deepened. "Why are you smiling?"

Oops. "No reason."

"Like to tell me what you were doing all this time?"

"I already told Mrs. Kelper. Percival got loose, and I chased him. That's it. Nothing more exciting than that." It had been, but I wasn't going to let him in on it.

"I got the call from her, telling me your van was sitting empty and open. When I got here, there was your purse and your keys sitting here for anyone to take. Do you think this is responsible behavior?"

I crossed my arms and waited. Once he'd blown his stack, he'd cool off and go away. Just a matter of time.

"It seems every time something is going on, you're right in the middle."

I shrugged. "Don't know what to tell you. Guess I'm a social butterfly."

"First, you just happen to be first on the scene of finding a dead body. Then, I find you in all sorts of situations where you seem to be causing some kind of disturbance." He narrowed his eyes and pointed his stubby index finger in my direction. "You watch yourself. Because I'm sure watching you."

I had an insane desire to either salute or curtsy but did neither. No use calling even more attention to myself. Mrs. Kelper had probably already called all her friends to tell them about the excitement of me being missing, possibly kidnapped, or worse. I waited until the sheriff had gotten in his car and driven away before climbing into my van. Once he'd turned the corner to leave the neighborhood, I was ready to go too.

Percival hopped onto my lap as soon as I got into the driver's seat. I held him close for a few seconds. "Honestly, what got into you? You've never run away from Mama like that before." He turned his head until our eyes locked. "Wow, cat, I'm starting to believe your kitty-sense really is in high gear."

He purred and shut his eyes.

As I petted his soft fur, I thought of all the reasons Wilma had to have killed Durbin.

How she'd been shocked to learn she hadn't been in his will. She'd buried the jewels in her garden to hide them when she found out the lawyer lied—she wouldn't have gotten them after all and didn't want Candi to get them.

And what Candi and Wilma had said to each other. And about Wilma's pointy nails. The scratches on Candi's face. Her just now threatening to choke Candi. That along with Wilma wanting her husband dead to get his insurance money and the fact he'd been killed with her left-handed gardening tool.

Wilma had to be the murderer. The only way justice would be done was for her to go to jail. How to convince the sheriff when he was still intent on proving Russ was the murderer?

Chapter Thirty

Thoughts of what I'd overheard Wilma say the day before still rattled around in my mind. She was the most logical person to have killed Durbin. The sheriff had disregarded my theories so far that someone besides my uncle was guilty. If I told him about the latest conversation I'd heard, okay, overheard, would he finally believe me? After work today, I'd just march myself down to the station and make him listen.

I put the phone in my purse after leaving Candi a text message. Guess I needed to check around the base of my counter more often, since it's where I'd found what I was sure belonged to her. Who else would have a key chain with a red heart and Candi spelled out in sparkly pink letters? I looked at it again. Yep, a small link of the chain had broken, leaving this part alone. Candi must have her actual keys. Otherwise, how had she been getting around town? Maybe she didn't realize where it had come apart. Then somehow, it had gotten knocked beneath my counter.

As I dangled the key chain's red heart in my fingers, a small thump came from my left. Percival had jumped up on the counter and was making a beeline right for me. Wait, not me, the heart. He pounced, trying to smack at it, tugging it with his paws to get me to let go. It slipped from my fingers.

"Hey, stop that."

Percival knocked it over the side, peered down at it as if he couldn't believe he'd done it, then gracefully landed on the floor next to it. By the time I crouched down to his level, the heart was batted under the counter.

Ah, mystery solved. Too bad all the mysteries I was trying to figure out couldn't be so easy. I reached beneath the wooden structure, which was raised a good six inches from the floor on wheels for easy movement when needed. My fingers came in contact with… I grimaced as I tugged out the object. It was a catnip mouse, soggy from kitty saliva and covered in dust.

Blech.

Must clean under there soon.

I brushed off the mouse and tossed it to Percival, who licked it until it was soggier than before. Trying again, I reached under the counter and grasped the heart with my fingertips to tug it out. It was now covered in dust bunnies. Well, great.

I stood, grabbed a paper towel and cleanser, and gave it a good scrubbing. If Candi got my message and came to pick it up, I didn't want it to look like it had sat in someone's dusty attic for a year.

Percival and I were holding down the fort. Veronica had a doctor's appointment and wouldn't be back for a little while. Our first clients weren't due for an hour, so I'd decided to get caught up on some cleaning around the entrance area.

The front door opened. Candi rushed toward me, hand out.

Wow, that was quick. "Hi, glad you got my message. I—"

She snatched it from my hand. Whoa, what got into her?

"What are you doing with this?" she snarled.

"Um…I just now found it. It somehow slipped under my counter."

Her eyes were wide, with a wild quality I hadn't noticed before. "I've been looking all over for this."

"I guess the key chain broke one time when you were here. Can't think how else it would have gotten here."

She frowned as she studied it. "Why is it damp?"

"Oh, um, my cat got a hold of it and knocked it on the floor. I cleaned it off and—"

"Don't touch it ever again."

My mouth dropped open. "Sure. Sorry. I didn't realize it was something so important."

She pressed it to her chest. "It was a gift."

"Oh. Was it from Durbin?"

Her eyes narrowed, and she glanced away. "Yeah. From Durbin."

"Well, I'm sorry you didn't know where it was, but glad we found it." Percival was now back on the counter. I patted his head. "Good job, buddy."

Candi was eyeing the key chain, eyebrows lowered.

"Is something wrong?"

"Wrong? No. It's…"

"Did something happen to it? Gosh, I'm sorry if it got scratched or something on the floor."

"Scratch?"

"Yeah. I thought maybe it got scraped up."

"You do know then. About the scratch?"

I frowned. "What?"

She glared at me and took a step around the end of the counter, no longer opposite me. What was she doing?

Candi tapped her fingernails—red today—on the countertop. "I should have known you knew more than you said."

"What do you mean?"

"When you were questioning me after Durbin's death."

I shook my head. "I was just trying to find out the truth."

Candi took a step closer. "No, you were trying to trick me into saying something."

"About what? About Durbin?"

"That's right."

I stepped back. Percival, now alerted by Candi's change in tone, crouched down, his tail lashing side to side.

"Candi, what's going on? Why are you so upset? Is it just about the key chain he gave you?"

"It wasn't from him. It was from Tom Peterson. But you already knew that."

"No. I had no idea. Honest." She had a gift she treasured from the guy giving her quotes for a construction job?

"Oh, come on. It was clear from things you said to me you suspected me of killing Durbin."

My mouth hung open. Had she known all the times we talked that I'd been fishing for information? "You accused Wilma of scratching your face. And insinuated she killed Durbin. I... overheard you arguing with her. She threatened to kill you."

"No. I knew who murdered him. Because it was me."

My mouth went dry. "You?

"That's right. Used Wilma's left-handed implement. Wasn't it good thinking on my part?"

I thought back to Candi, seeing her write down information for the sheriff with her right hand. "But you're not left-handed."

She shrugged. "I'm ambidextrous. Use the left when I need to but not on a regular basis. It worked out great, too. Took suspicion from me. Afterward, I heard you'd been snooping around about Durbin's watch with the scratch on it."

"You'd scratched it?"

"It happened during the murder. With the sharp garden tool. Guess it scratched his watch face."

"Was that your nail polish on the watch face?"

"Stupid Durbin. Tom and I had this whole plan to kill him in his sleep. Maybe a pillow over the face or something. He was old. We figured it wouldn't take much. That day he told me he'd figured out I was lying about my relationship with Tom. Said he knew I didn't really love him."

I glanced behind Candi, hoping someone, anyone, would pop in. I'd even welcome Buford at this point.

"He had to go and ruin things, so I had to kill him on the spur of the moment. I'd just had my nails done! A couple of them still had damp places because I hadn't wanted to wait for them to dry at the manicurists. It was my favorite color. I texted him to meet me at his house when he'd left me a voicemail earlier, saying we needed to talk. I knew something was up."

Ah, the text he'd gotten at my shop was from Candi. The one where he said it wouldn't take long and he'd meet me back at his house when I was done grooming Jasper.

My purse sat on the other end of the counter. My phone was in there.

Could I somehow rush to grab it and dial nine-one-one before Candi could take it from me?

Candi knocked on the counter, getting my attention. "You know what?"

I shook my head, not sure if I should say anything or not.

"Since I heard you were so interested in Durbin's watch—oh yes, a few people saw you pointing at it at the funeral home, gotta love small-town gossip—I could no longer wear the lovely pink shade in case you would notice it. That made me mad. It's my favorite color. Goes with so many of my outfits. Then when you called and left me the message about the broken part of my key chain, I thought you saw a similar scratch and pink polish on it.

I hadn't noticed it, so it must have been small. Either that or, not thinking Candi had been the murderer, I hadn't been looking for anything to point guilt in her direction. "All this time, you truly never loved Durbin?"

"Of course not. His witch of a wife didn't care about him either."

I thought back to Wilma's admission of hating her husband. And Florence and Lottie telling me about Wilma's fling with the lawyer. Hadn't Candi told me about it also? "You said Wilma attacked you. I saw the scratches on your face when I was with the sheriff. Why would she care if you were with her husband if she didn't even want him herself?"

"It was all a ruse to implicate her. The closer you got to discovering the truth, the more I needed someone else to take the blame. Since Wilma had those ridiculous pointy nails, and word had gotten out I'd been having an affair with her husband, she was the perfect patsy to take the fall."

I shook my head. "Those scratches were real. I saw them."

"Nope." She grinned. "I can give credit to Tom for that. When he'd been in college, he'd been into the drama club. Knew how to make something look like it was real blood. He'd done a good job, right?"

"I...."

She laughed, pointing at my face. "Ha, I knew it. You never suspected the scratches were fake. Neither did the sheriff. Once I got an apology from Wilma for something she'd never done, I acted like it was all okay."

"You'd wanted the sheriff to see your scratches?"

"You bet I did. I didn't know you'd be with him when I ran up to show him. The fact you believed me too was icing on the cake."

I'd helped her in her ruse while I'd been trying to discover the truth about who killed Durbin. What a fool I'd been.

She came a step closer. I backed up again. What should I do? Alone in the shop with a murderer who knew that I was aware of the truth.

"Candi, look, um, why don't we call the sheriff and let him sort this out. I'm sure you didn't kill Durbin on purpose, right? I mean, you loved him. Maybe you were just mad when you did it. I can't believe you were making it up with all those tears of grief after he died."

"I'm telling you, I hated the man. Never loved him. Not a bit."

I stared at her. She sure had been convincing talking about him as the love of her life. The tears. The grief-stricken expressions. What an actress she was. I'd had all those talks with her, unknowingly giving her information about what I suspected.

Candi placed the key chain on the counter. "I'll tell you a little secret. See, Tom gave me this key chain because we're in love."

"You are?"

"That's right. Why would someone my age be interested in a grumpy man old enough to be my father?"

The thought had occurred to me there was a wide age gap, but not so much to think it wasn't true. May-December romances happened all the time. I hadn't doubted it.

She reached into her jeans pocket. Was she getting her phone? Instead, she pulled out something long, shiny, and sharp.

A knife!

"Candi! Wh-what are you doing?"

"I can't let you go on telling people things about me. It would ruin everything for me and Tom. He and I have plans. It all hinges on getting Durbin's money. Guess I was convincing to the old coot that I loved him, so he left his money to me."

"But you didn't know about the will when I told you."

"Of course, I did. I was his secretary. I typed up the draft myself."

225

This couldn't be happening. I'd been so sure Candi had been the grieving lover, lost without the man she'd loved. I'd listened to her, comforted her when she'd cried. I'd felt guilty about talking to her with false pretenses to get more information about Durbin.

Well, no more.

Now she faced me, a glint in her eye and a gleam reflecting from the lights above from the knife she held. The one edging closer to me!

She took another step. I backed up. My backside hit the wall. There was no place to go. I was trapped between her and the counter.

And she had a weapon.

A loud hiss came from the counter. Percival, fur puffed twice its normal size, crept up behind Candi. Was he going to scratch her?

He leaped and landed on her head.

He was a cat hat again!

Candi screamed, flailing her arms, trying to remove what I knew to be painful sharp claws from her scalp.

She still didn't drop the knife.

I grabbed her arm, trying to grasp the weapon. The blade angled sideways, scoring the flesh on my palm. I screeched in pain.

Percival hissed again as Candi smacked at him with her hand. No way I could let her get the knife near my baby. I grabbed her wrist, hoping she'd let loose of the knife, but her grip was like iron.

Candi reached up and hit the cat in the nose. He yowled and fell to the floor.

Percival! Was he hurt?

Candi shook her head as if dizzy, shaking away cobwebs. Then her glare focused on me. "Now, let's finish this, shall we?"

I tried to edge to the side, hoping to slide against the wall to escape, but Candi pressed closer, the knife edging dangerously close to my throat.

A hiss. A growl.

I blinked. But Percival was still prone on the floor. So, who—

Jasper sailed through the air, landed on the counter, and climbed up Candi's shoulder to take Percival's place as a hat. He went one step further than

Percival, digging in his claws so deep, a trickle of blood ran down Candi's forehead.

The knife hit the floor as she desperately tried to disengage the talons of death from her scalp. Jasper hung on. Candi had almost succeeded in undoing his claws when Percival reappeared, landing on Candi's shoulder.

The cats, working in tandem, growled, hissed, scratched, and kicked.

Candi smacked against them with both arms, then, giving a mighty yell, tore them away and tossed them to the floor.

My babies! I reached for them, but Candi lunged at me.

In the back of my mind, I heard a noise. A squeak?

The door opened. It was Hank!

"Molly?!"

Footsteps pounded across the floor. Hank appeared behind Candi, grabbed her arms, and pressed them to her back. His eyes were wide. "Molly, are you okay?"

My nod was shaky.

"Call the sheriff," said Hank.

My legs were rubbery as I hurried to grab my purse. It took me three tries to punch in the right numbers. I somehow garbled out for help and tossed the phone aside.

The cats were under a nearby table. Not hissing or growling at each other. They were huddled together like a big, frightened ball of fur. Thank goodness they seemed unhurt.

Hank tilted his head toward my shelves. "Grab a leash."

"Huh?"

"To tie her hands. I can't hold her like this forever."

I ran, stumbled, then reached the shelf, grabbing the first leash I saw. It was pink. How appropriate.

Rushing back to Hank, I tied Candi's hands behind her while Hank held them steady.

Candi took a step back. She'd get away.

"Oh, no, you don't." I retrieved the knife from the floor and handed it to Hank.

He looked from it to her, to me. His gaze lowered to my hand. "You're hurt?"

I touched my palm coming away with a smear of blood on my finger. "I… I'll be f-fine." Was shock setting in?

Hank forced Candi to march in front of him toward the door. I hurried after them, reaching the door right as the sheriff burst in.

The man's eyes widened as he took in the scene. "Holy cow. Does this have to do with Durbin? What you were trying to tell me about his murder?"

I blew out a long breath. "Yes, Sheriff. Candi here just confessed to me she killed him. And Tom Peterson was in on the plan to kill Durbin too."

The sheriff shook his head. "And I thought today was going to be boring." He tugged on her arm, raising his eyebrows at the leash her hands were tied with. "Come on, Candi. We're going to the station." He looked at me. "Are you all right?"

Hank stepped to me and placed his arm around my shoulders. "She is now."

The sheriff blinked. "Good, um… I'll talk to you in a bit, Molly, to get your statement. Right now, looks like you maybe need to sit down." He left the shop with Candi in tow.

Hank tightened his hold on me. "You look pale. Come on." He led me to a nearby chair.

My heartbeat hadn't slowed down yet. Was it really over? Suddenly, my body felt drained. I allowed Hank to help me get comfortable, but my thoughts were sluggish, like life was in slow motion.

Hank hurried to the counter and reached for something behind it. I was suddenly so tired, it barely registered when I heard him speaking to someone.

Then, I sat there for several minutes with Hank beside me. He didn't say much, mostly just held my hand.

The front door opened. If it was a customer, maybe Hank could ask them to come another time.

He released my hand and stood. "Oh, I'm so glad you're here."

Who was he talking to? I turned my head.

Russ stood there, his eyes wide. "Molly? You did it." He rushed to me and knelt on the floor beside my chair.

When his arms enveloped me in a warm embrace, I relaxed against him. After a couple of minutes, I pulled away. "Wait, how did you know?"

"Hank called me. Told me about Candi. And that you were injured. Do you need a doctor?"

In all the turmoil, I'd nearly forgotten the wound. Maybe shock took away pain temporarily, because right at that moment, my palm throbbed. But the cut itself wasn't large, and Hank had cleaned and disinfected it for me as I sat at the table. "No, I think it's all right."

Russ rose from the floor, then took a seat next to me. Hank had stepped a few feet away to give us privacy, but Russ waved him over.

Once Hank was settled, Russ again took my uninjured hand. "Molly, I don't know how to thank you." He looked at Hank. "Both of you. Hank, Molly told me you were helping with the investigation too."

Hank shrugged. "I'm just glad it's all over now."

I sighed. "So am I. "

Russ watched me for a second. "What you did was above and beyond, my girl."

"No." I shook my head. "It's what family does. For love."

Chapter Thirty-One

People poured into Fabulous Felines throughout the day. Well-wishers. Looky-loos. Nosy Nellies. While I'd admit trying to people-watch and listen to all the gossip I could, at least it was for a specific reason. However, it was nice to know so many people cared about me and about Percival and Jasper. Once folks heard how they saved the day, the kitties got lots of attention and, even better, treats and catnip.

I somehow managed to groom three cats while chatting with those who dropped by. Veronica was working in the back, having told me I needed to be out front for anyone wanting to see how I was. The number of people doing exactly that shocked me. She'd been right.

It was still hard to believe Candi had been the one to kill Durbin. I'd missed clues, had believed her lies. I'd had Wilma as the probable murderer but hadn't suspected Candi at all.

I had to admit, the girl was a good actress, though. Those tears were real. Maybe Tom wasn't the only one with interest in the drama club when he was younger.

The sheriff strolled in, waving to everyone as if he'd won the Olympics. Sure, he'd arrested Candi for Durbin's murder, but I thought I, as well as others, cats included, had a little bit to contribute too.

He smiled, accepting pats on the back and handshakes from the people milling about, and then reached me at the counter. "Hi."

"Hey, Sheriff."

"Doing okay today? Your hand healing up?"

I held up the bandage, which I'd made to cover my whole palm. Not that the cut was so big, but while grooming cats, I didn't want any of the pet parents to think I was getting something icky on their cats' fur. It would have been nice to have worn a glove to groom, but I'd found it awkward to get proper use of my fingers when wearing them. "Doing fine."

"Glad to hear it." He leaned one elbow on the counter. "Thanks for stopping in earlier to give your statement."

"No problem. Betsy and I got through it okay." When I'd gotten to the station at the time he'd requested, he'd been nowhere to be seen. Not wanting to return later to do it, I'd asked his second-in-command, Betsy, if she could take over. She'd done so gladly.

He had the decency to look down for a moment. "I wasn't there because, um, the folks at the newspaper wanted a photo op."

Photo op? Wow, the arrest had gone to his head more than I'd imagined. "It's fine. I had other things to do anyway." I patted an orange and white cat's back. She looked up at me and closed her eyes in a kitty version of a hug.

He made eye contact. Did he have something else to say? I had to lean forward in order to hear him, as more people crowded into Fabulous Felines.

"Uh… see, when you first told me there was no way Russ could have killed Durbin, I thought you were protecting him because he was family. I didn't, well, believe you."

"Yes, I remember."

"What I need to say is…well, I was, um…."

I waited a few seconds. When nothing else happened, I ventured, "You were wrong?"

His face reddened. He glanced around. Was he hoping no one else was listening? Normally someone would have been, but they were all too excited talking to each other. And it was getting louder.

He shrugged. "Yeah, that's right. I was wrong. So…" He held out his hand. Was it supposed to be an apology? Knowing the sheriff, that was the best I'd get.

I nodded, letting him off the hook.

He smiled. "Okay, great. Uh, see you later?"

"Sure. Later." Though I hoped it wouldn't be in any official capacity. I'd had enough of his scolding, people's rumors, and a murderer.

With an added spring in his step, Sheriff King once again was happily greeted by people as he made his way to the door.

Veronica, who'd been trying to do crowd control, joined me. "How long do you suppose they'll all hang around? It's not like the majority of them are waiting to have their cats groomed."

"Not sure. They'll get bored at some point. Or remember they have jobs to get to. Or homes."

She grinned. "True. At the very least, some might get hungry and wander down to Paula's Pastries."

Jillian made her way through the crowd. "Hey, there. I know we talked on the phone last night because it was late by the time you'd been to the doctor for your hand." She looked pointedly at my bandage. "But I had to come see you were okay for myself." She rounded the counter and gave me a hug.

Veronica patted her back. "Glad you're here, Jillian. She tries to do it all herself. See what I put up with?"

Jillian laughed. "Yeah, I do see." She studied me. "You're okay? Really okay?"

"Yeah. It was tough getting to sleep last night, thinking about Candi, and what she admitted to."

Veronica held up her hand. "Don't forget the knife."

"Yeah, Thanks, Veronica. Don't think it's possible."

She chuckled. "Sorry. I'm just so relieved everything worked out, that you weren't hurt even worse than you were. You know I resort to humor at the most inappropriate times."

Jillian smiled, and I laughed. Giving Veronica a side hug, I nodded. "It's why we love you."

She winked. "So true." She headed back into the fray of onlookers, trying without much luck to suggest maybe some of them might have someplace else to go.

Jillian took my un-bandaged hand gently in hers. "I won't stay long. I have to get back to the library soon, and you have work to do." She glanced at the people standing around and back to me. "Honestly, just checking to make sure you're all right."

I nodded. "I am."

"Oh, there is one other thing."

"What's that?"

"I heard a rumor floating around. Something about you? And Hank?"

My eyes widened.

"And sitting in a car."

I cleared my throat.

"And you're dating?"

My face heated. "See, it's not really.... We aren't actually... It was all a ruse. There was a stakeout to watch Buford. Then he found us, and Hank blurted out—"

"Yeah, yeah. I figured it was something like that. Because I know, as your best friend, you would have told me if you were dating someone." Her eyes narrowed.

"Yes. Of course."

She winked. "I know. Giving you a hard time. Too bad the rumors weren't true, though. About you and Hank."

I shrugged. "Yeah."

She patted my hand gently and released it. "Okay, girl. Just had to see for myself you were fine. I need to head out. Call me later?"

"You got it."

I watched as she left. While she had I had talked, Veronica must have had some luck, because the crowd had thinned, and few more were trickling out when the door opened again. When would it end? Was everyone in Whitewater Valley going to pop in today?

The next person who came in was Hank.

My whole body heated up, thinking about what Jillian said, how she'd heard the rumor. Which meant everyone else in town most likely had heard it too. To prove the point, the remaining folks in the room began to elbow each other, watching Hank as he approached me.

Veronica waved her arms. "Thanks for stopping by, everyone. Always glad to see you. Hey, I hear Paula is serving Blueberry scones today. Sounds good, right?"

People's salivary glands must have acted on impulse at her suggestion, because the rest of the people, even the pet parents waiting to have their cats groomed, gave us waves and told us they'd be back shortly. When I glanced at the cats waiting in their carriers, they were all napping, so they wouldn't mind waiting anyway. How had they not woken up with all the mayhem going on around them?

Who needed to sleep like a baby? I'd rather sleep like a cat.

Veronica lifted one of the carriers and headed to the back room. The fact that she closed the door to give me and Hank privacy spoke volumes. If she was busy working, she might not even be able to hear our conversation.

But what would the conversation even be? My hopes had been dashed so many times. It was only when Jillian mentioned the rumor that hope rose in me, wishing Hank had stopped by for something more than to check on me. *Get a grip. He's a friend. Stay calm.*

I'd managed to finish the grooming for the cat, so I gently coaxed her into her carrier. I doubted Hank would be here long, then I could get to work on the next cat in line.

He came around the counter, much as Jillian had done. I didn't expect him to hug me, as she had, even though he'd done that very thing when he'd come in during Candi's attempt to stab me.

"Molly." He stood close but didn't reach out. "I'm so glad to see you. That you look… okay. You are okay, aren't you?"

I smiled. "Yeah. I am. Thank you again for what you did yesterday. Without you…" I shuddered.

"Believe me, I'm so thankful I walked in here at the exact moment yesterday you needed me."

My heart warmed. Even if we were just friends, I had a feeling after what we'd been through yesterday, it would be a close friendship. A thought occurred to me. "Hey, why were you coming in here yesterday, anyway?"

He pulled a folded paper out of his pocket. "I'd found a couple more articles I thought would maybe help with Percival and Jasper getting along."

I let out a happy sigh. "Believe it or not, last night, they didn't fight, hiss, or growl."

"That's great. What changed?"

I pointed to the shelf beneath the counter where my two cats were curled into one big furry ball. They were smiling. "I'm not sure. It all happened after Candi had been here, and they'd jumped on her in my defense."

His eyes widened. "That's it."

"What's it?"

"Your cats needed a reason to unite. To come together. Until yesterday, they hadn't found their common ground."

"And what might that be?"

"They both wanted to protect you. And now..." He tilted his head toward the cats, who since the noisy crowd was gone, could be heard purring. "...they have a common goal."

"You think so?" I shook my head. "Wow. If I'd known weeks ago they needed me to nearly get killed for them to be friends, I would have—" I realized what I'd said. "Well, maybe not."

He took my uninjured hand. "No. definitely not."

I waited, still wondering what he might say or do. Would he wave and leave, like usual, after he'd stopped by? I wanted to say more to him, to tell him how I felt, but my tongue froze in my mouth. How many times had I been hurt by someone I'd come to care for?

"Listen, I know people are spreading rumors you and I are...."

"Um, yeah. Jillian told me she'd heard about it."

"I'm thinking," He lifted one shoulder in a shrug. "Why not?"

"Why not what?"

"Let's make the rumors true."

My eyes widened so much I wasn't sure they'd return to normal.

"What do you say? How about a real date?" he asked.

My ears buzzed. Had I actually heard those words, or was I dreaming?

His smile fell. "Oh, Maybe I read the signals wrong."

Say something before he takes back the offer. "Oh, yes. I do. I would. I mean, yes."

He grinned. "Great. How about we—"

Thumps came from near my feet. The cats had left the comfiness of their shared sleepy ball and were both standing on the floor, each stretching and yawning. Percival jumped up on the counter, sat down, and tilted his head as he watched me. Jasper appeared next to him and began licking Percival's ear.

Hank moved closer to the cats. "Amazing. What a difference."

I patted Percival on the head, then Jasper. "I think you're right about why they're getting along now. Not as if I'd want a repeat of what I went through, but I am so thankful these two seem to be friends now."

"So am I." He rubbed Jasper's fur. "And this little guy has a good home too. Anyway, as I was saying, how about you and I have a real date?"

"That sounds awesome."

"I had a couple of cancellations. Maybe we could go get some coffee?"

"Oh, now?" I pointed to the two cats still sleeping in carriers, waiting for their grooming appointments. "I couldn't...see I have to—"

The back door opened, and Veronica rushed in. "I'll do those groomings for you."

I shook my head. "No, that's not fair. Too much work for you and—"

She planted her hands on her hips. "I said go. I'm older than you, so it means you have to do what I say."

Hank's eyebrows rose. "She has a point."

"I think you guys are ganging up on me."

Veronica nodded. "In a good way. I hear Paula is having a special on blueberry scones."

I narrowed my eyes. "Didn't you make that up to get other people out of here earlier?"

"Yeah, but who's to say she isn't?"

"She has another point." Hank grinned.

"All right, you two. You win. Hank? Let's go get some coffee, just the two of—"

The cats left the counter, their paws pattering against the wood floor. Then Percival reappeared. A few seconds later, Jasper joined him. They stared at me as they sat by my feet.

Hank glanced down. "So glad to see these two getting along. Guess you won't need those articles I found after all." He patted his shirt pocket.

"Guess not, but I appreciate it anyway."

Percival made some sort of scratching noise. What was he doing? I bent down to see. He'd dragged something off of the bottom shelf. It was a leash.

"Uh, Molly?" Hank pointed down to his feet, where Jasper was pushing another leash with his paw right up to Hank's shoe. "I think maybe they want to come with us."

I laughed. "Lottie and Florence get away with it because they tell everyone their cats are emotional support cats. How would we get away with doing the same thing?"

Hank shrugged. "Hey, I'm the town vet, so if someone asks you why you have your cats in a public place, you send them right to me. Don't worry. I have your back."

As I gazed into his warm dark eyes, I could see he really did.

Acknowledgements

Thanks to my agent, Dawn Dowdle, who always believes in me. And thank you to Level Best Books for this start to a new series.

About the Author

Ruth J. Hartman spends her days herding cats and her nights spinning mysterious tales. She, her husband, and their cats love to spend time curled up in their recliners watching old Cary Grant movies. Well, the cats sit in the people's recliners. Not that the cats couldn't get their own furniture. They just choose to shed on someone else's.

Ruth, a left-handed, cat-herding, farmhouse-dwelling writer, uses her sense of humor as she writes tales of lovable, klutzy women who seem to find trouble without even trying.

Ruth's husband and best friend, Garry, reads her manuscripts, rolls his eyes at her weird story ideas, and loves her despite her insistence all of her books have at least one cat in them. See updates about her cozy mysteries at Ruthjhartman.com.

SOCIAL MEDIA HANDLES:
  https://www.facebook.com/ruth.j.hartman
  https://www.amazon.com/stores/author/B00355AV1U

https://twitter.com/RuthjHartman

AUTHOR WEBSITE:

www.ruthjhartman.com

Also by Ruth J. Hartman

The Bookshop Kitties Mysteries
Dial M for Meow (Book 1)

The Kitty Beret Café Series
Hairballs and Homicide (Book 1)
Felines and Fatalities (Book 2)
Meows and Mayhem (Book 3)

Ring of Death

www.ingramcontent.com/pod-product-compliance
Lightning Source LLC
Chambersburg PA
CBHW050202120726
47903CB00002B/722